Chris van Wyk

Chris van Wyk was born in Soweto in 1957. He lives in Riverlea, Johannesburg, where he works as a freelance literary editor and full-time writer. Van Wyk has published poetry, short stories, children's books and stories for newly literate adults. His first poetry collection, *It is Time to Go Home*, won the Olive Schreiner Prize in 1980. His books for children include the well-loved *A Message in the Wind* and *Petroleum and the Orphaned Ostrich*. *The Year of the Tapeworm* is his first novel.

The Year of
the Tapeworm

Chris van Wyk

Ravan Writers Series

Published by Ravan Press
P O Box 145 Randburg 2125
South Africa

ISBN 086975 469 6

Cover design: Centre Court Studio
Cover illustration: Lois Neethling
Typesetting: Maxwell Avenue Design

Acknowledgements: The poem on p. 58 is I. Choonara's 'Piccaninny
Dream', published in *Seven South African Poets,* edited by Cosmo Pieterse,
Heinemann African Writers Series, 1971. The story on p. 147 is adapted
from Obed Musi's 'Broken Shoe Casey', published in *Casey & Co —
Selected Writings of Casey 'Kid' Motsisi*, edited by Mothobi Mutloatse,
Ravan Press, 1978.

Printed by: Sigma Press, Pretoria

Contents

For
my wife Kathy
and
my friend William

Ordinarily a tapeworm has a double life history
— *The New Modern Medical Counsellor*

1

Strange Visitors with Familiar Faces

The knock on my door woke me at 2.30 on that Saturday morning. At first my liquor-addled brain refused to register the urgent banging of bone on wood. I had only been asleep for about two hours and, to put it mildly, I was a sick man. But the knocking persisted and I knew there was no other way to deal with this problem but to get up and open the door.

It occurred to me that it might be someone seeking help. I had a car. Perhaps some boy or girl, lying wounded in a gutter nearby, needed to be rushed to hospital. The township had been in flames for months now, and hundreds of people had been injured or killed.

I suddenly remembered, incongruously, my unfinished short story lying in the bottom of a desk drawer at work: it was a satirical piece in which the government tries to pass a law forcing black students to learn all their school subjects in Afrikaans. My inspiration to complete the story had dissipated after my friend and colleague, Gus, convinced me that it was too far-fetched — even as a satire — to be an allegory of the government's proposed Dagga Bill, which would prohibit blacks from smoking the weed. Weed! You see, already these endless reams of government propaganda were taking effect. Dagga is no weed, it's a medicinal plant with spectacular properties and very few drawbacks; indeed, every time you draw back you're closer to heaven (ha ha ha).

More impatient knocking.

It might be the henchmen of a very angry and ruthless mashonisa. I had borrowed money from a certain Mr Mtolo — quite a large sum from a fairly powerful Sofasonke tycoon — and the solemnly promised date of repayment had long since come and gone — day, month, and, I believe, year.

Then again, it might be Gus or one of my other colleagues from the *Black World*. Maybe there was some street corner I had to rush to, strewn with bodies from which I would have to extract another gruesome story for our readers to digest with their mealie-meal porridge and sour milk on Monday morning.

The impatient rapping again. My wife stirred beside me. I struggled out of bed and limped on my bare feet to the front door, my curiosity and indignation quickly sweeping away any fears that I had. The tiles underfoot were warm as I padded from the red and white ones in the bedroom to black and white in the passage to red and white in the lounge, making sharp little L-shaped turns: Scara the black knight. It was a warm January morning.

'Okay, okay, I'm coming,' I grumbled, rattling the bunch of keys which I had picked up from the sideboard to prove it.

I opened the door and stared cautiously into the darkness, weakly lit up by the myopic orange light of a streetlamp that shone onto my doorstep.

I could not believe what my eyes revealed to me. The sputla I had drunk at the Black Widow shebeen only a few hours before must surely have been laced with a demonic potion. Otherwise these two men would not be darkening my doorstep — or, in this case, I should say lighting it up.

'May we come in?' one of them said, but I rubbed my eyes and stepped back for they were already shuffling their way into my tiny lounge before I could utter a word.

'Who is it, Scara?' Khensani croaked sleepily from the bedroom.

A word without the letters of the alphabet slithered out of my throat like the tapeworm that had been feeding off my sanity, the same species of tapeworm, possibly, that had caused the death of the ninth President of the white minority government a few years ago. My mouth went dry. What does one say when the President of your country (albeit of a minority government) is standing in your little lounge facing you, flanked by the Minister of Mines? Was he the eleventh or twelfth President of our Republic, I wondered. I had lost count.

'Friends, tell her we're your friends!' said the President in the same authoritative voice I had so often heard booming from my black and white TV on a familiar range of subjects: 'total onslaught',

2

'majority rule, never' and more recently 'blacks cannot be allowed to use marijuana because, unlike whites, they are immature, irresponsible and prone to outbreaks of terrible violence when under the influence of any carcinogen' — the last word replaced with 'hallucinogen' in subsequent reports in the papers. It was a voice that over many years had grown louder and more and more self-important from being listened to attentively, quoted throughout all Christendom and heeded by friend and foe alike.

'Friends, honey,' I stammered self-consciously in my see-through underpants and tattered white vest.

Well, you know, this is the Calvinist Republic where blacks — meaning, I suppose, about twenty million adults — don't have the vote. And I must have said it a thousand times if I've said it once, in shebeens and other such primordial places where men gather to beat their chests, that if the President ever crossed my path I would tell him in no uncertain terms what I thought of his laws of tyranny and terror. But it's a very different story when the man of your nightmares stumbles into your house in the wee hours of a Saturday morning and you have the mother of all hangovers. And when I say a very different story I mean exactly that. The next couple of months of my life were going to be very, very interesting, as sure as there is a prison called Robben Island.

'What do you want?' I asked foolishly. Well, what does a man say?

'Shut the door, man!' the President demanded.

Obediently I shut the door, meaning of course that I was now harbouring the township of Sofasonke's most wanted criminals. What the hell would I say to two million fellow Sofasonkans when they learnt that this rascal had been in my house? 'Sorry, comrades, I didn't know it was President De Vries. The man looks different in the flesh. Okay, that bald patch which seems to have been a prerequisite of the presidency for decades can't be missed anywhere, but you know that in Sofasonke the light is poor and I really did not recognize him.'

'Oh come now, Scara wena,' they would say. 'What about those cold blue eyes?'

'Ah, by the spear of the nation, I had no idea the bastard had blue eyes. I've got a black and white TV, comrades. I thought his eyes were a dark shade of grey.'

'But that accent, Scara, surely you must have recognized the settler's accent! You are a learned man, Scara, a reporter of news; a man who gets around . . .'

'I know, I know, gents, but that guttural voice was a mere whisper in my lounge. He had somehow found himself in Sofasonke, in the midst of his most fervent enemies and finally come face to face with the most dangerous of them all; that blustering roar was hardly a whimper,' I would lie desperately. 'He was hoarse, choking with fear, croaking . . .'

'What are you standing there for!' De Vries snarled. He was out of breath — definitely on the run, I thought. I heard a car speeding into our street from Madibane Street. My house is on the corner of Khumalo so the headlights beamed through my lounge window from an angle which gave everything in the room — the furniture and ourselves — a fleeting italics of shadows.

'Vervlaks!' the Minister of Mines cursed in pure Afrikaans — a definite first in my house.

I froze and watched the two men sink deep into my couch.

'It's okay,' the Minister reassured De Vries. 'Just don't move.'

'Sê die kaffer moet wegkom van die venster af!' De Vries hissed.

This was too much, I tell you; I had been called a kaffir in many public places, by shopkeepers, a family of festive whites on their way home from a picnic, raucous youngsters passing me in their parents' car, even by a woman in a whites-only procession of born-again Christians, for God's sake! But never in my own house! This was definitely another first.

'Wat sê jy daar?' I demanded. But I knew that my Afrikaans wasn't strong enough to convey my anger, so I opted instead for: 'Masipa, De Vries!'

Swearing was strictly forbidden in my parents' home. My father is Zulu and Mama is Xhosa, and anybody who has even a scant knowledge of these languages knows how vile profanities are in both of them. And so I settled for a compromising 'shit' in Sesotho.

Mr President scowled at me from behind his thick lenses but chose to ignore my justifiable anger, just as he had chosen to ignore it for the last three and a half centuries.

I still did not know what was going on and was about to open the door again and tell them to voetsek. But the President seemed to have read my mind.

'Don't do anything drastic,' he said. 'We know your father. He owes us a favour. We want you to take us to him.'

'You know him,' I said weakly. This man De Vries earned his living by telling mammoth lies — 'I get fan mail from blacks every day',

4

'A man who lost his passbook once wrote to me personally asking how soon he could get a new one as he could not live without the document', 'A witchdoctor told me that blacks who protested against apartheid were bewitched' — but I knew he was now telling the truth.

You see, I happen to be the son of the eminently revered and prodigious Sizwe Ngomezulu Nhlabatsi.

'I'll draw you a map,' I offered. 'It's very easy to find his house, it's right down here, turn left into the next zone, the house has orange perspex over the stoep and . . .'

'We don't have a car,' De Vries said.

Then how the hell did they get here, I wondered.

'I don't go to my parents' house,' I said. 'I haven't been there in months.' But this was too personal so I tapered off into silence.

'Do you have some brandy here?' De Vries asked, his tone just a little too demanding for my liking. He had removed from a pocket of his dark suit a handkerchief so huge that you could have used it to shroud one of the bodies that would inevitably be discovered in this township come daybreak. He wiped his almost hairless head, his forehead, his face, the deep fissure that divided his fleshy chin in two, and his neck. I observed all of this with a perverse fascination — I had never seen a President perform these very ordinary ablutions before. I suppose if I was lucky I might even hear him give one whopping fart, right here in my little house.

'Brandy,' Mines asked me impatiently.

'No brandy,' I shook my head. Did they think this was Tuynhuys where the cellars were awash with the stuff?

'Ask him what he's got?' De Vries told his cabinet minister.

'Coffee and tea,' I said angrily.

'Coffee, coffee,' De Vries said.

'Coffee,' Mines told me.

I went into the kitchen wondering what the hell this Mines fellow's name was. Kriel or Cruywagen, Van Wyk or Verwey, some stupid name like that. And what did they want with my father? I had an idea.

I put the kettle on to boil and my mind flew all the way back to my childhood.

2

Under the
Orange Awning

I'm ten years old, thin, quirky, and tall for my age. And on this particular day in my young life, I'm fidgeting on the tattered green leather seat of a Putco bus with a burden which my bowels cannot bear for much longer. The frequent emission of very stale gases is ample proof of my encumbrance and has sent windows flying open and provoked a flurry of complaints through pinched noses from the other young passengers — my peers, as I learnt later in life these unhappy people were called.

In my short grey flannels and grey jersey I shift uneasily on my seat. The world outside is no longer interesting. The men rolling gigantic reels of newsprint into the building housing the *Daily Star;* the women bustling and haggling at the Indian market-place piled high with pyramids of apples, naartjies, oranges and tomatoes, and the sphinx of an oversized Indian mama who has long since given up on the flies that buzz around her spicy condiments; the babel of sweaty workers on scaffolding stabbing arrows into pulpy concrete with their trowels and catching bricks that fly skywards into unerring hands, again and again and again . . . All these daily wonders of my world, which usually kept me staring out of the bus window, had now lost their enchantment.

The robots, the robots! Every one was catching us! Did this always happen? What was I going to do? There was no way out!

Eventually, after what felt to me like an expedition rather than a mere ride home from school, the bus lumbered up a hill towards Sofasonke under its cloud of smoke manufactured by two thousand Ellerines and Welcome Dover coal stoves.

I was the first to jump off the bus. But in my haste I must have deactivated my sphincter; a stream of shit came cascading down my legs in a warm, smelly lava. I stood still for a moment, allowing nature to run its course, so to speak, while everywhere children sniggered and gasped and pointed. One particularly sensitive soul even threw up.

And as I squelched sombrely forth a path was quickly made for me. I knew then what it was like to be utterly alone.

The following day I was clean and spruced up. Something of the characteristic spring had returned to my step. I was wearing a clean white shirt and crisp grey pants and I could still inhale faint wisps of the aromatic Lifeguard soap with which I had been sanitized.

But nobody on the bus had forgotten the shit of the previous day. When I sat down the two seats before me were immediately vacated. And a shuffling behind me alerted me to the fact that a similar evacuation was taking place there. Everyone, including my close friends, had decided that it was better to stand at the back of the bus all the way to school than to sit within breathing distance of me.

Even at the tender age of ten, as I was then, I knew that I was being unjustly persecuted. Yesterday they had had all the justification to give me a wide berth, to snigger and laugh at my misfortune. But I had been thoroughly scrubbed — and slapped — by Mama and all that was left of my accident now was the embarrassing memory.

I stood up on my seat, holding onto the ceiling of the bus to prevent myself from falling. Facing my detractors at the back, I launched into an eloquent and emotional speech castigating them all for treating me so unkindly and beseeching them to take their seats — especially Thabo, whose actions I likened to those of a traitor since he and I spent each morning of our journey to school sitting together and watching the world go by.

But nobody budged. Instead they laughed and sneered and made rude splattering noises through their pursed lips.

Now I had always been one of the more confident and assertive lighties at school; not the kind who took shit from anybody. But this was not easy. If I didn't convince them soon then I would be ostracized for the rest of my life — or at least my primary school days.

I sat down again and decided on a plan of action. If things did not improve on the return journey then the only solution left open to me was to call in Tata.

Well, things did not improve on the return journey — otherwise I

7

wouldn't be telling you this story — and so I had to turn to my father. Now before you think I was some kind of cry-baby who ran to Mama or Tata whenever things got a little heavy for me, let me explain. My father is one of the finest, most respected witchdoctors in the country. And I went to him for help in his capacity as an inyanga and not as my Tata. I decided that I was being unfairly ostracized due to an unfortunate but unusual occurrence — shitting in my pants. I therefore had the right to correct matters in an unusual way.

After school I approached Tata. He was sitting on our stoep, which had been converted into his consulting room by means of three brick walls and a corrugated roof of bright orange perspex.

The perspex inadvertently created what seemed like a propitious atmosphere for Tata's work; the African sun shone through the translucent roof, imbuing the skin and the clothes of all who sat in this makeshift room with an eerie, brindled hue and enveloping everything — the mat on the floor, the ancient, sagging settee, the dining-room curtain that fluttered onto the stoep — in warm orange stripes.

Well, as you know, atmosphere invariably gets around and Mabandla, an inyanga who practises in Zone 17, also erected orange sheeting over his consulting rooms. And his practice has grown from a trickle of patients with such mundane problems as piles and indecipherable nightmares to a steady stream with more illustrious concerns, including: 'Will my ancestral land be returned and, if so, how much blood will be spilled before that day?' Soon after this we heard that yet another sangoma in Mabopane had also ordered a few sheets of orange perspex.

Before long there were copycat inyangas and sangomas all over the place. The corrugated perspex manufacturers made a killing. Mama must have thought about all this long and hard, because one day she stopped stirring a pot of thick porridge, looked up at Tata with one hand on a bulging hip, and said, 'This thing with the plastic was your idea. You should be getting money from amaplestiki.' Illiteracy has not impeded my mother's sense of propriety and, in this case, her instinctive attitudes regarding copyright law. But Tata couldn't be bothered with the white man's laws of patent and ownership. He said the orange sheeting is a good trade mark because now people know where all the medicine men and women live. 'It's just like the striped pole that shows white people where the barber-shops are,' he explained.

Besides, at the end of the day it is reputation that counts. Because that afternoon there was the usual queue in our lounge when I got home from school. About eight people were waiting to have their marriages saved, their money problems solved or their long periods of unemployment brought to an end, or simply to have a malignant boil lanced or appetite restored.

I did my homework at the kitchen table, and ate some pap and morogo, while I waited for Tata to see patient number nine: his own son with the shit problem.

Eventually it was my turn.

'Good afternoon, Tata,' I said, with a note of formality, and went to take my place on the mat which was still hot from all the other butts that had been receiving advice and muti from Tata all afternoon.

'Ah, my little man,' Tata said, smiling warmly. 'And does he know more about this strange and wonderful world than he did yesterday?'

It is a mystery to me still why my father sometimes spoke to me in the third person.

The crow's-feet that spread out from his eyes seemed deeper to me than usual. I recalled, fleetingly, many years before, sitting on Tata's lap, inhaling his pleasant body odour and warning him that his face was cracking up.

'I have a problem with some friends,' I said.

'But why do you not answer my question?' Tata said, packing his poultices, roots and bones into a little wooden box that had been built in a school woodwork room to hold shoe brushes and polish.

'Because I don't want Tata to put Tata's medicine away,' I explained desperately.

Tata held a Vaseline bottle, filled with what looked like rotten avocado pear, in mid-air. When I had come to sit on the mat, cross-legged like the eight men and women before me, Tata had regarded me with some amusement, probably believing that I was aping his patients. But now he eyed me with some suspicion, thinking, if I knew my father, that I was up to some little juvenile trick like trying to play truant from school or something.

'What's the matter?' he said.

I told him.

'And they still think you're full of shit?' he said with supercilious amusement.

I nodded.

'Maybe it's because you didn't wipe that speck of shit off your

9

forehead,' he said, glaring at a spot above my eyes.

Instinctively I wiped my forehead and gave my hand a few dog-like sniffs. There was nothing there that smelled even remotely like the previous day.

Tata grinned at me. 'Here.' He handed me the Vaseline bottle filled with the avocado pear stuff. 'Rub this onto the palms of your hands with a few drops of your first urine tomorrow morning.'

'This, Tata?' I said, a little disappointed. He was giving me the very potion I had found him with when I sat down as patient number nine. I just wasn't convinced. I suppose I had expected the full ritual: delving into my past, the two of us speaking about this and that, throwing the bones around a bit, invoking the ancestors, and then telling me to come back in a day or two for a dose of muti that would prove difficult to concoct the first time around.

Tata nodded.

'On the palms of my hands?' This must have been the same stuff that Tata had given to his last patient. I wondered if that man — I had seen him hobbling out looking happier than when he came in — had also had a problem with shit. But it was against the inyanga code of ethics to discuss the problems of your patients with others — or to divulge to your patients that you were giving them a placebo for that matter, which I thought I was getting.

'You just do as I say,' Tata said, and rose from the mat, trying to shake the pins and needles out of his legs. That really put my faith in Tata's healing powers to the test. Surely an inyanga could prevent himself from getting pins and needles?

Anyway, I wasn't totally unimpressed by my dad. Besides which I was desperate and willing to try anything. I had become an outcast at school and I did not want to suffer the pathetic and lonely pain of the pariah for another day.

Of course, the next morning it was panic stations when I went to have my first pee. It just wouldn't come. But my anxiety didn't last too long. I had to pee on my hands before getting to that bus-stop. And I did.

And it worked! In fact, I think that I exceeded the dosage. Not only was I no longer a pariah among my peers but that day I became more popular than I had ever been. I was offered about two dozen different sandwiches even before I got onto the bus. Thabo gave me a friendly slap on the back and Matiso revealed the secret of a trick in which he would hide his arms underneath his jersey and create the illusion that he had three arms hidden there.

And Lerato just came over to my seat and gave me such a sopping wet kiss that for a moment I thought she had left her lips stuck to my cheek . . . ugh!

3

A Deal
with Tata?

'How's that coffee getting on?'

It was the President himself, his shadow looming large on the kitchen wall.

'It's coming, it's coming,' I said, startled out of my reverie.

'But that kettle has been boiling . . . !'

'Shut up, you'll wake my wife,' I snarled at the white leader in a surprising moment of self-righteous indignation, holding a finger to my lips.

And the man actually did shut up. But not before making a very rude guttural noise. Then he glared at me and disappeared into the lounge.

I thought, with some satisfaction, that I had put the President in his place. They had to realize that they were in my house, my bloody little Sofasonke pondokkie which they had shoved me into with their guns and their laws.

In one of my more inspired newspaper articles I had coined the phrase 'skull and crossbones' to describe the little township shacks that had proliferated all over the country since De Vries's Nationalists came to power many decades ago. The 'houses', all identical, were bleak, grey little structures. Each one had a central front door flanked by two tiny dark windows, and this configuration reminded me of the hollow skull and crossbones that warned us all against entering such dangerous places as power stations and dynamite factories.

The Nationalists had started out by putting our ancestors in barren reserves far away from the cities. Then they realized, on second thoughts, that they needed us to extract gold and coal from the bowels of our ancestral land, so they built these houses as temporary dwellings. They were built with many deliberately uncomfortable features — tiny rooms, walls as thin and rough as matzos, toilets in the yards, no hot water, no bathrooms, corrugated asbestos roofs with no ceilings, tiny yards — so that 'migrant' workers and other temporary sojourners would not be tempted to stay on permanently.

And Sofasonke with its twenty-seven zones and its population of two million people was linked to the name of Nhlabatsi in a legend that had begun before I was born.

My parents were the first people to move into Sofasonke. This was in the mid-fifties, at a time when the Movement was resisting the government's huge resettlement programme. Prior to that blacks — natives as we were called in those days — lived in the same neighbourhoods with whites, 'coloureds' and Indians. But then the government introduced its first apartheid policies, which meant that Indians, coloureds and natives would all be moved to their separate respective areas 'to develop separately'.

How did the government eventually get the natives to move to Sofasonke? Well there are two versions of this story.

Version 1: The eminent witchdoctor Nhlabatsi was visited in the middle of the night by high-ranking government officials at his home in the racially integrated suburb of Sophiatown. There was room for everyone in this bustling, cosmopolitan area. Men just home from World War Two, filled with hope for a better life of lasting peace and full citizenship. Wood and coal vendors on horse-drawn carts, leaving trails of horse shit in the dusty streets. Gangsters in hats and suits, jiving with their gals to new African music, and emulating the hoods in American movies. Fahfee runners and bogus priests. Washerwomen, shebeen queens and nice-time girls. An inyanga or two. In this crazy place a deal was struck with my father in which he was paid the princely sum of ten thousand pounds in return for moving to Sofasonke. The logic was that if he moved first, the people would follow suit as they were in need of his services.

Version 2 is rather different. The people were given an ultimatum: move by such-and-such a date or be bulldozed. After the houses had been razed to the ground, the various 'racial groups' were then marched off at gunpoint to municipal offices. Here, one by one, they were subjected to government tests, both oral and physical, to determine who was coloured, who Indian, and who African. The physical test consisted of pushing a pencil through the hair of the candidate. If the pencil slipped out easily then he or she was obviously a coloured. If the pencil stayed put then the hair in question was clearly tightly curled and therefore African. The oral test was just as ingenious. The candidate was asked to pronounce certain English or Afrikaans words thus:

EXAMINER: Vereeniging.
CANDIDATE: Vrenegeng.
EXAMINER: Teacher.
CANDIDATE: Teeshar.
EXAMINER: Ship.
CANDIDATE: Sheep.
EXAMINER: You are a native.
CANDIDATE: You are — I mean I am ay nayteev.

These two versions have plagued me for many years. It is ridiculous to believe that my father could have accepted a gift from the government for selling out the very people whose ailments he treats, whose nightmares he interprets, whose demons he sends scuttling. But if he didn't, then Version 2 has to be believed.

Today there are ten times more temporary sojourners than 'permanent' whites in any Republican city.

I poured the coffee, finding it difficult to go about it quietly even though I had just warned De Vries not to disturb my wife who was sleeping less than two metres away, separated from the kitchen by a wafer of brick and concrete!

But the two men in my lounge had not learned their lesson. When I carried the two cups to them they were waiting for me, ready to pounce, their eyes glowing with rage in the early morning sunlight that had begun to filter through the curtain. I had never known humans so desperate for a cuppa.

'And what is der meaning of dis?' Mines asked me, thrusting a newspaper under my chin. So it was not the smell of coffee that had steamed them up after all.

'What's the matter with you, man!' I hissed, spilling coffee from both cups into their saucers. 'See what you made me do now!'

'So this is what you people do to me while I'm spending every

14

hour of every day trying to give you a better life!' The President sounded genuinely hurt.

I really didn't know what this man was on about now. I assumed that one of my stories in the newspaper had angered him. Some black leader or other had probably made another statement deploring another death in detention and rejecting the official explanation with that well-worn phrase, 'with the contempt it deserves'. So what!

But De Vries shoved the newspaper, a three-month-old copy of the *Black World*, into my hands the moment after I had dropped the cups on the table. He had found it on a side-table amongst other yellowing newspapers and magazines.

Mines angrily jabbed a fat finger at the offending page. And so outraged was he that he sent specks of spit flying through the air and splashing onto my neck and cheek!

'You're fucking messing in my neck!' I told him, slapping and wiping as if I were engaged in one of my protracted nocturnal battles with bedbugs.

He made the same guttural noise that had issued from the presidential throat in the kitchen a few minutes ago. I had never heard such an expression from a human before. Maybe it was a party slogan or some war cry they chanted in parliament whenever they heckled the official opposition — a lone, liberal Jewish lady who held a northern suburbs seat in the name of the United Liberals.

I looked down at the page and saw the reason for their outrage. Staring back at me was a black and white picture of De Vries taken by my friend and colleague, Gustav Kinnear. It had been shot at a press conference after the President had signed a historic bill in parliament declaring that all black Republicans would soon have their own independent states. The caption beneath the full-length photograph quoted him as saying: 'And I have achieved this today with a drop of ink and not, as is the habit with so many natives elsewhere in Africa, with a torrent of blood.'

The picture had most probably been taken as De Vries uttered those very words; the President is seen pointing proudly at himself — an inversion of his usual manner, which was to jab at the world. His mouth is open. A beam of light from a chandelier shines onto his forehead giving him the look of a mad demon.

But that's what the picture looked like before I got hold of it one Sunday afternoon after lunch.

Khensani and I had enjoyed a very satisfying meal of chicken curry, rice and potatoes with bread pudding and custard for dessert. Afterwards I had gone to lie down on the couch — exactly where De Vries himself was sitting now, snarling at me — with two cold beers. Khensani had taken the Volksie and gone off to a Sofasonke Education Crisis Committee meeting. When the Committee was launched the previous year I had asked her if she could ever recall a time when there had not been a crisis in education.

I opened the Sunday edition of the newspaper and began to read about how all the different ethnic groups wanted their own home-lands. De Vries had consulted extensively with all the ethnic leaders in a range of 'multi-ethnic summits' and according to him this is what we all wanted.

None of us blacks belong in this country. And this comes from a man who was born in a small town somewhere in the Netherlands!

I found a red pen and went to work on the white leader. I gave him a pair of Raybans and a tiny Hitler moustache. Then I rewrote the caption to read: The tapeworm will never get me.

And this is what was making these Afrikaners so angry. I decided that enough was enough. I turned to them.

'Hey, look here,' I said, trying very hard to keep my voice down, 'you know that you were talking shit at this press conference. And all I did was vent my spleen for all the things you've done to us. This is the first time you've ever been to Sofasonke — am I right or wrong?'

'What has that got to do with it?' De Vries asked, tilting his head towards me as if inviting me into a rugby scrum with him.

'Well . . . if you made these surprise house calls on a more regular basis then maybe I would've been too scared to do something like that to your picture.' This was not quite the point that I wanted to make, but nobody who mattered was listening to me so I kept quiet.

The two politicians glared at me as if this was the biggest load of bullshit they had ever heard. And they glared into their murky coffee cups as if it was the worst rubbish they had ever drunk.

'Van Riebeeck Instant,' I said.

'Go to hell!' De Vries cursed, spilling some of the coffee.

His reaction was harsh, but not surprising. I was now trespassing on the hallowed ground of white national symbols: flags, national braaivleis holidays, the image on banknotes and, yes, even on coffee tins, of the long-haired Dutch sailor and ex-convict who had 'dis-covered' the Republic way back in 1652 . . .

4

Tata,
I Presume

In the meantime the sun had risen on another Saturday morning in Sofasonke. It would be nice to say that we heard the dulcet throaty chirp-chirp-chirping of birds outside and that kind of thing. But Sofasonke is a bit short of flora and fauna, you know, the trunky/leafy and feathery/beaky stuff you find in the suburbs. I don't think old De Vries and his illustrious line of predecessors had planned specifically to do us out of mossies and doves and oak trees, but it's one of those side-effects of apartheid, of which there are many — but I don't want to go into that right now.

I drove De Vries and his partner to 970 Mapetla Street, the house with the original orange awning. The sky had a tinge of red on that summer morning, as if the killings in this huge (sprawling, as all good journalists like myself liked to say) township the night before had been so violent that the blood had spattered against the sky.

The identical skulls and crossbones stood in quiet, brooding rows on all sides. Dogs barked in backyards, smoke billowed out of chimneys. In the distance I could hear a train dragging its steely clamour further and further away.

I drove past the decrepit ruin of a beerhall. Before the riots this had been a popular watering-hole with festive laughter gushing out of its windows. Now it was simply a scorched shell, littered with glass from smashed windows and broken beer bottles, the hollow creak of defeat emanating from the hole where a door once was.

Scraps of paper fluttered down the streets until they were caught like hapless fish in sagging garden fences. Against the wall of a bombarded municipal office was scrawled the rebellious cliché:

What wouldn't they pay? School fees for an education that would turn blacks into hewers of wood and drawers of water, the poll tax, rent . . . Underneath this sign someone had added the legend:

VIVA SIBISI VIVA

The first time I had come across this slogan was hundreds of Saturdays ago as a six-year-old hoisted on my uncle's shoulders. Uncle Nimrod had taken me along to a shebeen on one sweltering Saturday afternoon.

The trip to Uncle Nim's favourite watering-hole passed without incident, but the journey back home, which was long overdue, was much more exciting. For one thing he seemed to be mistaking shadows for old friends, tripping over imaginary rocks and slipping down phantom dongas. This was very entertaining for me as I sat perched high on his shoulders, precariously clutching his sweaty forehead.

And all the time Uncle Nim was singing a scurrilous song as he swayed down the dark Sofasonke streets. It was a ditty about his calabash of beer and his woman. He sang:

'I take them both with both hands,
and draw them to my lips.
I taste them both with equal passion,
and that is why the one cannot stand the other.'

He staggered around a corner and walked smack into a riot. Police sirens and men running everywhere. Stones, gunshots, police dogs barking in the back of police vans, then being unleashed on screaming crowds collapsing on each other, a palisade of clenched fists perforating the sky and chants of

VIVA SIBISI VIVA

Uncle Nim flung me off his shoulders, gripped my arm and ran, sweeping my feet off the ground. As we neared home, I turned to my uncle who seemed to have sobered up considerably.

'What do those letters stand for, Uncle Nim?' I asked.

'What letters?' He was trying to get his breath back, but I could tell that his mind was preoccupied with what we had just witnessed.

'CBC.'

'Sibisi,' he explained, in gasping monosyllables. 'It's a last name. Do you know what a last name is?'

'Yes I do,' I nodded.

'Tell me.'

'Mandla,' I said proudly. We were speaking English and I was very proud of my precocious progress thus far.

'No, it's not,' Uncle Nim shook his head, smiling. He was still struggling to get his breath back.

'Well, the last time somebody called my name they said, "Mandla!"' I shouted into my cupped hands to demonstrate this point.

Uncle Nim laughed so much in that dark, lampless street that a few curtains were irritably swept aside and shadows grunted at us.

'Your last name is Nhlabatsi,' he told me. 'Your first name is Mandla.'

'Why were they shouting this name Sibisi then?'

'Because it is the name of a leader.'

'A leader?'

'A man who is fighting for our freedom, the freedom of black people.'

'Was he fighting there too tonight?'

'No, he is in jail.'

'Then how can he be fighting?'

Another twenty or so questions followed before I was satisfied with my first real political lesson. Uncle Nim died in a police cell before my eighth birthday.

My two companions were literally lying low: Mines, beside me in front, collapsed into his creased pinstriped jacket, and the President at the back, kissing my back seat with its effluvia of old leather, sweat, and antediluvian vomit (before the floods that followed when my love for alcohol increased). And no matter where he is these days and what his vicissitudes may be, that fugitive, cramped-up moment spent in the back of my Volksie must surely have been the furthest he's ever been from the hallowed portals of the plush Presidential Residence.

Finally we arrived at the home of my childhood. The sun glowed from the orange roof. I saw that the curtains were drawn closed, a certain sign that my strange but beloved parents were still asleep, dreaming the weird dreams that they would later translate into omens and portents of events still to happen. I knocked on the door, flanked by the two white men who kept looking around furtively and shifting about from one dusty shoe to the other.

The bedroom window opened and I saw my mother's face, veiled by the Terylene that I used as fly-traps in the endless boring summer afternoons of my boyhood. She smiled at me, her one and only son. Then she looked down quizzically at my two companions, flung the curtain aside like a bride suddenly distressed by an unpleasant memory of the best man, and stared balefully down at De Vries. I did not need Tata's clairvoyant powers to know that trouble was fast approaching.

'Last night I swept the rubbish into the yard, when I should have swept it into a corner in the kitchen,' Mama told me with a querulous wail in her high-pitched, asthmatic voice. 'I knew I should not have tempted the tokoloshe. Now look what has happened!'

I groaned. It is considered bad luck (by Mama and other Sofasonke souls) to sweep dirt out of the house after sunset. And the ominous advent of none other than De Vries was the result of my superstitious mother's reckless oversight.

'Mama, open up,' I said as if there was a toilet in the house and I was bursting to pee, 'these men have come to see Tata.'

Mama ignored my entreaty. She waved a petulant finger at De Vries. 'You,' she said, 'what do you want here?'

'Nyalabutsey the witchdoctor,' the President said, rendering the worst mispronunciation of our surname I had ever heard.

'Hah! Nyalabutsey!' my mother cackled.

'Mama!' I cried desperately.

Mama ignored me. 'You remember March nine? March nine?' she asked De Vries, arching her eyebrows into imperious little twin bows. When Mama's questions echoed there was trouble abroad, as in: 'Why did you shit in your pants? Shit in your pants?'

De Vries scowled at me and at the Minister of Mines as if we were the cause of this audacious inquisition.

'I'm asking you,' Mama insisted emphatically. This was no mere hypothetical question.

The Minister of Mines whispered something in the President's ear. De Vries nodded and looked up triumphantly at Mama.

'Oh, the day the women came to parliament,' he said disdainfully, 'to make a bit of noise and wave some banners abyout.'

'A bit of noise!' Mama scoffed. 'That March nine was the biggest March nine since we have been fighting you in this country, Mr President . . .' The last expressed with a contemptuous sneer.

'Mama!'

'. . . the day we came to tell you where to bury your passbooks and all your other ugly dirty laws . . . but you couldn't even come out to meet us, could you?'

'Mama, please,' I begged. I heard a car starting up somewhere, the unmistakable rasping noise of someone vomiting in a backyard near-by (I sympathized with the anonymous brother as I too was sweating profusely and feeling queasy), a door creaking open. Sofasonke was waking up. We couldn't be seen standing in a yard while the President of the country received a tongue-lashing from the wife of an inyanga!

'Twenty thousand women! And where were you? Hiding in a cup-board, hey? Making wee-wee in the lavatory! You strike a woman, you strike a rock.' Then Mama burst into a political song which the women had sung on that day to taunt the President:

'Wathint' abafazi
Wathint' imbokodo'

The door opened and Tata's long, gentle, unassuming frame filled the doorway. When he rested his sleepy eyes on his two visitors, his face showed not a flicker of surprise. He wore a vest and shabby, faded-pink pyjama pants. Some blanket fluff nestled in his black and grey beard.

Tata greeted his visitors courteously and invited them to step underneath his orange roof — with an equanimity that bordered on indifference! Maybe Tata had been involved in some secret conspir-acy with these white people after all. Would the two gentlemen excuse him for a while, he wanted to know. Then he left the room — for the ritual of bathing and drenching himself in aromatic herbs and spices — yes, like a Kentucky Fried Chicken, I suppose, but without the batter.

Tata's latest two patients sat beside each other on a two-seater sofa. I sat on the remaining easy chair and stared at the dusty tips of my Florsheim brogues.

Mama's tirade a few moments ago had not been out of character at all and, truth to tell, I had expected something like it. Only a few years ago, a couple of weeks before I moved out of the house, I had witnessed a similar attack on two Jehovah's Witnesses. The couple were dressed up to the nines (he in a tailor-made powder-blue pin-stripe suit, she in a navy-blue two-piece with red hat and shoes) and sporting such incandescent smiles that their invisible haloes must have been switched on to maximum.

After a few dire warnings about the imminent advent of God, the gentleman dug into a suitcase and brought out the latest copy of:

'The *Watchtower*, madam. Yours to keep for just a small donation.'

And where was I while all this was going on? Sitting exactly where I was sitting now, listening to Nina Simone. Mama had her ample back to me and was blocking out the gorgeous angel and her male crusader. But with a few strategic movements on my part — craning the neck to peep over Ma's shoulder, ducking low to peer under her arm — I was able to catch brief glimpses of her and was using those precious moments to communicate to her that she was gorgeous, that I was impressed, and that I liked her. How could one not have liked those big shining eyes that gazed, I could see from my vantage point, from Mama to her companion, to Mama, to her companion, as he spoke about the beauty and wonder of heaven? Lose the girl, was my mental advice to him. Not many Sofasonkans are going to want to head for this super suburb in the sky while there are such mortals as she sauntering down their own dusty streets.

A brooch no bigger than a fingernail flashed from her left breast. What was it? A little golden fish, a cartoon character, some biblical emblem, I knew not what. But at intervals the sun caught it and reflected its beams straight in my eyes.

'Watch the hour,' Mama was saying. 'Watch the hour! I go to church every Sunday to pray to my God. I help the poor people. I am kind to everyone. I am kind even to a dog which I hear barking in the latest hours keeping me awake and remembering all my troubles and my asthma and my feet that swell like magwinya . . .' Mama paused for a moment to catch her breath, wheezing indignantly. She turned slightly and pointed a fat finger inside. '. . . My food it is burning on the stove and you want me to watch the hour — for a little something!' She shoved the magazine back into the man's hand and, before I could step in and save the Nhlabatsis from further embarrassment — and get a chance to speak to the girl — Mama had sent them both fleeing through the gate and down Mapetla Street.

De Vries had got up to resume the restless, and irritating, up and down pacing which he had begun in my house. But my parents' little skull and crossbones, like mine in Zone 3, did not provide much room for this nervous behaviour. So after a while he abandoned it and went to sit beside his pal again on the sofa opposite me. The two immediately began to fill each other's ears with frantic whisperings — a little like two schoolboys in the principal's office while the principal is out.

'When do you think De Jong will announce it?' De Vries said.

'Today, tomorrow —' the Minister shrugged his shoulders. 'They will want to make an announcement before the rumours start. But the country has to know that the process of democracy and the rule of law has been tampered . . .'

'The bastards!' De Vries cursed, shaking with rage. 'But this witchdoctor will do something, Ockert, he's the best on the continent.'

Ockert! A Christian name! This was real soul brother stuff. But what was Ockert's surname? I gazed at his solemn face, but it wouldn't come to me.

'My philosophy is the only way, Ockert,' De Vries said, his voice suddenly quivering with conviction. 'This continent is a cruel one and for us to survive' — at this point he glanced at me — 'we, I had to release their leader.'

'Of course,' Ockert agreed, placing a consoling hand on his companion's shoulder. 'But . . . will this Nyalabutsey understand?'

'He understands already,' De Vries said. 'Didn't you see it in his eyes just now? He knew years ago we would be coming here today, he knows why we're here . . .'

I sat as still as possible, mesmerized, taking in every audible word of this strange exchange. What was it all about? Then:

'Why didn't you take them to Mosotho's house? That malalapipe would've given them what they deserved.'

This suggestion came from behind the closed door of my parents' bedroom, from my mother's sharp tongue to be more precise. It was uttered in Xhosa so I doubt if the two white men understood what Mama had said. And even in English it would have made no sense to them at all — unless they knew that Mosotho was a dissolute, malevolent, disreputable witchdoctor who, it was widely rumoured, turned all those he detested into cats and set them loose in the Sotho section of Sofasonke (where this animal is highly regarded as a culinary delicacy served with pap and tomato gravy). And malalapipe? Well, this meant that Mosotho was a troglodyte who sometimes chose to spend his nights in subterranean slumber in the labyrinth of stormwater drains and sewers underneath Sofasonke.

But the two men did pick up the menacing edge in Ma's voice. They glanced in my direction, expecting me to reveal something of what my mother had said. But, like a stubborn boy who refuses to disclose the whereabouts of his insolent cohorts, I looked everywhere — at Mama's cluttered display cabinet, at the plaster-of-Paris birds on the wall that were cast in small, smaller, smallest to represent comparative and superlative distance — I looked everywhere but in their fleshy faces. There was a photo of me and my buddies on the wall and I decided to concentrate on that to pass the time.

It was a picture of me, Tshepo, Matiso and Gus, taken at St Christopher's in Swaziland many years ago when we were all doing our O levels. The picture hung crookedly on its hook and it seemed as if the four of us were aware of this and were desperately trying not to fall: we were all laughing, showing off rows of teeth like newly harvested mealies. Tshepo was holding onto me, I was pulling Matiso's tie, Matiso was bent double trying to get my hands off his tie, Gus was giving the Black Power salute. What was the joke? Who had taken the picture? I was surprised to realize suddenly that I could remember neither of these pieces of personal history.

The white statesman and his sidekick had followed my pensive gaze until their ice-blue eyes rested on the framed photograph.

'Who's the one on the end?' Mines asked me.

He wanted to know about Gus. Now it suddenly came back to me: until a recent cabinet reshuffle, Ockert had been Deputy Minister of State Security!

'Who's this De Jong you're talking about?' I countered.

De Vries's jaw dropped in disbelief. What an uppity kaffir! I could hear the thought ringing loudly in his head.

Just then my father came in. He was wearing a red and black checked shirt underneath a brown pullover, despite the heat of the morning. His greying curls were gleaming with Kamillen and its redolent aroma filled the room.

I sat forward in my chair, marvelling once again at Tata's composure: there was no evidence at all of surprise in the soft brown eyes that twinkled between the deep imprints of his crow's-feet.

But Tata was used to having unusual patients. The most memorable until today had been a migrant worker from central Africa who worked many years ago as a miner at Western Deep Levels. This miner had resolved to go back home to lead his people to independence from British colonial rule and he wanted Tata to concoct for him a muti that would give him 'the courage of a lion' to fulfil this noble ambition. Tata must've given him some very potent stuff to swallow, sniff or smear on his body, because thirty years have passed and the man is still president of his starving, oppressed country. Indeed, his self-proclaimed, official designation is 'President for Life'. I really think Tata overdoes it with the muti sometimes.

But enough of that.

Together with the sweet smell of his hair-cream, Tata seemed to have brought a palpable aura into the room. The two white men rose solemnly, in the same way they do when they sing their national anthem. I suppose it had something to do with Tata's reputation as well as his demeanour of grace and self-respect. He nodded benignly at the two men, waiting for me to introduce them formally.

I rose and made a gauche gesture to Tata to take my chair. I had had no formal training in introducing Presidents and other cabinet ministers to inyangas. Whenever whitey meets whitey in Africa that moment is so profound that their first words are immortalized. One thinks of the well-known 'Dr Livingstone, I presume!' or the more general 'By golly! I thought the tsetse flies had got you too, old chap!' Well, only time will tell if this meeting between Willem Adriaan de Vries and Sizwe Ngomezulu Nhlabatsi will be remembered. But if this should ever chance to happen, let me record my father's words for posterity. He said:

'Yebo, it is the big makulu baas this one.' And then, turning to me: 'And how is Khensani?'

Enquiries as to the health and welfare of loved ones! Had I not been so flabbergasted by his question I would have said something like, 'Okay, I guess, we just need to catch up on some lost sleep.' But I nodded and said, in Xhosa: 'She is well, Tata.'

De Vries and Ockert indicated, with a series of grunts, that they would like to speak to Tata alone, and, with a pair of glowering stares, tried to relocate me to some distant homeland. I uprooted most eagerly, like some gullible bantu who had been promised ten cows, a BMW and a chieftainship.

5

On a
Mission

I left without a word of gratitude from De Vries and Ockert for the favour I had done them. But then why should they be thanking me for anything? They had just given me, a small-time Sofasonke journalist who drank a little too much sometimes and smoked the medicinal leaf a little more than he should, the scoop of the decade! The next thing was to fetch my friend and *Black World* colleague, photographer Gustav Kinnear. I swerved expertly out of a den of dirty Sofasonke kids and headed for Ma Dikeledi's — I needed two beers to wash down some dust first before I wrote the story of the century.

The headlines flashed about in my head like those flash cards which my Sub B teacher used to hold up before the class:

PRESIDENT VISITS WITCHDOCTOR

No, far too bland. Well, how about:

DE VRIES IN SECRET PACT WITH SOFASONKE INYANGA

Better.

I parked my car outside Ma Dikeledi's skull and crossbones in Zone 4. Someone peeped out at me from a parting in the lounge curtain — for the second time that day and it wasn't even eight o'clock yet. It was Ma Diks herself and she had a worried frown on her face.

I got out of the car and was about to wave to her but the face was no longer there. Now what's going on here, I wondered. Ma Diks had already opened her front door before I reached it. Two thumb-sucking toddlers tangled themselves around her legs, tugging at her dress. She shoved them back into the house with an impatient, 'Suka!'

'Good morning, Ma Diks. How's it going?' I said, already salivating at the thought of the two cold ones I was about to sink.

'What do you want here, my child?'

Awu, what was this? 'The same thing Van Riebeeck wanted from the Khoi when he landed on our beaches,' I said. But Ma Diks had not spent much time at school so I had to elaborate: 'Refreshment, and to stay a while.'

Ma Diks looked at me as if I was speaking High Dutch. 'Haven't you heard, my son?' she said with the same grave look on her face as when she had first announced to the world many years ago, after her husband's death, that she would be opening up a shebeen to compensate for the monthly widow's pension which she would not get because she was black.

'Heard what, Ma Diks?'

'There's trouble — the police are all over in Sofasonke again today, making their roadblocks and searching the cars . . .'

'What for?' As if the police ever needed a good reason.

'The comrades they say the whites they are fighting amongst each other and the right-wings have taken over — I don't know . . .' She shrugged.

'Damn!' I exclaimed. The news of De Vries and Ockert had already reached the township. And, just as I thought, there had been some kind of palace coup! I had to know more: 'When did you see the comrades?'

'They were here early this morning. They're going around to all the shebeens. They are telling us not to sell liquor to anybody. They say the war is on.' Ma Diks had a look of distress on her face. She showed, as kindly as she could, a reluctance to talk to me and, from her tiny stoep three metres away from where I stood at the fence, spoke just about loud enough for me to hear, all the time glancing nervously up and down the street.

Damn and blast! The De Vries government did not want us to smoke dagga and the comrades were prohibiting alcohol — quite undemocratically! My head throbbed now, with indignation as well as babalaas. I just had to have that beer!

'How about just one cold one,' I said, swinging my car keys around my finger as a sign that I would make for the hills if my request was granted. 'Take-away.'

'Hawu, the police and the comrades, Scara.' Ma Diks, like any other inhabitant of Sofasonke, had good reason to be afraid of the cops: about ten years ago they had killed her husband, Spooky.

Spooky — so called because of his eyes, which popped out of their sockets like big marbles — was a happy-go-lucky man who worked hard and spent his spare time with his pigeons and his weekends in shebeens drinking — but never lived to sit in one of the most famous Sofasonke shebeens: his own house.

Spooky was a household name in Sofasonke for his hobby: breeding pigeons. This was unique in the township as it was a pastime indulged in mostly by white youths in the suburbs. Spooky was seen as both the wrong colour and the wrong age for a pigeon-fancier. And, more importantly, he was also in the wrong income group. But despite all these adverse factors, the pigeons took to the skies above Sofasonke, breasts pushed out proudly, gizzards propped to the brim with mieliepap and other delights, plumage glowing on most days, wings flapping to the rhythms of the bustle below. Spooky's flocks of birds saw everything that Sofasonke had to show as well as those things it did not want the world to see. The birds perched on fences listening to housewives gossip, they hovered over drunks swaggering home to the accompaniment of their own maudlin monologues, they watched workers rushing for trains, buses and taxis, children trudging to school, washing fluttering on washing-lines. They gawked at lovers making love in alleys. They watched when the students gathered outside their classrooms chanting songs and marching and tumbling down when the first shots were fired from police rifles. They circled the skies when the first army convoys rolled into Sofasonke to restore order, or more appropriately, to halt the incipient revolution before it grew in determination or spread to other townships in other provinces.

Spooky's pigeon hok was the height of a man and took up half his tiny yard. In the other half there was a pine tree, which towered above the roofs of the township, with a ramshackle toilet in its shade. What was left of the yard was carpeted in pine needles and cones, downy pigeon feathers and pigeon shit. The latter also provided a certain odour that came to be associated with the Spooky residence and its surroundings.

How many birds did Spooky have? Some said five hundred, some a thousand, while others argued that there were at least ten times that number. But how could Spooky indulge himself in such an expensive hobby? It was common knowledge that pigeons strayed from white suburbs many kilometres away and came to make a new home in Sofasonke. Other pigeons found their way to Spooky's hok in much more mercenary and secretive ways: stolen and stuffed under the shirts of little boys who came and dared to bargain with Spooky. A typical deal would go like this:

'Where did you get this bird, sonny?'

'Where the white people live. It was walking about on the ground.'

'Do you know why it was walking about on the ground?'

'No, Ntate Spooky.'

'Look underneath this wing. See the blood there.'

'I see it, Ntate.'

'I will give you fifteen cents.'

'Awu, Uncle Spooky, eighty cents.'

'It will cost me two rands to fix it up.'

'Thirty cents, Uncle Spooky.'

'Here's twenty. Goodbye.'

Spooky worked as a messenger in the city of Johannesburg, rushing about on a scooter every day between white men's offices, delivering architectural drawings in long cardboard tubes. One day he was on his way to the bank to deposit some cash for his employers, when he was accosted by three tsotsis in Eloff Street. They stabbed him in the neck and made off with the 'loot', as the *Black World* put it, an amount of about fifteen thousand rand.

Spooky was rushed to Baragwanath Hospital. He was discharged two days later with six stitches in his neck and a throbbing head.

Ma Diks was happy to have her husband back home alive. He always called her his biggest, loveliest pigeon and on that day she cooed and flapped around him. Immediately she arranged a weekend party to welcome him home and to give thanks to the ancestors by sacrificing a sheep.

Mama and Tata were among the guests. Tata officiated at the slaughter with his usual solemnity, but afterwards got slowly tipsy along with Mama and all the other guests. The old folk caroused deep into the night, ululating and swaying to songs from the Transkei and Zululand. When I came to fetch my parents the party was sounding like a cross between one of Mama's revivalist meetings and a Sofasonke stokvel.

Who does not know the incredible mess that greets the host and hostess the morning after the night before? Early the following day Spooky stumbled into his yard to bury a heap of sheep's entrails — the discarded leftovers of the previous night's thanksgiving party. While he was digging a hole the cops appeared from nowhere and pointed their guns at him. It turned out that they had suspected Spooky of being involved in the robbery and thought they had caught him burying the money.

Spooky, of course, could not reveal the whereabouts of the missing cash. They hung him in his pine tree and beat him up. Ma Diks screamed until she fainted. The birds screeched and flapped their wings. Later, the neighbours revived Ma Diks and told her that Spooky had been dragged into a police van and taken away.

The next day they knocked on Ma Dikeledi's door to tell her that her husband had died in his cell after slipping on a bar of soap in the shower.

'Look, Ma Diks,' I said, 'just give me a cold one and I'll be on my way. I tell you I need it badly today.'

'Hawu, Scara,' she sighed. Then, without turning her head, she ordered someone inside the house to bring me a cold Castle. The woman was being very cautious; an arm protruded from the door and passed the beer to her. She told me to come closer and to unzip my windbreaker. Then she deposited the bottle against my bosom and I zipped up again, gripping the cold beer with one hand.

So furtive were these actions that if anyone, cop or comrade, had been keeping an eye on the shebeen from a discreet distance the exchange would have gone unnoticed.

I took out some cash but Ma Diks shook her head vigorously. 'Some other time, Scara,' she said, shooed the toddlers inside and disappeared into the house herself.

I drove a few blocks down the road and, on a quiet corner, opened the beer with the buckle of my seatbelt. Wet beads dampened my hands and a foamy crown emerged from the mouth and subsided again, playing peekaboo with me. I took about five huge, delicious gulps and felt, I am not ashamed to say, irritated when I ran out of oxygen to carry on guzzling. I should've asked for two, I told myself, enjoying the rumbling explosion of an appreciative wind.

After Spooky was buried, Ma Dikeledi started the shebeen in order to feed the children and pay the rent. 'The House of Tears', as it was called, became a popular drinking place.

Just three weeks after Ma Diks opened her door to the eternally parched residents of Sofasonke, two men arrived to slake their thirst. They sat and drank for a few hours, buying generous rounds of beer and brandy for everyone in the joint. And when their tongues were well oiled they told Ma Diks and the other patrons how they had acquired their wealth: they had robbed a messenger on a scooter in Eloff Street a month ago. Coincidence plays its sleight-of-hand tricks on the rich as well as the poor, skulks in the mansions of the gold and diamond magnates of Sandton as well as in the skull and crossbones shebeens of Sofasonke.

Ma Diks's shebeen soon acquired legendary status, thanks to the late Spooky's pigeons. After virtually watching the death of their keeper, they were set loose to seek new masters. Ma Diks had the hok chopped down and burnt, and with a hose which she bought especially for the operation she had the tiny yard douched of feathers, birdshit, and her husband's blood. But this cleansing ritual proved only partially successful: Spooky has been dead for years but still the feathers remain, and every man or woman who stops by at Ma Diks's for a pint leaves with a feather stuck to his or her shoe, cuff, lapel like a brooch or a downy talisman.

There were shadows around the car, blocking out the sun. Then there was a knock on my window. I looked up. About eight youths had surrounded the car.

'Open up,' one of them said, miming the motion of rolling down a window. I complied, thinking, dammit! Ma Diks was right, and all she was trying to do was protect me. Why do some of us prefer to learn the hard way?

'Hey how's it, guys?' I greeted them all, putting on a brave, friendly smile. One of them held a blood-soaked handkerchief against his temple. He was squatting on his haunches, shifting uncomfortably on his tackies as the pain swung about in his head. He gritted his teeth as he dabbed at his temple with the bloody rag.

Two or three amandlas were shouted back at me. The youth at the window greeted me with the familiar township 'Heita.'

My mind was racing. How should I handle this one?

'Comrade, we are calling on the oppressed masses of our country to stop drinking the white man's liquor and to support the call for a stayaway until our leaders are released.'

With the cold beer in my hand I didn't feel at all like an oppressed mass, but I nodded anyway.

'Hand it over, com.'

The humiliation of handing over your liquor to kids! The bastards! But what could I do? The youth took the bottle from me and, without taking his eyes off me, handed it to a comrade behind him. This fellow held the bottle upside down and the good stuff ran into the dust of Sofasonke like horse piss.

'Do you have any more, com?' He raised his eyebrows and gave me the kind of gaze reserved for a stubborn child who won't hand over a bottle of poisonous disinfectant. He scanned the back seat and the floor of the car. His breath whooshed past my face and it was obvious that he was also boycotting the white man's toothpaste.

'No more, com.' I couldn't believe what was happening to my beer — beer I hadn't even paid for yet! And these so-called radicals were probably all half my age!

One comrade at the rear of the pack, who had not been distracted by the Spilling of the Beer ceremony as the others had been, lowered his head to give me his full gaze. A sparse moustache ran across his upper lip. 'Ask him where he bought the beer,' he told their spokescomrade in Zulu.

'You heard the question,' the leader said with a languid sigh.

'I bought the beer in town, com,' I said. 'Before I knew about the boycott.'

'Such a cold one, com?' The youth who had spilled the beer offered the bottle to anyone who wished to corroborate his opinion.

I cast a discreet eye around for Ma Diks's trade mark, the tell-tale feather that would be fluttering about somewhere in the car or on my person. I could see nothing.

'Show him his mother, he's lying!' the injured youth snarled impatiently. I suppose he was tired of being the only one in pain.

'That's the truth, com,' I stuck to my story. Ma Diks had had more than her fair share of grief. No ways was I going to get her into trouble.

Their leader still kept his face in my car. He stared hard at me, trying to reach a verdict. Eventually he exhaled another gust of foul breath and decided to give me the benefit of the doubt. But that did not mean that I was now free to go on my merry way.

'What do you do, com?' he asked me.

I do many things: I write stories of fantasy and imagination, I drink beer, I make love to my wife — more often than is normal for my age and race, if the whitey magazines can be believed. I clean my car about once a month — and in this I am well below the national average. I ferry beleaguered presidents of minority governments to my father's mat of bones and charms. But I assumed that he wanted to know what I did for a living.

'I'm a journalist.'

'For which paper?'

'*Black World*,' I said and waited for the customary response in much the same way one flings a door shut and waits for the bang.

'That reactionary paper!' the wounded comrade shouted, coming closer. 'I won't even wipe my arse with that reactionary nonsense!'

Reactionary. That word again. I tell you if these comrades didn't like a football team it was a reactionary team. Or a goal for that matter!

'Hayi, wait now, Comrade Vusi,' the leader said. 'We are trying to find out something here.' He turned to me. 'We want you to take us on a mission, com. You are a fortunate somebody because the struggle has chosen you for a very important mission.'

'No problem,' I said, which was a lie. I didn't like the idea at all. These comrades had interrogated me, threatened me, and spilled my beer — and I was determined to get myself another one, more out of mutinous spite than to slake my thirst.

Just then another car approached and the pack encircled it. It was a canary-yellow Corolla, a little beaten up and suffering from a severe rash of rust.

'Can we wait for our comrades, com?' the leader asked me. A hypothetical question if ever there was one. He came to sit in the passenger seat while the bleeding Vusi shifted his arse into a comfortable position behind me — where the President had sat hardly an hour ago. I watched the action around the other car from behind the wheel, feeling a little like one does after the cops have laid into you for not having your dompas handy and are now working your friends' case: a little pity for your buddies, but also a little relieved.

There were two men in the Corolla. Questions were being asked and the boot searched. I chose this moment to ask my new comrades a question of my own:

'What's going on here?' I made sure that my tone was inquisitive rather than demanding.

'You're a reporter but you don't know fuck all!' the bleeding Vusi shouted from the back seat.

The leader chuckled and turned to me. 'Our country is having a right-wing take-over,' he said. 'People are saying they've killed De Vries but we don't know for sure.'

'A coop, Mr Reporter,' Vusi called snidely from behind me.

'Oh, you mean a coup,' I said sarcastically.

'C-O-U-P — coop,' he said.

One of the comrades detached himself from the group around the Corolla. He ran across a small patch of veld towards Radebe's store on the street corner. He was shaking his fist as he ran, and bounding along in his tackies which put some extra buoyancy into his already springy stride.

The side of the store was a huge face-brick wall marked with scraps of bills and posters advertising stokvels, township plays and old karate films. The bouncing youth came to a standstill at the wall, raised his fist, in which he had been clutching an aerosol can of paint, and sprayed this message in large canary-yellow letters:

STAYAWAY MONDAY 28 JANUARY — UNTIL FRY (abbreviated because he was beginning to run out of wall space) 9 FEB. NO WORK NO SCOOL NO STRONG DRINKS AMANDLA

A cry of 'Amandla!' thundered through the air. And suddenly people — kids, men, women — their fists raised in the salute of the oppressed masses, appeared from behind rickety fences, in dark doorways, on the stoep filled with shoppers and indolent kids.

The youth signed off with the customary:

VIVA SIBISI VIVA

Then he cantered back proudly to the Corolla. As he passed us he shouted to the leader, whom he called Machel, that they would follow us in the other car.

'Let's go, com,' Machel instructed me, pleased that they had made their mark on a tiny fraction of the masses of Sofasonke.

And so off we went in convoy, my pink and black Volksie leading the way while the two bewildered men in the yellow Corolla obediently repeated every swerve, bump and turn I made.

A police siren whined in the distance, like a deadly mosquito declaring its thirst for my blood.

'System!' Comrade Vusi declared, spitting the word out with

venom. 'Maybe the same pigs that kicked me. But today is the day they join their ancestors!'

What the hell did he mean? A glance in the rear-view mirror revealed all. He had produced a huge gun from underneath his shirt and placed it purposefully on his lap. When he caught my disapproving eye in the mirror, he told me gruffly to concentrate on my driving.

Dammit! I could be in prison before lunch-time. Languishing on the Island before next weekend! What the hell was happening to me today? Very likely more than happened to some septuagenarians in an entire lifetime. And I was only thirty-four.

At least my navigator was evidently as eager as I was to avoid the System; I could tell by the directions he was giving me, trying to keep as far away from the sound of the siren as possible.

This precaution was small comfort to me though. Not all cops who roamed the streets of Sofasonke heralded their coming with flashing blue lights and screaming sirens. There were the Buffels and Casspirs, those lumbering anti-riot behemoths, like some species of African wildlife awoken from hibernation to kill all who threatened the white man. It was surely only a matter of time before we turned a corner and drove straight into the path of one of these predators.

'Com,' I asked desperately, 'what about the Buffels?'

'You a driver in de struggle, okay?' Vusi reminded me. 'When we promote you to adviser we'll let you know.'

This young man was on a high. I could tell by the way he shifted about on the seat, rearranging the weapon on his lap and dabbing at the wound in his head. As far as he was concerned this struggle, begun three and a half centuries ago, would be over before midnight tonight if he had anything to do with it. His comrade sitting beside me was more realistic.

'Com Vusi, shove the weapon,' he said.

But Vusi ignored him. The yellow Corolla was still following us obediently. We drove down a backstreet in Zone 4. A trio of little boys wearing floppy pants made of old mealie-meal sacks scattered out of the dust raised by the two cars and called out to us, cheering and trotting along in our wake for a few metres.

On we drove, past the Black Star Beauty Salon where a handsome black couple, crowned with grand Afros, smiled at us from a signboard, unperturbed by the dust settling on their faces and hair — or by the fact that the Afro had gone out of fashion two decades ago.

We drove past a hostel where migrant workers basked in the sun.

They looked up from their game of morabaraba. One of them nudged his friend and pointed at us. We turned a corner and were about to drive past a shop when Machel told me to pull over.

'Weekend Special' blared from a loudspeaker. Under the crackle and hiss you could just about hear Brenda Fassie complaining about a lover who only came around on Saturdays but was never seen during the week. About six youths were dancing to the beat, their tongues lolling, their tackies squeaking on the stoep worn smooth and shiny grey by this impromptu Saturday morning discothèque. And when Brenda stammered her heartbreaking chorus, their tongues disappeared as they all joined in, shouting:

You're my weekend, weekend spesh-ul
You're my weekend, weekend spesh-ul

We observed the action from the car for a while. My friends in the commandeered Corolla waved at me and flicked friendly smiles at the comrades. They didn't seem to mind this slight interruption to their day as much as I did. I suppose that if I was giving you the condensed, *Reader's Digest* version of my story I could have cut them out altogether. But they were there and I'm telling you everything.

'Are they your friends, those guys?' Machel asked me.

'I think I've seen them before,' I said, although I wasn't sure where.

But the comrades were not too interested in my friendships at the moment. What they were preoccupied with was attention. And at Mohapi's Cash Store in Zone 4 they were getting almost none. The spotlight was focused entirely on the dancers on the stoep. So light-footed were these performers that their tackies, which were not laced up, were like birds which took them on short flights across the stoep in a routine of pirouettes and perfect landings that had even me forgetting my woes for the moment and looking on spellbound.

All this entertainment came to an abrupt halt with a loud bang that zinged through my head and paralysed the entire festival for about ten seconds. Comrade Wounded had fired his gun into the air from right next to me!

My first instinct was to turn around and punch a hole through the other side of his temple. I thank my ancestors that I resisted the impulse.

He ordered me out of the car 'Quick-quick!' so that he could get out himself to take charge of the moment while everyone was still stunned.

The music stopped suddenly.

'People . . .!'

Cometh the hour, cometh the man. As I stood beside Vusi I suddenly realized that I must look like his sidekick. I took a few unobtrusive but definite crablike steps away from him to dispel this impression. His wound had stopped bleeding and a brownish crust had begun to form. He held both hands in the air, the real gun in one hand and its imaginary pair in the other. He had obviously taken time off from the rigours of the struggle to enjoy a Western now and then.

'Bruddas and Seestas of Afrika!' There followed a long pause bristling with suspense. Then: 'We are bleeding!'

Of course, this was meant as a metaphor for the suffering masses, the struggle for freedom, the centuries of oppression under white rule, the many who had fallen, fled into exile, died in detention. But a little girl sucking pensively on an icy choopa failed to appreciate the rhetorical flourish, and stepping forward with a worried look at Vusi's ugly wound, she said earnestly: 'Ntate, Baragwanath is that way.' And she started giving him directions to the hospital.

She was barefoot, and had so much dust between her toes that she could have started her own ant colony there. But what sweet innocence!

Comrade Wounded didn't think so. He directed a fierce stare at the sympathetic child which drove her back into the crowd as effectively as a policeman's Alsatian. Then he continued: 'Our muddas and fuddas are being killed in de factories! Dey are killing us in de schools. Dey have taken our country from us and made us slaves in our own land of Afrika.'

There was silence as everyone listened to this potted but tragic history.

'. . . And what do we do? We dance like monkeys on de stoep of a shop, like clowns!' This last was spat out with unequivocal scorn.

In the meantime, the youth with the spray-can had sauntered up to the stoep and was choosing a space on the wall amongst Coke adverts and announcements of discounts and 'specials' in condensed milk and washing-powder.

'De township is crawling wit de System. Yesterday dey shot Comrade Kehla — he's dead, comrades, dead!' He glared at me as if it was *my* fault. I turned away and concentrated instead on the notice which was being sprayed onto the wall. The message was the same as the previous one, spelling mistakes and all.

Comrade Wounded went on: 'De struggle is almost over, we can say in its final stages. De forces of evil have at last been brought to deir knees. Dey are fighting among demselves. Dat pig Deepfreeze is on de run from dose even to de right of de evil right-wing regime. Now is de hour to strike. Mayibuye!'

'iAfrika!' came the automatic response from the stoep.

I wondered what these comrades would do if they knew that the very same Deepfreeze had been sitting in my lounge this morning, while I carried coffee to him like a waiter.

'Amandla!' Comrade Wounded screamed in my ear and I knew that this was my cue — or else.

'Awethu!' I shouted, a few decibels louder than anyone else, wondering when the cops would come screeching around the corner, voorlaaiers blazing. I started thinking seriously about losing the comrades.

Suddenly there was a distracting shuffle on the stoep. Comrade Wounded stepped forward, his gun at the ready.

From the crowd of shoppers and loiterers, an old woman emerged. She was a gogo of about seventy — definitely not a day younger. Her hair was a grey mop which she hadn't bothered to brush or comb, as grannies sometimes don't: strands of hair pointed in all directions. She had not known a set of teeth for years and her face was a mass of wrinkles.

With her right hand Gogo clutched a gnarled walking-stick. Her left hand had two tasks: it was carrying a packet of groceries and keeping up a frayed skirt around her bony waist.

Gogo shuffled to the edge of the stoep, teetered, and would've fallen off and tumbled to the ground and broken a hip-bone and ended up in hospital and been a burden to her family for another thirty years — there being no such thing as homes for the aged and infirm in this neck of the woods — if Machel had not shouted: 'Help her, clowns!'

One of the agile dancers skipped over to the ancient woman and showed her how to get off in three easy steps. She found some breath to thank the youth, her jaws first moving up and down endlessly before she uttered the words, like a badly dubbed television soapie. Then, without another word, and looking myopically at the ground, she hobbled past Comrade Wounded and, with some effort, shuffled into my car!

In one moment we went from soap opera to sitcom. Some of the people on the stoep dared to giggle. Comrade Wounded could see his serious speech — and not a bad one I thought it was too — ending in laughter. He shot another bullet into the air and everyone shut up.

'Amandla!' he shouted again.

'Awethu!' came the automatic response from everyone including — or rather, especially — me.

'Viva Sibisi viva!'

'Viva Sibisi viva!' we all hailed the legendary leader of the people's liberation movement.

Meanwhile Machel had gone over to the car and was conferring earnestly with the old mama. Then he walked back to Comrade Vusi.

'She thinks this is her nephew's car,' he said, trying hard to stop the grin that was spreading across his face. 'She heard nothing you said here. She's half blind, three-quarters deaf and one hundred per cent stupid.'

'Where does she want to go?' Wounded asked. He didn't think it was at all funny.

'To the Plaza in Fordsburg,' Machel said. 'It's Thembi's birthday today and she wants to go and buy her a white hat.'

'But now who is Thembi?' Vusi asked as if the outcome of the struggle rested on unravelling the true identity of this mysterious person. The guy had as much of a sense of humour as a neglected Sofasonke horse.

(And let the record show that it was *my* car he was so indignant about!)

Machel ignored the question and, with sudden and renewed resolve, ordered Wounded and me into the car. He beckoned to my two Corolla friends to get ready to follow us.

'What's happening?' one of them asked.

'We'll tell you everything in front!' Machel shouted to them.

We sped off with our new but very old passenger who had relegated Machel to the back seat. 'Please hurry, my child,' the old woman pleaded, giving me a filleted smile. Her toothlessness had killed the clicks and zeds of the Xhosa that she spoke. 'Thembi's party is at three o'clock and there is still too much work to do.'

Unfortunately I could not oblige. I was still taking my orders from Machel and Vusi. And the only place I was going was the Black Star Beauty Salon, which we had passed earlier on.

Our arrival in the salon was announced with another gunshot which sent staff and patrons to the floor or dashing for non-existent doors. I still had no idea what we were doing here. But this time Machel was in charge and I should have known that I could expect something more imaginative than a mere speech.

There were about ten women in the salon. By now they were all writhing and groaning and crying on the floor, each pretending (possibly believing) that she had been the target of Vusi's one bullet. A trickle of cement marked the spot where the bullet had really lodged, high up in a wall.

'Get up all of you!' Machel commanded. 'We are friends, not whites.'

(What a refreshing face-lift of a well-worn antonym. I made a mental note for a future short story.)

After a gunshot it's not all that easy to convince anyone of your peaceful intentions. The groans continued from behind chairs and underneath tables. But eventually Machel persuaded everyone to come out of hiding.

'Have you heard about the country-wide boycott which the forces of democracy have announced?' he shouted.

A hairdresser wrung her dye-stained hands in the air. A hair-drier buzzed like an insect unconcerned about the unfolding drama. A woman with her hair in a sticky mousse that looked like Tata's muti stared nervously at a wall-to-wall mirror which duplicated the entire frightened room.

'Have you!' Machel shouted with such menace that it was immediately followed by a desperate, 'Y-e-sss!'

The painter of announcements had run out of paint, but, enterprising fellow that he was, had found some red lipstick, and the mirror proved a perfect surface. This time he managed to spell 'stayaway' with three y's.

'And that sign stays there until the boycott is over,' Machel warned the women, who were trembling in terror. 'You,' he pointed at the woman with stained hands.

She gasped.

Machel pushed Gogo forward. 'Give her one of those perms of yours, make her look nice, like Miss Sofasonke, dye her hair, make her look number one.'

'No,' Gogo resisted feebly, finally realizing what was going on.

'Shut up!' Machel told the crone. 'We spend the whole day

fighting the enemy, but you are throwing parties for your stupid bitch of a daughter and pretending you don't know there's a boycott in place . . .'

I realized then just how lightly I had got off earlier that day.

Gogo was led to a seat and held down by none other than my two friends of the corroded Corolla. And the hairdresser went to work on her.

'It's because you did not fight the boers when you were young that now we have to resort to this,' Machel continued his stern lecture.

'This is not a nice thing that you are doing, my sons,' the old woman sobbed.

Machel ignored her crying. He grabbed her handbag and fished out three crumpled ten-rand notes. 'What does this job cost?' he asked the woman who was transforming Gogo's aluminium streaks into jet black.

'It's free for you, com-comrade,' she stammered tearfully.

'What does it cost!'

'S-six rands . . .'

He pocketed one of the notes and put the rest back in the purse. 'For the struggle,' he said.

I failed to understand the logic behind these calculations. But nobody, it seemed, was too concerned about the finances of the struggle while Granny was being revitalized. And after a few more protests, which included such utterances as 'Oh, my children' and 'Jesu Christu', she more or less settled down to her facial and coiffure.

And what a transformation it was too! Right before our eyes, under the magical hands of a more composed hairdresser, we saw twenty years whittled off young Thembi's ancient and senile — and missing — grandmother.

First her face was plunged into a foam of soap that made the whole place smell like a northern suburbs garden in springtime. This was rinsed away to reveal a face smarting from unaccustomed cleanliness. Then a thick white mask was smeared on. While this formed into a crust the woman set to work on Gogo's hair. It was washed with a pink shampoo, a jet-black gel was applied, and then it was brushed and combed into a sparkling perm. Finally her face was washed, rouge, mascara and eye-shadow were daubed into the right places, and voilà!

Granny looked a little like Phumzile, a pretty neighbour who had

41

been runner-up in the Miss Sofasonke beauty contest three years ago.

The comrades were cheering and clapping, while the staff of the Black Star smiled nervously. Comrade Wounded helped Granny out of her chair.

'Sixteen valve!' someone shouted. This was a compliment usually reserved for girls under twenty who were well-built and beautiful.

My two friends had escaped! While Granny was being renovated they must have sidled out and driven away, leaving me to the devices of the humourless Comrade Wounded and the imaginatively menacing Comrade Machel.

After the Beautification of Gogo I thought that the mission for which I had been chosen had now reached its end. I thanked the comrades for choosing me for this special assignment, expressed my heartfelt gratitude for having been given the opportunity to make such a unique contribution to the struggle . . .

'But I really have to go now. My father's sister's daughter was run over by a Casspir in Mabopane and I promised my father that I will take them to . . .'

'Shut up and drive!' Wounded told me.

I acceded to both his requests.

Machel was more conciliatory. 'You haven't fulfilled your mission yet, com. But don't worry, we're almost at the place where we want to be.'

'Are you from here?' Vusi asked me, his tone interrogative and scornful.

'What do you mean?' I replied, not bothering to look at him any more. I knew what this was leading to.

'Are you from So-fa-son-ke?'

Hearing it enunciated like that, syllable by chilling syllable, I was suddenly reminded what the word meant: 'We all die together.' I shook my head to dispel the portents that had entered.

'Born and bred,' I said.

'And school?'

'Funnily enough, I actually liked school a lot.'

But the good Comrade Vusi was impervious to sarcasm. 'I am asking where did you go to school?' he said.

'Swaziland.'

'I knew it,' he said triumphantly. 'I knew you were somewhere far from the action, I can just see it in your style. When we were engaging the enemy at school your parents took you away! That's why you speak funny and you think this struggle is a waste of time.'

Hah! Engaging the enemy! I supposed he was referring to all those books they burnt in huge bonfires. Well I too had been known to set alight the odd school book in a moment of incendiary rebelliousness. But only *after* I had read it. And *he* spoke funny too. But since he was the one with the gun, I decided that bruddarly love was more important than arguing about accents.

The Mission
Continues

I had been driving for about twenty minutes when Machel ordered me to stop the car. We were on one of those lonely, isolated Sofasonke backstreets. A row of skull and crossbones lined one side of the road and veld stretched away on the other side, with two or three creaky zinc shacks jutting out from the long grass to mark the beginnings of another squatter community.

I glanced at my watch. Five past six! Well, well, well, how time flies when one is on a mission.

Machel scanned the surroundings. Vusi got out, strode a few paces into the veld and had a long pee. In the hot, quiet, African afternoon, listening to the comrade relieve himself, I remembered my spilt beer, and then felt disgusted with myself for having made such a crude association.

Two men materialized from far away in the veld. They strolled along, coming nearer and nearer, their voices growing louder and louder. They were chatting away, deeply engrossed in their conversation, which was conducted in Xhosa. Just when I thought they were going to walk right past the car, they stopped and greeted us.

Machel got out and spoke to them. And Vusi, after he had shaken himself dry, joined the trio. They spoke in undertones, and moved a few paces further away from the car to make sure that I wouldn't hear their little secrets.

Why didn't I just drive off? Because Comrade Machel had my car keys dangling from his fingers. And my name on his lips, which made me prick up my ears to hear as much as possible. I heard the words 'reporter', '*Black World*' and 'Swaziland', as bits of my CV gusted closer on the wind.

This little indaba lasted less than three minutes. Then the two new-comers took the places of Vusi and Machel in my car. Machel had given one of the men my keys and he handed them to me. My two erstwhile friends waved me goodbye — Comrade Machel chuckling at the utter bewilderment my face must have betrayed — and my new companions told me to drive.

Enter Jack and Joe, two men of about my age.

Jack sat beside me and became my new navigator. He had a gravelly voice that sounded like it belonged in a smoky American jazz bar. Joe might've been the proud owner of such a voice too. But he was determined to keep it a secret. He sat in Vusi's place and this seemed to envelop him in Vusi's unprepossessing ill humour. He bore a passing resemblance to Rodwell Mazibuko, the sports reporter at the *Black World*, but he did not seem at all like someone who would be interested in the sporting life of the Sofasonke community.

This leg of the 'mission' took us through more backstreets until we reached a house near the station in Zone 17.

'Flick your lights once,' my navigator told me.

I did as I was told. A door across the road opened and two figures emerged, one tall, the other of average height. They made straight for the Volksie and I saw that they were both men.

'Everything okay?' the tall man asked Jack. The collar of the man's coat cast angular shadows on his face, but I could see that he was elderly, an impression supported by the rasping timbre of his voice.

'Everything's working according to plan,' Jack crooned, nodding vigorously. 'Meet Scara, he'll take us to the place.'

'Pleased to meet you, Scara,' the man said. 'I'm Jerry.'

'Oh,' I said with a sarcastic note in my voice, 'so now I get to meet all the Js.' They might have shown a bit more originality with their aliases, I thought.

Jerry had no comment to make. He and his companion shook hands. Then they embraced warmly, cheek against cheek, and gave one another a few gentle slaps on the back, as if they did not expect to meet again for a long time. The old man eased himself into the back seat.

I still did not know what was going on — apart from the obvious and ridiculous fact that every time I picked up new people they were older than the ones before.

This Jerry was the epitome of patience, politeness and dignity. His eyes twinkled with warmth and he looked at me with kindly concern when I glanced at him in the rear-view mirror.

'Are you okay, Scara?' he asked, holding my shoulder and leaning forward to look at my face as I answered his question.

'I'm okay, Tata,' I said, sounding deliberately unconvincing.

'The young men, did they not give you any trouble?'

I assumed he was referring to Machel and Vusi. What avuncular benevolence! What bloody self-important audacity! As if he himself was my guardian, rather than another scoundrel commandeering my car.

I was tempted to do one of those sarcastic little sketches for which I used to be quite popular at college and in the news room. But there was something about this statuesque old man, his manner, the tone of genuine concern in his voice that stopped me. Besides, as we turned the corner, we were rudely interrupted in that good old Republican way.

I counted three, four, five police vans and a police car, their blue lights making a merry-go-round of beams and shadows in the dusk. Conspicuous camouflage was all over the place: swaggering across the street in tightly laced brown boots, wagging fingers at motorists, searching cars, shining torches into faces, shouting Bravo! Charlie! Delta! over two-way radios that crackled *ggg gg gggg* like a phonics class in an Afrikaner preschool. And enough hardware to wipe out half of Sofasonke.

'Shit!' Jack cursed. 'All that waiting and planning . . .' This time his crooning was a little off-key.

'Don't panic, boys,' Jerry said. 'There's nothing to worry about.'

A policeman wagged a finger, ordering us to pull over. 'Out, out, out!'

Jack and I — like a nursery rhyme gone bad — fell out of the car. Joe came tumbling after. But Jerry stayed just where he was.

'Whose car is this?'

'Mine, sergeant.'

'Lisensie, jong.'

I took out my licence and gave it to him. It disappeared into hands as huge as spades. He glared at my photo as if I had the ugliest face he had ever set his blue eyes on, which, I can tell you right now, is not how my Khensani and my Mama usually gazed upon it.

I looked up into the sergeant's eyes. But it was his red nose that caught my attention; his nostrils were stuffed with a forest of thick black hairs that bristled with every one of his exhalations. The effect was quite eerie in the flashing blue light.

The sergeant looked down that very same nose at the old man who was still sitting in the car, and spewed out the automatic abuse. 'So, why are you still sitting there like a Zulu king after a feast? Didn't I say out?'

'That's what you said,' Jerry answered. And then he peered out of the window so that the young sergeant would not miss a syllable. 'But I think I will sit right here until you let us go, young man — or take us to one of your many jails.'

I could not believe my ears. Nor could the sergeant.

'Gert!' he called, not taking his stupefied eyes off Jerry. 'Gert!'

Along came Gert.

'Listen to what this kaffir is saying!'

'What did you just say, young man?'

But the sergeant would not repeat the insult — or anything else for that matter. Gert had come up to the car and made a quick decision.

'Jong, let them go if they've got nothing to hide.'

The sergeant waved us on with a rude flick of his thumb.

We drove out of Johannesburg, heading for the town of Rustenburg, and then for the Botswana border which lay beyond it.

Jerry was talkative and friendly, and even moved to the front so that we could chat. He asked me much about myself. He was not at all contemptuous of the fact that I had gone to school in neighbouring Swaziland during the turbulent years in which so many people had died, been detained, or fled the country to be trained as guerrillas.

'Education is itself a mighty assegai, my son. Even if you do not know it yet, you have been trained to play a part. You have been born with a skill which not many of us have. Teach yourself to write well, to write the truth.'

The truth. Well, what would he think about some of my tales of fantasy and imagination? Gus and I have endless debates about them. I was always on the lookout for people I could include in my survey. Jerry seemed like a better than average candidate to provide a political perspective on the issue.

Jack leaned forward from time to time to speak to Jerry in coded, cryptic phrases to which I obviously could not be privy. But the old man seemed to understand my discomfort, and perhaps this made him receptive to what I had to say.

'When I'm not being a journalist I write tales of fantasy and imagination.'

He knew it was his opinion I was after, but he took his time to give it, outstaring a kilometre of cat's-eyes before turning his head to respond.

'Yes, that method of storytelling also has its place and its relevance.'

'What do you mean?'

'That not everyone will appreciate what you are doing in your writing. Many are too oppressed by the reality to understand the links between their daily lives and the stories that spin from your pen.'

After a while I ventured to ask: 'Why is it that you could get us past that roadblock?'

'Oh, that is simple, my son,' he answered. 'These people who oppress us, they have been taught to believe that we are not who we really are. And we in turn, quite unconsciously, have done a terrible thing: over the many oppressive decades, we have moulded ourselves into what these people want us to be. We leap out of their paths, we clean their houses, we eat what they believe is good for us, we live where they want us to live. But this conception is often so fickle, so, er — tenuous, that one word from me convinced that young white man that we are not the people he was taught to believe we are . . .'

'Young white man,' Joe sneered, provoked out of a long silence, 'they are racist pigs!'

'And that too is not who they are,' Jerry said.

Joe was not convinced. And nor was I for that matter.

I liked the old man. Let me tell you why. When I was about sixteen years old I had a friend called Simon. I saw Simon shot by a white policeman when he and I were caught fishing illegally at a dam near Sofasonke reserved for whites only. One of these days I'll put the whole story down on paper — but now I want to tell you about Simon's dad. Only last week I bumped into him. I still thank my ancestors that I was sober at the time. He looked at me with probing, yearning eyes, and I knew why. He was looking at the man Simon would have been if he were still alive: I represented the age, the interests, the education of his son. Jerry looked at me with the same eyes, as if he saw in me all the millions of people of my generation.

I didn't know who Jerry was. All I knew was that everything in the world outside the car amazed and delighted him as it would a child: a row of modern townhouses on the edge of a white suburb, neon lights in the shape of a boy sipping fruit juice through a straw, even the robots! But what really got him going was a billboard advertising Lifeguard soap. As we drove past the huge hoarding he shouted out to it as if in greeting. Then he made me stop the car and reverse. He stared long and hard at the hoarding: a picture of three feet peeping out of an old-fashioned bath-tub, with the slogan 'Cleans you no matter who you are'.

'Aha, they still make it,' he said, smiling. 'I sold thousands of bars of Lifeguard for them once a long time ago, sometimes I can still smell the soap on my clothes.'

I cannot recall all the turns and journeys our conversation took, but somehow he ended up asking me if I was married and what Khensani did for a living. I told him that she wrote an advice column for a newspaper.

'Hah!' he chuckled. 'An agony aunt — that is what they are called, not so? I too had a girlfriend once who used to be an agony aunt. That was . . . what? . . . thirty, thirty-five years ago now.'

At about half past eight that evening I dropped the threesome off near the border, in the bush far away from civilization. Of course, I knew what was happening. I was helping these people flee the country, a crime which could get me ten years in prison!

I half expected to pick up another two or three men; indeed, I waited for the crunching footfalls above the nocturnal chirping and screeching and croaking from the dense bush. But Jerry and his two friends were eager to see the back of me and bade me a pleasant journey.

'Write about tonight's experiences,' Jerry told me. 'In your newspaper or in one of your stories of — what do you call them? — fantasy and imagination.'

'Which category will tonight's story fit into?' I asked him.

He thought about this for a moment while his fellow fugitives coughed and jumped about in the dark underbrush to convey their impatience. 'You decide,' he said eventually.

'And who are you?' I ventured.

'I can tell you who I am . . .' he said. His two friends froze. '. . . But if you're a good journalist — as you've been suggesting — you'll find out anyway. Do some investigating before I return. And when you see my girlfriend . . .' He thought for a while. 'Gwen.'

'Gwen?' I frowned.

'The agony aunt. Tell her I love her and take her a bunch of flowers from me.'

'Who shall I say it's from?'

'She'll know.' He laughed and his voice carried far into the bush. And then he was gone and I sat in my Volksie listening to the croaking, the irritable sounds of disturbed birds, the distant gurgling of water running over smooth stones. I climbed out of the car and took a long pee.

On the long drive home I decided that I was going to find out who Jerry really was. It shouldn't be too difficult. I also thought about Khensani, waking up to find that I had disappeared, with nothing to account for my hasty departure in the middle of the night but the foul smell of the lounge, the coffee cups, an untidy kitchen. What would I tell her? That I had to take the President to see my father? Nobody, least of all Khensani, would believe that.

'Oh Scara, why don't you stop the dagga and that drinking of yours.' Advice from Dear Khensani, Agony Aunt of the *Calabash*, the magazine for people who have time for their hearts.

And after a long argument and an even longer period of frozen silence, she would eventually come up to me, put her arms around my shoulders and say: 'Scara, we need a child. Why not go to a doctor and let us see —'

'No white doctor is going to touch my balls and count my sperm!'

'But there aren't any black gynaes . . .'

To get my mind off my domestic problems, I turned my thoughts back to Jerry. So he had suggested that I write about him in one of my stories. Well, let's see. He had been around in the fifties, and I had a feeling he was a jailbird. That's quite commonplace if you're black and living in the Republic. He worked for some kind of soap company. Most interesting was that, like me, he'd had a girlfriend who was an agony aunt. I still had about an hour's travelling to do before I reached Sofasonke. I began to compose a short story which went like this:

DEAR GWEN
BY MANDLA NHLABATSI

Jerry was lying in bed tuning in to the voice of his wife Lineo as if it were a partially interesting radio station. It was ten o'clock and the township was still full of its usual Saturday night sounds: cars driving past the house, an errant child being summoned home by an anxious mother, the stampede of running feet, dogs barking . . .

The shebeen across the street was jumping, and tinkling musically with the sounds of bottles clinking against glasses, laughter and jazz on a turntable that had seen better days. But a voice crooned on bravely:

Are the stars out tonight?
I dunno if it's cloudy or bright
Cos I only have eyes for you . . .

Their tiny connubial room was filled with the aroma of Palmolive soap and Ponds Beauty Lotion, which he got free as sample stock from the cosmetics company where he worked as a sales rep. Through this fragrance wafted the stale smell of his cigarettes and the ghosts of their supper: burnt porridge rising from the depths of a pot in the kitchen and beans billowing from under the bedspread, urging him to pay a cold and comfortless nocturnal visit to the toilet in the yard.

But then the sensuous silhouette of Lineo's breasts and the perfect arc of her bum found form between the candle on the upturned bucket that served as his bedside table and the candle that turned a corner of their room into a bathroom.

'We are supposed to be brothers and sisters,' Lineo was saying with a sigh, concluding a story about how a gullible northern suburbs domestic worker — who had signed her tearful letter 'Angry Maid' — had been liberated of her life savings by an old man who claimed to be a prophet, the descendant of a Shangaan rain queen, and had convinced her that he could cure her mother's gout. This was just one of the many weird problems that Lineo had to help solve as the Agony Aunt or Dear Gwen of the *Bantu Herald*, ensconced between 'Your Bantu Stars' and a pen-pal column which appeared under the bold italicized legend: 'A stranger is just a friend you do not know.'

'It's called "Come Softly",' Jerry told her.

'What d'you mean, "Come Softly"?' She had been rubbing cream on her elbows but stopped in mid-stroke, four fingers sensuously encircling her arm, her other hand pointing over her shoulder, making a perfect shadow puppet of a long-beaked bird. In the flickering light she gave her husband a puzzled look.

'Gout,' he explained, chuckling. 'It reduces your speed from ten miles per hour to about one . . .'

'Jerry!'

'Shh.' He did not want her to wake up her mother in the other room.

'How can you be so cruel?' she berated him.

'Me cruel?'

'Yes, I'm telling you how a woman lost all her money and all you can tell me is that her mother's affliction is named after a song by . . . by Otis Redding.'

'Percy Sledge,' he corrected her. 'Lady, know thy soul.'

'Oh, Jerry!' She flung the lid from her bottle of beauty lotion at him. 'You are incorrigible!'

'Come softly to me,' he whispered, grabbing her arm and pulling her gently towards him. Protesting feebly she flopped onto his chest. He slipped one hand down her silk nightie and covered, with his palm, her nipple, her areola, a hemisphere of her breast. For the umpteenth time he moved it slowly up and down, then rested it in his hand, marvelling at the liquid ounces that once again belied its marshmallow lightness.

Lineo drew in her breath, enjoying the sensation. She found his mouth and kissed him, feverishly moistening his lips with her tongue.

They both grappled with the intrusive bedspread until it lay on the floor in a defeated heap. A new, earthier fragrance now assailed the warm air, wilting the bouquet of soap and lotion.

Outside, a drunk slurred, 'I've had enough.'

'Speak for yourself,' Jerry said. Beads of sweat took up their position on his forehead.

The candle on the upturned bucket gave up more of itself to the intense flame at its tip.

Dear Gwen,

Me, I am nineteen years old. I am too much in love with my boyfriend, Joseph. But now my problem is this: Joseph he is scared of white people. He comes to visit me sometimes here where I am working. My master and madam they have a nice bedroom sweet which has got big pillows and nice patterns with a big mirror that shows your whole self. Now I want that me and Joseph must lie down on this bed because the madam and the master they are all of them overseas, but Joseph, oh Joseph, he is to scared. What I must do?

Nice Lady
Northcliff

'So what do you think I should tell her?' Lineo asked Jerry the next morning. She was going through the same motions as the previous night. Only this time she was adding lipstick and rouge.

Jerry grunted over a dish of water where he was brushing his teeth. They had been married for almost a year now and still his wife insisted on asking him questions in the mornings when he had toothpaste in his mouth.

'Hey, sweets,' she asked again, 'what advice should Aunty Gwen give the poor girl?'

A year of marriage had also taught him to know the familiar sounds that issued from the room: the *zzz* of a zipper would make him look up suddenly to catch the dark symmetry of her shoulders as they disappeared into a dress; splashes of water could alert him to the erotic possibility that she was squatting over a dish of water, lathering her legs with dripping soap. This time a gentle exertion in her voice made him turn around to look at her. She was lying back on the bed, with her legs stretched over the side. One of her long dark-brown limbs was already sheathed in a black stocking. Her other foot was in only toe-deep.

Jerry's erection was instant.

'Lineo!' he spluttered, the frothy toothpaste in his mouth causing him to pronounce the L in her name, instead of saying 'Dineo' the way a Sotho-speaker would.

'Jerry!' she cried softly, clamping her thighs together, pushing him away.

'Five minutes,' he pleaded, 'five minutes.'

She stared at him as if he were a madman, as if this was the first time he had made such a desperate, early-morning overture. His eyes were all over her body; her breasts quivering like Maltabella porridge left in a bowl just a little too long, her legs, one now darker than the other, courtesy of Arwa, her creamy hips, oiled as if to lubricate the seductive sway that had first caught his attention the minute he set eyes on her.

'We can't do it in the mornings . . .'

'Who says . . .? Has the white man passed another law that I don't know about?' rubbing a knee against her leg.

'Look at the time, mshana!'

Mshana! The night before they were lovers, in the morning he became her cousin!

The green Vauxhall swerved onto the main road, emerging from Sofasonke's grey morning cloud of smoke and taking its place in the long line of second-hand cars and commercial vans making their way to Johannesburg and its industrial surrounds.

Jerry's eyes darted from the van ahead of him to Lineo's legs to the van and back again to her legs.

There were three men in blue workmen's overalls on the back of the van. They were sharing a cigarette, taking a couple of puffs each. Two of them balanced precariously on the tailgate to catch the morning sun, the third was buried deep in the van, partly obscured by shadow.

Jerry found himself becoming engrossed in the men's antics. The two who leaned out began sparring with each other, bob, weave, bob, weave, duck, one on the jaw, a left hook, two on the gloves, duck, ah too slow . . .

and all the while the three of them were engaged in an animated conversation.

'What are these guys doing?' Jerry said. 'They'll get themselves killed!'

'If they lose their hold on that door . . .' Lineo agreed.

One or two motorists in the other lane had spotted this spectacle too and hooted, but the men ignored them. Indeed, they were spurred on by the attention.

Two jabs on the chin, duck, one on the imaginary gloves . . .

'Aha!' Lineo laughed, 'I know what they're doing, Jerry.'

'Playing with their lives, showing off.'

'Killer Khumalo won his Commonwealth title fight and they're acting out the whole thing for their friend who probably didn't listen to the broadcast.'

'Lineo!' he slapped her thigh. 'You're right!' Jerry remembered that the fight had been on the radio the night before. He'd meant to listen himself.

'What I don't understand though,' Lineo said, 'is how they know exactly who hit who and how the knockout happened simply by having listened to it on the radio!'

'Theatre of the mind,' Jerry explained. But Lineo had suddenly lost interest in this conversation. She began to speak about her job, her mother, and her mother's back problems. She fidgeted about, enjoying the luxury of being driven to work. She searched her bag for her chewing-gum, pouted her lips in the rear-view mirror and gave them a final coat of lipstick.

Jerry kept his eyes on the three blue-collar boxing enthusiasts. One of them looked into the Vauxhall and his eyes came to rest on Lineo's legs. He shared his discovery with his sparring partner. When the two of them had had their fill of ogling her they even called their friend from the shadows.

'Look at these silly guys,' Lineo said, clicking her tongue and trying to hide her legs with a length of her black dress that actually did not exist.

'I'm watching them,' Jerry said, 'I'm watching them.' Probably rating my wife now, he thought, giving her nine, maybe ten out of ten — doing exactly what the guys and I do to other women.

The van indicated left for Industria. The men all gave a grateful wave.

'Shameless!' Lineo scowled and shook her head. But Jerry wasn't sure if she was really cross. His guess was that she actually didn't mind the attention she had received, the same attention she had got yesterday and would get again tomorrow and the next day . . .

As he negotiated his way through the traffic his mind dwelt a little longer than usual on his wife's legs — and the effect they had on other men. But these musings produced in him, as always, a niggling feeling of discomfort. What was it all about?

Lineo interrupted his thoughts with a reminder that she needed more facial cream. And then he was dropping her off. She pecked him on the cheek, slammed the car door, and went towards the office. He watched for a few seconds, his eyes fixed on her buttocks.

And at that moment Jerry found the cause of his discomfort, located the unnerving hum in his engine, as it were: he, Jerry, was the fourth man who was being taunted by his wife's body. He swung back into the traffic and headed for Braamfontein. His feeling of discomfort had suddenly been replaced by a strange, liberating, happy feeling.

Last night's lovemaking had been far too brief, and instead of that long, subsiding, African sunset that should have beamed its warm rays through his loins, it had only made him hanker after more. This morning he should have felt smug, at least, that his wife's beauty had been so publicly and unashamedly admired, but instead he felt like one of the covetous blue-collar oglers himself — the fourth man!

It was just then that he heard a serendipitous flutter on the seat still warm from Lineo's bum. A quick glance from the corner of his eye revealed a crumpled sheet of paper. He picked it up and smoothed out as much of it as the busy traffic would allow. At first glance it looked like a little note, something his wife had forgotten. No, this was certainly not Lineo's handwriting. Here was an adolescent hand that took great care to slant all the strokes equally. 'Joseph . . . big pillows . . .' he read. What could it be? A red traffic-light provided a chance to read the page carefully. And when he saw the familiar 'Dear Gwen', he remembered the letter Lineo had read to him last night from a passionate young lover seeking advice.

As the lights changed to green, a thought slowly took shape in his head: this letter was a gift from the gods.

It was all so neat and obvious. Here was a kinky lady who wasn't getting enough of what she knew was good for her. She writes to Dear Gwen for advice. Dear Gwen, overzealous counsellor that she is, brings the letter home to her husband — a chap who is not getting enough of what he knows is good for him — and seeks his advice. Hubby fails to give desired advice but the little missive will not go away. Fate was surely giving him one hefty nudge.

He had an office — or rather a partitioned cubicle — in the 'Bantu' section of the firm. They were stuck on the ninth floor of a fifteen-storey building on Jorissen Street, overlooking a grim vacant patch that had been turned into a parking-lot in a street lined with gnarled old jacaranda trees.

When Jerry reached the office he found that half his colleagues had already arrived. He greeted them as he made his way to his own desk.

'Heita, bra Jerry,' he heard Robert's chirpy voice call out from within his little 'cell', as they called the tiny cubicles.

'Awu, bra Robbie!' he shouted back as if about to begin a praise poem in honour of their newest — and therefore most enthusiastic — seller of soap and perfume to shops in Sofasonke and other black townships.

He saw Chris's black satchel on his desk. He had arrived for work, Jerry surmised, but was right now more than likely perched on a seat in a cubicle in the non-white toilet, catching up on the news as presented by the *Black World*.

Jerry's cell was next to the one in the corner which belonged to Osbert Manyete. Now there was an arsehole for you. Osbert and Jerry were not on speaking terms since the poster incident. Lineo had appeared as a centrefold in some men's magazine, much to Jerry's embarrassment. She had not revealed much beyond her lacy white bikini briefs and satin brassière. But she was hugging a white kitten under her chin and staring at the camera with suggestive eyes.

After the inevitable ribald remarks in the canteen, Jerry's colleagues at Grant's Wholesalers had realized how embarrassed he was and decided, in a collective show of sensitivity and tact, not to mention the centrefold again.

Not Osbert. He stuck the picture up on the partition wall opposite his desk and told Jerry that it was there to give his manhood a daily exercise of push-ups! Jerry had no option but to punch the man's nose. He's probably used to having his nose flattened every now and then, Jerry said later. After all, he was born in KwaVindaba.

As Jerry approached his cell he heard his phone ringing. Could it be Lineo calling to ask him if he had found the letter, he wondered. Or to remind him about the cream she wanted.

'Hallo, Jerry Maluleka speaking,' in his courteous office voice.

It was indeed his lovely wife. 'Jerry, sweets,' she said, 'I left something in the car.'

'What?' He knew she must mean the letter.

'That letter . . .'

'Letter? What letter?' Don't overdo it now, he warned himself, spiralling the telephone cord around his forefinger. Feigning total ignorance might make his beloved suspicious.

'The one I read out to you about the naughty domestic worker who is wanting advice about . . .'

'Oh ja, I remember the one.'

'I think I left it in the car.'

'You checked everywhere?'

'Everywhere,' she said.

'You want me to go and look in the car?'

'Please. I wouldn't have bothered you but it's deadline for copy today and . . .'

'No problem,' he said. 'If I find it, I'll call you back.'

He replaced the receiver and withdrew his finger from the cord. Of course, he didn't have to go back to the car for the letter: it was right there in the top pocket of his jacket. He took it out and felt a tiny fraction of the thrill that pickpockets must feel when they go about relieving people of their money. He unfolded the letter and read it again. He noted that the address was in the northern suburbs — Northcliff. Obviously a maid who slept in.

He reached for a pen and was about to write down the address when an agitated shadow appeared at the door followed by Chris with a newspaper in his hand.

'Check this out, bra,' Chris said, spreading the black tabloid across the desk.

Jerry followed his friend's finger, which exuded a whiff of familiar liquid toilet soap, to an article headlined FAKES FOR BRAVERY, with a sub-head that read: 'Black heroes get fool's gold while white hero gets pure gold.'

Jerry (who had surreptitiously refolded the letter and returned it to his pocket) just had time to read the introductory paragraph in bold type before Chris, spluttering furiously, told him the full story.

Two black workers on a boer's mealie farm had pulled a drowning white mother and her two-year-old son from the swollen Vaal River. On the same day, in another act of bravery, a white postman had entered a house engulfed in flames and dragged a ten-year-old coloured child to safety. The postman and the two farmworkers had all been awarded the De Jager Medal for Bravery (it was named after a legendary eighteenth-century horseman said to have rescued a family of peaceable Voortrekkers from a hostile Zulu impi).

At an august ceremony, the bald white State President draped the orange, white and blue sash — from which swung the heavy gold medal — over the proud shoulders of the brave postman, a Meneer Potgieter. A week later, a white police sergeant bestowed the same honour on Alpheus Ngidi and Goodwill Mohapi. Mohapi and Ngidi waited a week before they tried to sell their medals, in the hope that they would fetch thousands. But the medals were valued at less than ten bob each. Now this exposé.

'So what?' Jerry said.

Chris frowned at his friend and colleague. 'What d'you mean so what?'

'How does this differ from all the other stories we read in the papers?' Jerry asked. 'Yesterday, for instance, we read about the white shopkeeper who beat an eight-year-old boy to death while his mother was forced to look on. Why? Because the kid was caught stealing five cents' worth of sweets. Last week there was the story of the black woman in the chemist shop . . .'

'What's your point, my man?' Chris hissed with pique in his voice and eyes, feeling decidedly that some cold water had been thrown on his justifiable indignation.

Well, what *is* my point, Jerry wondered. And then, jabbing a finger at the newspaper, he said, 'This is the government at play, at their least malicious. It's a joke, bra Chris . . .'

'Well, I'm not laughing, fana, I'm not laughing . . .'

'That's because the joke's not *for* you, it's *on* you — you as represented in this case by Messrs . . .' He looked for the names of the two heroes turned victims.

But Chris had had enough.

'Jerry,' he said, flouncing towards the door. 'I get your basic idea, but I've got perfume and soap to sell to the sweaty masses.'

'Chris.'

'Ja?'

'Your fly.'

When Jerry hit the highway to Northcliff it seemed as if his Vauxhall had acquired extra bounce. Which was the motorized version of the proverbial spring in one's step, since the roads leading to this opulent white suburb were paved with the good intentions of councillors, civil engineers and roadbuilders; the tar stretched forth boldly in long, black bands, the white lines were truly white and the jacarandas yielded their mauve blooms with such magnanimous abandon that they spread a carpet over the shady pavements.

Jerry cruised past the Northcliff supermarket, which bustled with activity; white housewives stocking up on wine, pool cleaner, magazines, icecream, Everysun Aquasport, T-bone steaks and meat-flavoured Bobtail.

A poem banked like a paper plane into Jerry's consciousness, blown in that direction by his joie de vivre and the conversation he had had earlier with Chris. The poem was a pithy piece of writing which expressed exactly what he was seeing around him. Only two lines long, it read:

Oh, to be white and free and twenty-one
Now that the jacarandas are in bloom.

Perfect. Banned by the state for publication and distribution.

In an impulsive moment, at a red traffic-light, he rolled down his window and smiled at the white woman in the car alongside him. He poked his head out of the window and she did likewise, her forehead furrowed with the kind desire to help the young native gentleman.

With an elegiac smile he said it loudly and clearly so that she would grasp the iambic pentameter, the metaphor and the sardonic implications all in one bold recital:

'Oh, to be white and free and twenty-one
Now that the jacarandas are in bloom.'

She stared at him as if he were mad. Then — her face changing from amber to red — she scowled and gave him the two-fingered motorist's cliché, uttered an exquisitely enunciated 'Fuck you', and drove off — in the motorized version of the flounce.

Jerry chuckled. He had just broken the white man's law. He had distributed a piece of undesirable literature. Much, much better than frisking your own jacket, he thought, but not half as good as what I'm about to do.

He remembered suddenly that this was a little bit of a detour: he was a long way from the run-down Sofasonke shops that he supplied with gels and lotions and creams and roll-ons — the black market. And so he had to remember to doctor the logbook.

He glanced at the back seat, where he had put the huge gift-wrapped parcel of soap and perfume. It was still there.

He swung the car into Prince Edward Drive and cruised through the cool, dappled shadows. Giant trees wore their crowns high above the security fences and walls. Driving past the wrought-iron gates, Jerry caught fleeting glimpses of placid blue swimming-pools and heard the sibilant whispering of automatic sprinkler systems.

'Unreal,' he exclaimed loudly, even though he had seen it all before. 'A far cry from Sofasonke.'

He drove slowly down the street looking out for the address. And there it was, the number 18 in large numerals.

Jerry parked his car, with premeditated confidence, right up against the gate. He got out and rang the bell, and waited.

Two women came strolling along the pavement through the patches of shade and sunlight. An old white woman and a young black one. Both were dressed in white. The old woman's frock and hat identified her as a member of a bowling club. The young woman's white apron and sneakers identified her as a servant.

Jerry was about to ring again when the intercom crackled into life.

'Hallo, can I help you?'

'The madam, please.'

'The madam, Mrs Rankin, she is not home now, can I help you?' A black woman's voice mouthing the courtesies taught in the literacy classes at the Centre for Domestic Advancement.

'I have a very important message and a parcel for her.'

A pause. Then: 'You want I must fetch the parcel?'

'Yes please.'

'Okay. Just wait there.'

'Thanks,' he said and felt his heartbeat accelerate. He would finally get to meet the writer of the ungrammatical but sexy 'My master and madam they have a nice bedroom sweet . . .' He leaned against the bonnet of his car, crossed his legs, decided that the amount of dust on his two-tone shoes was negligible for the occasion, and waited.

First he heard barking from somewhere in the huge double-storey house. Then he saw two Maltese poodles bounding up the long, winding driveway, one on either side like a pair of outriders. She followed behind the yapping dogs, almost running, eager to see another errand through for madam efficiently.

The two dogs leaped against the bars of the gate, growling and barking. He could not resist a quick 'Voetsek!' before she came within earshot. And then he watched her approaching. Her breasts bobbed beneath her apron. Two big brown eyes sparkled in a round, unblemished face. A little plump, he thought, but pretty. As she herself had put it in her letter: Nice Lady.

She was breathing heavily when she reached the gate, but immediately busied herself with calling the two dogs — Scraps and Scruffy — to heel, jabbing them with a white tackie until they went to lie on the lawn nearby.

'Hallo,' she greeted Jerry, pressing her body against the gate and trying to look as far up and down the pavement as the bars would allow. Her breasts came into sharp relief, poking their little points through the railings.

About nineteen, Jerry thought approvingly.

'What do you have for the madam?' she asked. But before he could tell her she said: 'The madam she's not here, she's overseas.'

'I know she goes overseas often,' he said, hazarding a guess.

'Yes,' she smiled, with not so much as a hint of suspicion as to how he knew this.

'To Greece?' he asked, choosing a European country at random.

'Yes,' she nodded, holding onto the gate with both hands. Greece, Germany, France, America, it was probably all the same to her — places that could only be reached by plane, where whites went to have a good time. 'What do you want me to give to her?'

'Nothing,' he said.

She laughed at this absurdity. A man with a message who has no message. 'Awu, why nothing?' she said, clapping her hands together and causing the poodles to growl.

'Well, let me explain, let me explain. You see, I've been sent to deliver a gift to your madam for being the most elegant — er — most pretty woman in Northcliff. My company has chosen her ....' He paused and sighed deeply, looking her straight in the eye. 'But I get here and I see that *you* are the most beautiful woman in Northcliff. So I think I should give *you* the prize.'

This enormous compliment embarrassed her so much that she laughed and had to avert her eyes and look at the dogs, the shrubs in the garden, a flock of sparrows flying overhead . . .

'Do you mean that?' she asked, searching his eyes for any evidence of mockery.

'I most certainly do,' he said. 'What is your name?'

'Nthabiseng.'

'We are indeed happy,' he said, translating the Sotho name into English. And then with a smile, 'Will you accept the gift, Nthabiseng?'

'It's cash?'

He shook his head, smiling at her childlike innocence. 'Let me show you what it is.' He opened the back door of the car.

'It's your car this one?' she asked, her eyebrows arched in obvious admiration.

'Yes, it's my car,' he nodded. He took the parcel from the back seat and asked again if she would accept it.

'I accept the gift,' she said with a coy smile.

He squeezed the packet of Lifeguard soap, cream and perfume gently through the grille and Nthabiseng received it with a mixture of excitement and grace.

'Well,' Jerry said, 'enjoy your present, you most certainly deserve it.'

'Thank you . . . your name is what?'

'Trevor.'

'Thank you, Trevor.' She beamed with embarrassment.

He was tempted to put Phase Two of his plan into action right there and then. But he knew that he could not risk asking her if he could stay a while. She was surely still suspicious of this generous and charming man and must have been lectured to over and over again about the dangers of inviting strangers into the house.

But there was still a parting shot. He paused as he was climbing into his car to say: 'I might even come back some day and pay you a visit.'

Her shy laughter gave no clue to what she thought of this prospect.

As he drove off he caught a final glimpse of her in his rear-view mirror, hastily tearing the wrapping off the parcel.

His plan was to call her back two days later. But his impatience got the better of him. There was no great risk, he decided, in bringing his plans forward by a day. Besides, he had to act before madam and master returned.

Before noon he found himself dialling the number which he had found in the telephone directory and easily memorized. As the phone rang he pictured Nthabiseng running from a far corner of the mansion which he had not yet entered, but which he desperately wanted to.

Then he heard her breathless voice: 'Hallo, it's Florence speaking.'

Florence? Then it struck him that she must be using her nom de domestique. 'Hallo, Nthabiseng,' he said deliberately, and waited.

'Can I help you?'

'Did the beautiful woman like the present?'

'Ooh,' she gushed shyly, 'it's you!'

'Can I come and see you today, Nthabiseng?' He spoke in Sesotho.

When he arrived at the mansion, she was waiting for him at the gate. She seemed to have washed and dressed for the occasion. She wore a low-cut, floral summer dress that ended midway down her thighs. And she was sporting a new hairstyle: she had combed a path down the middle and fluffed up one side, while the other side was combed flat — almost as if she had forgotten to fluff it up too.

She opened the gate for him to enter, and the squeak of its hinges triggered off a volley of yelps from somewhere deep inside the house.

As expected, the house was expensively furnished: a dining-room with a heavy oak sideboard, thronelike chairs and a long, gleaming table that could easily have seated the entire Urban Bantu Council. The room was so huge that it held, a quick count told him, altogether twenty chairs. And here the strange ways of whites were very much in evidence: one chair faced north, another looked to Sofasonke, while another two faced Germiston and so on.

'Where do you live?' Nthabiseng asked, standing beside him as he looked around.

'Sofasonke,' he said. Where else?

The walls were filled with huge paintings: a portrait of a white man in a floppy hat who stared contemplatively down at Jerry from behind a droopy autumnal moustache; a bowl of badly disfigured fruit; a woman with enormous breasts, stretched out languidly on a settee. No toothy black trio eating watermelon here, or green plaster-of-Paris birds arranged from far to farther to farthest.

'Did you like the perfume?' he asked her when they were seated in the kitchen drinking tea.

'I like it very much — but are you sure it's for me?'

'Of course it's for you. But what if it wasn't? Would you be able to give it back now?'

'Yes,' she nodded.

'Unused?'

'Not ever did I spray me,' she nodded again.

He put down the teacup, which made up in daintiness what it lacked in volume. He wanted to know why she was still unconvinced that he had intended the gift for her.

'I was once embarrassed when I tried to take something that was not meant for me,' she said, speaking now in simple, lucid Sesotho She told him the story — laughing and giggling at the memory of it.

'In Ladybrand where I come from, there in the Free State, we once had a variety show. They had it in the Methodist Church Hall and they had many nice things for us; singing contests, fancy-dress competitions, jokes, everything.

'The hall was packed with enough people to fill that church for two Sundays in a row. The end of the show was what we were all waiting for: that was when they were going to call the lucky winner of a prize . . .'

'What was the prize?' He helped himself to another cup of tea. He enjoyed listening to her Sesotho, which was almost untainted by the slang and quirks of Johannesburg. And while she spoke he could study her features at close range without embarrassing her. She was a shy young woman.

A shy young woman who fantasized about making love on her madam's nice big bed. He felt the thrill of suspense and anticipation surge through his body and he smiled at her.

'Ten pounds!' she said. 'The man on the stage asked for a child to come and join him there. A little boy came and drew a name from a big box with Albert's Bazaars written all over it while we all shouted, "Shop at Albert's and save save save!" about five times over.

'Then the little boy handed a ticket to the man, and the man called out: "Nthabiseng Sealoma!"'

'That's you!' Jerry said.

'Listen, I'm not finished,' Nthabiseng said, clicking her tongue in good-natured impatience.

Nothing like tea and a good laugh to get acquainted, Jerry thought, feeling very pleased with himself at that moment.

'I ran down the aisle. There was another woman racing down the opposite aisle but I wasn't sure why she was also running towards the stage. Although people often do that when there's big cash; they get excited on behalf of the winner.'

Jerry smiled at this quaintly expressed observation.

'This woman and I got to the stage together. By this time I was getting very much annoyed with this woman. I didn't mind her getting excited for my part, but I thought that she shouldn't get up on the stage with me too.

'The man was a little surprised when he saw us both on the stage. But he kept smiling, looking from one to the other, one to the other, like a man whose wife has surprised him with twins. The first thing he wanted to know was: "Who is Nthabiseng Sealoma?"'

'"Me!" I shouted. "Me!" the other woman also shouted.'

'Oh no!' Jerry could see what was coming.

'Our numbers were on our tickets and it wasn't my number, it was hers. Oh, I didn't know where to put my face.' Reliving the moment, she held her face in her hands.

Jerry, alias Trevor, stood up and put his arm around her neck.

'Let's go to the bedroom,' he said, lifting her up gently and kissing her. She responded shyly but warmly to his passion and led him to the back door.

'Let's go to the bedroom,' he said again, thinking that she probably had not heard him.

She nodded and opened the back door, which led to her servant's room off the kitchen. The room was small and cramped; underneath a window a child's discarded school desk, draped with a blue tablecloth and adorned with a chipped mirror, served as a dressing-table. Opposite it was a single bed which sagged deeply in the middle. Three pairs of high-heeled shoes — white, cream and black — stood in a neat row against a wall.

Overcome with desire, Jerry decided not to discuss the logistics of the desired venue. They sagged into the concave bed breathing heavily.

'You're a funny man,' Nthabiseng said after an hour of lovemaking.

'In what way?' He was putting on his socks, his thoughts on his job. He had been away for three and a half hours!

'You want to do it in my madam's room.'

'But didn't — I mean wouldn't you like to do it there too?'

'No,' she shook her head. 'But that's what Agnes did.'

'Who's Agnes?'

'She worked here before me. When madam is away, madam's sister comes here to check if everything is in order. She caught Agnes on the bed with another man. She fired Agnes on the spot and told me to come and work here tempry. I work for madam's sister, Mrs Leon.'

THE END

7

De Vries
on 'Spotlight'

I think old Gus is going to be truly knocked out by this new story of mine. I make the acquaintance of a mysterious old man. He is some fugitive from the white man's law and, judging by his age, has probably been causing successive white regimes a little bit of discomfort. I am commandeered to drive him to the border on some secret mission or to escape from some drag-net that is closing in on him. The old man and his comrades remain very secretive, but he can't help blurting out a few crucial and revealing little biographical titbits:

He mentions that he had something to do with a popular brand of soap. I take this soap and sculpt from it a working environment: desk, chair, a wafer-thin office, an old Vauxhall, a randy personality, the bustle of a city in the fifties.

I listen to the man's wisdom, to his deep laughter, and I give him youth, a sense of humour, a humourless colleague, dreams, the lusty appetites of a young man.

A throw-away remark about a beautiful girlfriend, an agony aunt, and what do I do? I dress her up in stockings, skimpy dresses and bouquets of sweetness and desire.

Gus Kinnear, read this one and die.

Johannesburg glimmered on the horizon. To which of its myriad lights would I be drawn? Khensani would not be too keen to hear about my antics at this time of night. Especially as I had promised to take her to a funeral in Soshanguve today. Nor was I going to creep back into the house and beg for forgiveness. What to do? What to do? I decided on a plan of action — or was it sheer impulse?

At about eleven that night I turned off Main Reef Road into

Riverlea. The coloured township lay huddled around a dark yellow mine dump like a large litter around a teat. The streets were as filthy as those in Sofasonke, indeed the ordered rows of skull and cross-bones, the dirty children, the swaggering Saturday night drunks, the shebeens bursting with the fizz of life, all this bore a striking resemblance to Sofasonke but for two things: there were no comrades spraying graffiti here and no cops patrolling the streets.

I prayed that Gus would be home. I had some amazing stories to tell him. And I needed beer. Lots of cold beer.

Gus and I go back a long way. Apart from being colleagues we were also school buddies at St Christopher's in Swaziland. Gus had a tongue that must have been dipped in a concoction of butter, nectar and honey. And during our schooldays he was forever putting it to good use talking the 'beadwork', as he so aptly put it, off a bevy of nubile Swazi beauties. But once his gift of the gab really saved our necks when a group of us — about ten matric boys — were thrown into the Mbabane police station for smashing up the Happy Hut, a local discothèque.

That night we had stuffed our beds with clothes to make it look as if we were fast asleep. This must be the oldest trick in the boarding-school book and the only reason why anybody ever gets away with it is that the teachers don't bother to check if you're there anyway. My theory is that no teacher on late-night inspection duty wants to go into a room in which forty farting teenage boys have taken off their sweaty tackies.

But we certainly made our presence felt at the Happy Hut. Watching strip shows, dancing with prostitutes and bribing the waiters to sell us liquor when we couldn't convince the bastards that we were twenty-two-year-olds from Jo'burg holidaying in Swaziland.

Then we got drunk, smashed up some multicoloured lights, over-turned a few liquor-filled tables. When our waiter refused to get us more liquor, Enoch Mabuza, a strapping middleweight, gave him one of his prize lefts to the jaw and broke his dentures.

We were bundled off to the police station. And if we were not going to be sentenced, we were all facing certain expulsion at least. The shame! What would my father say? All that bone-throwing to give his only son a good education. My dear mother! I pictured her then, almost as if I had suddenly acquired some of my father's clair-voyant powers. She is standing in the yard when she sees me coming down Mapetla Street dragging my big suitcase. She drops her broom in the dust and clutches her heart tightly with both hands. 'Modimo! What have we done, Jesu Christu! My son has been fired from the school! Something is not as it should be . . .'

But good old inimitable Gustav prevented all this High Noon in Sofasonke stuff. How? He convinced the arresting officer, through a genealogical peroration delivered from behind bars, that the man had veritable streams of royal Swazi blood coursing through his veins.

I watched the expression on the policeman's fleshy face change from indignant disbelief to mild interest to fervent conviction that he was indeed destined to spend the rest of his life not among felons, mercenary lawyers and corrupt magistrates but holding court with erudite diplomats, idle princes and pubescent ladies-in-waiting.

The man freed us — unconditionally — in gratitude to Gus for pointing out his illustrious ancestry and thus giving him the opportunity to claim his rightful place in society in the Kingdom of Swaziland.

'Is he really a Swazi royal?' one of the boys asked Gus as we skipped our way back to the college early the next morning, the sun peeping over the mountains.

'Don't be so gullible, man,' Gus said with disdain. 'The only royal stuff that clown's got running through his veins is that beer he imbibes at the Royal Swazi Spa.'

Gus was married to a local girl, Charmaine, and they lived in a caravan in the backyard of Charmaine's parents' skull and cross-bones. They were on a waiting-list for a house. Only last week he had told me of yet another rumour that the government was going to flatten the mine dumps to make way for Riverlea Extension Three. He had been on the waiting-list for five years now and joked that he was thinking of paying my father a visit to see if Tata could somehow 'strengthen the possibilities', as he put it.

'I'll take anything he gives me,' he said with mock desperation, 'root of plant, bark of tree, claw of animal, no matter how bitter, my bra.'

Well, let's see what he thought of Tata after what I had to tell him about his very distinguished visitors.

There were about eight cars parked outside the gate of 213 Colorado Drive where Gus and Charmaine lived. A party maybe? But it couldn't be; the place wasn't jumping.

As I walked up the short path, Charmaine emerged from the house and stood on the stoep. She peered into the darkness and called out, 'Scara?'

'Hi, Charmaine.' I could see into the tiny lounge behind her, men and women, all dressed up in dark suits and dresses, drinking tea in a rather sombre atmosphere.

'He's in the caravan,' she said. 'I'll take you there.'

I followed her — to 213B as Gus called the caravan, listening to the slap slap slap of her slippers against her heels.

In the short walk from the front of the yard to the back, I remembered what Gus had told me about a recent argument with his pretty wife. She was tired of living in the caravan and wanted to move to Fleurhof, a new coloured housing scheme rejected by whites because it was too close to the townships.

'And where's the money gonna come from?' Gus had asked.

'You can make a lot from taking snaps at weddings,' she had pointed out, already having done some preliminary feasibility studies.

'Wedding photos!'

'Or are you planning to spend your whole life taking pictures of dead blacks for a few cents?'

'You know, Scara,' Gus said afterwards at the office, 'she wears these slippers all the time, morning, noon and night, and I swear one of them sounds like it's saying "more money, more money" and the other one, "big house, big house".'

As I walked behind Charmaine now, in the dark, I tried to work out which slipper was saying what.

Hearty, uninhibited laughter issued from the caravan; it was really jumping here in contrast to the house we had just come from. And there, through a lit window, I saw Gustav, his thin frame behind the brown bottles of beer, stabbing the air and holding his head back as he made a point to a laughing, appreciative audience. His left eye was half closed from years and years behind the camera lens. But this enhanced his good looks: women regarded it as a permanent wink.

Charmaine slap-slap-slapped up to the caravan, flung the door open and snapped: 'Do you have no respect for the dead?'

'Ag no, Charmaine!' Gus groaned.

Scara, I told myself, your timing is seriously out. Any fool could tell that there's been a funeral here today. Then I suddenly remembered Gus telling me that some uncle of his or Charmaine's had died.

'Scara's here to see you,' Charmaine said. Then she turned to me and said with a sneer, 'What are you doing with a feather in your hair?' I brushed at my head and a little grey feather floated down to the ground. She turned on her heel and flounced off as if I had no respect for the dead either, slap, slap, slapping away, her heels like two receding half moons.

'Hey, Scara, you come to tell me you know where De Vries is?' Gus asked as he dragged me up the two steel steps into the caravan and poured me a cold beer.

Now what the hell does one say to that? I tell you, I was quite stunned.

A Leica rested proudly on a shelf. And every square centimetre of the walls was plastered with images of Charmaine and their little boy, Derek.

I downed the beer in two gulps, taking in Gus's guests as I did so. Spotty had a thick ginger moustache that clung to his freckled face like a snail on a mottled rock. Lennie boasted a scar which began on his right cheek but ended I know not where: it disappeared under a grey skullcap. I pictured a knife in one of his pockets somewhere.

'Welcome to the blacks-only Wimpy Bar,' Gus repeated his now stale joke. The caravan did indeed resemble a Wimpy Bar — although it was about ten times smaller.

'Verder?' I said. This was Afrikaans for 'furthermore', and in the lexicon of current slang it meant: 'What's new?'

'We went to plant Charmaine's uncle,' Gus explained with as much solemnity as if he had said 'I went to buy some cigarettes'.

I nevertheless offered my condolences.

Spotty and Lennie began to snigger and, instead of reprimanding them, Gus joined in. I looked on, more irritated than confused. What do you do when your best friend has just told you that he has been to bury a loved one and then starts laughing in your face? Maybe this was one for 'Dear Khensani'. Or more likely, I had come too late for an inspiring dagga session.

'We're laughing because of the way the man died,' Gus explained: 'On a toilet seat from a heart attack. When these guys here broke down the door they found him with one hand on his prick and a copy of *Playboy* spread open to the centrefold in front of him. He was busy jerking himself off when he died.'

Then we all filled our glasses and drank a toast to the good Uncle Marcus.

I had come to tell Gus about my eventful day. But with Spotty and

Lennie around that would have to wait. I didn't mind. The beer was flowing without any comradely interruptions. And after a while the conversation turned to matters of, well, shall we call it 'interracial teasing'.

Spotty starts it by telling us (me in particular, I think, by the way he keeps glancing in my direction) about a black caller who phoned a black deejay on a state-run black radio station.

'So it's a request programme and a guy phones Dan the Boogie Man . . .

CALLER: Hallo, Dan, is that Dan the Boogie Man?
DAN: Hi there, my man. You wanna send a request?
CALLER: Not really.
DAN: Not really? Ha ha ha. Well, why did you call then, brother man?
CALLER: To tell you that you're a big poes.

Before you can say Shaka Zulu, Dan's got a record playing. When that number is finished, another caller is waiting.

DAN: Hi, my man, how's the going?
CALLER: Aye, Dan, okay, okay.
DAN: So what Dan can do you for?
CALLER: Huh?
DAN: Would you like to send a request?
CALLER: Ja, I would like to send a request.
DAN: To . . .?
CALLER: To that guy who just called you a big poes.'

Lennie also has a radio story for us, which he begins in the form of a question: Why, he wants to know from me, do black people send dedications over the air to their wives, boyfriends and gogos when these family members are in the next room?

DEEJAY: Hi. And who am I speaking to?
CALLER: Is James, James Mazibuko.
DEEJAY: James Mazibuko, what took you so long to call man?
JAMES: Yes, I try long time but it engaysh.
DEEJAY: Oh, James, James, James. James from?
JAMES: Huh?

70

DEEJAY: Where are you from James — Alex, Sofasonke, Zeerust?
JAMES: Not any of those places.
DEEJAY: Which place then, James?
JAMES: Brakpan.
DEEJAY: Aaaah, Brakpan! So, James from Brakpan, who would you like to send a request to?
JAMES: My belovard wife Nokuzola.
DEEJAY: And what do you want to tell your beloved wife tonight, James?
JAMES: I love her very, very mush.
DEEJAY: Oh, James you really are a romantic somebody, aren't you now?
JAMES: Too mush.
DEEJAY: So, where in this world is Nokuzola tonight?
JAMES: She ironing in the keeshun.

'Now there's something I don't understand about coloureds,' I said. Things were beginning to roll in quite an ethnic direction in Gus's house-on-wheels, but everyone was being very good-natured about it.

'Tell us, tell us,' Gus pleaded, 'we'll be only too happy to explain.'

'Why is it that when coloureds phone in to Radio Sofasonke they ask if they can send a "delegation"?'

Poor Lennie was looking very confused. 'What's your point, my bra?' he asked.

'De-dee-cay-shin, my good man,' I explained. 'A request is a dedication, you get it?'

'Then what the hell is a delegation?' Lennie asked.

'That,' Gus explained, 'is what coloured people send to the government when they don't want to be thrown out of their homes. These are opposites: a dedication is *never* turned down, a delegation is *always* turned down.'

Lennie decided that it was actually not important to know these terms anyway.

Gus turned on the portable TV set. I suppose he was worried that things were getting out of hand. At first the state channel made a valiant effort to evade us, but then it decided to stay if we settled for a compromising bluish-grey view of the national news.

Suddenly, without warning, the tiny screen was filled with portraits of De Vries and Ockert. They were side by side, exactly as they

71

had appeared on my doorstep early that morning — De Vries on the left and Ockert on the right. For a fleeting moment the words 'ominous' and 'coincidence' flitted into my mind, understandably enough when you consider that I was raised by an inyanga. But then my St Christopher logic reminded me that there were not a great many permutations in which two men could stand side by side.

A title materialized on the screen:

DE VRIES AND VILJOEN: QUISLINGS OR REALISTS?

Viljoen! That was the bastard's name!

'Hey, a special edition of "Spotlight",' Gus said excitedly. 'That means an extra special dagga skyf.' He fished out a parcel of the wonder weed from underneath his mattress and began to roll an extra fat zol. Whenever Gus and I watched 'Spotlight' together we lit up. It seemed to lend an extra dimension to the absurdities of the government.

There was a deafening fanfare and, without wasting breath on honorifics or titles, a familiar voice began to speak:

VOICE-OVER: De Vries and Viljoen: Quislings or Realists? Tonight, this special edition of 'Spotlight' attempts to answer the question. We do so by putting under the political spotlight two men who have played a crucial role in shaping the course of political events in our country. But last night they came face to face with the realities of their often radical and reckless reforms . . . *(A drumbeat booms out ellipses.)* Who is this man Willem Adriaan de Vries . . .?

The voice-over, bristling with urgency, began to assail our ears with a potted history of the life of De Vries, while our eyes were treated to a series of fuzzy black and white stills of the former President taken from a family album:

A naked, bald-headed De Vries on the lap of a very fat, very unhappy-looking black maid.

GUS: At last, the alternative photo album.
ME: The President training to shit on us.

A fourteen-year-old, barefooted De Vries enveloped in a halo of smoke as he braais coils of boerewors and piles of T-bone steaks. A

72

hand squeezing a concertina is caught in the foreground.

LENNIE (*smacking his lips*): Ooh! Too nice.

De Vries astride a shimmering black stallion called Swart Storm.

VOICE-OVER: Willem Adriaan de Vries's skill as an orator rested on his ability to appropriate the homespun wisdom of the very people whom he despised. But one significant African adage he was never heard to utter is the one which says: 'When you put a man on a horse you cannot expect him not to push out his chest.'

Long before De Vries mounted the powerful but fractious steed of government, and let the hooves of power drum out a warning to Africa, he showed an arrogance that set people a-tremble in his own backyard.

Look closely at this photograph. It was taken on the family farm, 'Beloofde Land', when De Vries was a twenty-one-year-old boereseun, brimming with confidence and ready to change the world. And immediately after this picture was taken he set out astride Swart Storm to do just that.

On the De Vries farm lived a family who, for reasons which will be explained later in the programme, had overstayed their welcome. This was during the harsh years of the Depression and the family had nowhere to go.

De Vries senior, or Oom Jannie as he was affectionately known in the Pietersburg district, had issued the poor family with several final warnings which they did not heed, begging to remain on the farm until they found other lodgings.

Young De Vries decided to evict the family himself — but before he did so, realizing the historical significance of what he was about to do, he posed for this photograph.

When he arrived at the tiny house, the family were not in. They had gone to visit a sick relative on a neighbouring farm. Without dismounting, De Vries kicked open the front door and steered Swart Storm into the house. He went about breaking every piece of household furniture, glassware and crockery. And as he did so, the horse between his legs, as if sensing its rider's malicious intentions, began dropping pile upon pile of green manure in every room. De Vries exited through the back door.

Tonight we have in our studio the family who bore the brunt of early De Vries anger. Welcome to 'Spotlight', Marietjie and Kerneels van der Merwe.

ME *(shocked)*: Whites! He did that to his own people!

The Van der Merwes, a self-effacing old couple, blink in the glare of the lights as they try desperately to lift themselves out of a soft leather couch, raising a cloud of dust around them. In one particularly fine geriatric movement the old man falls so far back in his seat that we catch a glimpse of the soles of his scuffed velskoene.

ME: Last Stand on the Gomma Gomma.

Oupa Van der Merwe stares into the camera as if he has only just become aware of its presence. Then he scratches one wrinkled cheek, gazes at the greasepaint on his fingertips and says for all the world to hear, 'Watter kak is dit dié op my gesig?'

GUS: The power of the camera.

ME: The power of the spoken word.

LENNIE: Power to the people.

De Vries, his glasses reflecting the light from a packed hall, caught in an earnest pose, jabs the air with a finger as he makes a point.

VOICE-OVER: De Vries began a chequered career in politics when he joined the Suiwer Wit Party. He took the oath of office at the age of fifty-five, becoming this country's youngest ever President.

Footage of old De Vries in parliament; in Latin America signing trade agreements; pumping flesh with Paraguayan and Uruguayan dictators, while they pin medals to his chest; on walkabout among his white constituents.

Then the background music took on a gloomy tone.

VOICE-OVER: Two years ago, things suddenly took a turn for the worse. De Vries seemed to forget his constituency, his mandates, and began to fill his diary with appointments and plans that at first alarmed and then shocked all freedom-loving Republicans. He began to hold secret talks with the radicals, the communists and the terrorists. Those madmen who are hell-bent on bringing centuries of carefully nurtured civilization to an abrupt end.

But our ever-vigilant intelligence network and security forces were always there to monitor this strange turn in the leader's behaviour. Every handshake with a black terrorist, every clandestine whisper in a communist leader's ear, every secret meeting with a pressure group was recorded.

Our President, to our shame, was sleeping with the enemy, was committing adultery, was satisfying his own perverted fantasies after having sworn an oath of allegiance, of eternal loyalty to his party and his country. How could we explain this unaccountable behaviour?

Eighty years ago, the very first President of the independent white Republic fled to Switzerland with ten million pounds in gold bullion. A few days previously his doctors had diagnosed a tapeworm, and it is this which probably led to his madness.

Twenty years ago, the beloved founder of the Suiwer Wit Party and father of apartheid, died when a deranged assassin stormed into the houses of parliament and butchered him. The madman claimed that he was ordered to commit this evil deed by a tapeworm lodged in his gut.

Recently De Vries has complained about a pain in his own stomach.

The Bouncing
Bear

I heard singing. An a cappella choir, singing to the rhythm of what felt like a moving train. The voices were distinctly female and the song was derisive, taunting, with every refrain exploding into ear-splitting laughter. Convinced that it was another of my crazy nightmares, brought on by alcohol and dagga, I turned over and tried to sink back into sleep, but the refrain persisted:

Ngeke ngishade nothishela
Ugula njalo
Ubanga usizi

I opened one eye a fraction and looked around. The singers were women, seven or eight of them, in white tackies, white frocks and mauve capes! My mother! This was her church group, the March of Africa to Zion Church. Even though I could not see the backs of their capes, I knew there would be large white crosses embroidered upon them.

Laughing and wagging their fingers to the beat of their song, they sang again:

Ngeke ngishade nothishela
Ugula njalo
Ubanga usizi

Then they all tumbled into each other like happy, bloated tiddly-winks in a ridiculous animated cartoon.

I knew where I was: on a train bound for Sofasonke. And I knew why these stupid women were taunting me: I wiped away the spittle festooned between my chin and my collar, which advertised my drunken state like a length of bunting. Then there was the pen in my top pocket which also played a part: these overgrown chorus girls believed that I was a teacher! I took out the pen, aimed it at them and went 'bang!' They all ducked and collapsed with laughter; then they began their silly ditty again, to the delight of all the other late-night and/or early-morning commuters.

But it was more than the drool and the pen that had caused this lampooning of my person. My first piece of award-winning investigative reporting, about two years ago, had been a story about them, the March of Africa to Zion Church. I had written an article on their 'frantic, ritualistic chanting and stomping about in the veld like Apaches' and their chief apostle who lived in extreme wealth off the contributions of 'poor, illiterate gardeners and domestic workers'. Every year in November millions of them trekked from all over Southern Africa to the church's headquarters, which were no more than a huge open space in the bush. Each worshipper was obliged to bring a fifty-cent coin as a contribution to the church. All these coins were thrown into an armada of stainless-steel baths that surrounded the holy ground, and when the baths were full the apostle navigated them straight into his bank account.

My editor was delighted, but not my Mama. She summoned me to her house and told me that while she herself would forgive me this sacrilege, the good Lord would punish me for it, one day when I least expected it. This taunting, I suppose, was the retribution that Mama had promised.

I opened my eyes, leaned out of the window and vomited into the hot summer night.

No more liquor for me ever again, I promised myself.

Beer and Dagga, those two great freedom fighters, had formed an unholy alliance against me. No conventional warfare for them, but acts of internal terrorism and destabilization. The result: red eyes streaming with tears, a runny nose, a stomach that churned and lurched with every nauseous bump and rattle of the train.

I shuffled out of my seat and went to find Gus. He was sitting in another carriage, listening attentively to a friendly ticket examiner whose khaki-uniformed butt swayed to and fro as the train trundled on through the night. He had a funny story to tell which he punctuated with clicking sounds from the little gadget he used to punch holes into tickets.

'I'm telling you,' he was saying, 'my wife wants a divorce' — *click-click, click-click* — 'Some nights I'm making love to her, and as I reach the point of no return, I shout: "Tickets! Tickets!" The first time I did that she thought I was funny. But I've been doing it for six months now and she says she's had enough!' — *click-click, click-click* — 'So what do I do? Get a divorce or chuck this job?'

'Ah, you're back,' Gus greeted me, offering me a shot of the brandy he had been sharing with the ticket examiner. 'I heard some beautiful music coming from over there . . .'

'Beautiful music!' I coughed out a cloud of cigarette smoke and sagged down next to him. 'Those singing sisters were making a bloody fool of me.'

Gus frowned.

'The sooner you learn my language, the better for you,' I advised, and translated their song:

> I will never get married to that teacher
> Because he is always sick
> He causes me sorrow

I was about to ask Gus what, in the name of my ancestors, we were doing on a train. Then my aching jaw reminded me. After watching that 'Spotlight' programme in Gus's caravan, we had decided that more liquor was in order. We had all had more than our fair share, but we felt that if we'd ever had a good reason to buy more alcohol, we had one tonight. For a while, thanks to De Vries's aberrant behaviour, there had seemed to be something volatile in the country's usually stagnant and oppressive political atmosphere. Now De Vries had been ousted and the right-wing was in power once more. They might decide to reintroduce their prohibition laws of not so long ago, which meant that we blacks would not be allowed to buy and drink alcohol.

I reminded my drinking companions, slouched around the table in Gus's caravan, about the Years of Thirst. I recalled how even our liquor had to go underground when hundreds of shebeen queens buried their potent and frothy brews in tins to keep them from the law. And I acknowledged the contribution made to the culture of drinking by Mfundisi Madingoane of the African Church of Hope and Glory, a Bible-punching priest from Sofasonke well known for his sermons. 'Like our beer,' he declared once at a revivalist meeting on a Sofasonke football field, 'Jesus will rise again.'

Well, these legends convinced my companions that we needed to get to the nearest watering-hole before the new regime got there, and so we all piled into my car.

The shebeen was a skull and crossbones like any other. But it was in total darkness and there was not a murmur of life inside. Hardly surprising, even for a shebeen, at two o'clock in the morning.

We knocked.

No response.

We knocked a little louder.

No response.

We knocked as loud as we could. The greed for more alcohol and our advanced state of drunkenness had deprived us of any sense of civility that we may once have had. We swaggered about on the stoep, calling out the shebeen owner's name and begging him to open up. 'Just three cold ones. We'll pay double. Pass it through the window. Then we'll be off. Won't pester you again. Shit!'

Knock, knock, knock, knock.

Eventually a gruff, sleepy voice from inside: 'Fuck off! We don't live here anymore!'

No amount of pleading could convince the voice to serve us, even from the bedroom window. As soon as our curses subsided we heard music: some jive song that was sending every township in the country into a frenzy. Yes, you've guessed it:

You're my weekend, weekend spesh-ul
You're my weekend, weekend spesh-ul

This was all par for the course in the Republic, coup or no coup: in some skull and crossbones yard people were braaing away their week's rations and dancing up a cloud of dust as if nothing had happened.

'There must be some alcohol there,' Lennie gurgled, trying to remain vertical.

'The cleverest thing you've said all night,' Gus congratulated him between hiccups. 'Let's go get some.'

So off we drove to do some serious gatecrashing.

'It's the Garcias' place,' Gus said. 'Old buddy of mine from primary-school days. There'll be no problem getting in here.'

As we approached the house, a heady cloud of braai-smoke and a whiff of beer drifted our way to tempt us nearer.

And then, from a car in the driveway, a male voice warned: 'No kaffirs allowed in here.'

I had been spotted and found unwelcome.

Without a moment's hesitation, Gus stumbled towards the car and countered: 'Will the rude bastard who said that please step out of the car so that he can get his body panel-beaten.' Gus was chewing his bottom lip and I knew he was angry, drunk but the moer in.

There were four or five indistinct figures in the car. One stepped obediently out and materialized into Richard 'The Bouncing Bear' September, coloured light-heavyweight boxing champion of the Republic.

TALE OF THE TAPE
Age: 26 years
Height: 1.8 m
Weight: 79 kg
Number of fights: 27
Wins: 27
KOs: 27
Race of opponents: Coloured
Previous experience: Rape, car theft
Distinguishing marks: Two front teeth missing (claims he knocked them out himself)

The Bouncing Bear was the only 'non-white' athlete to have received a handshake from President De Vries at last year's Ethnic Games (established after the Republic's expulsion from the Olympic Games because of its racist policies). That handshake had become famous when, at the very moment the President clasped the Bear's massive paw, a powerful bomb, which had been planted by the Movement for the Abolition of Ethnic Sport, exploded in the stadium. The front page of the *Coloured People's Herald* carried a photo of the handshake with a cloud of smoke and dust billowing in the background. Underneath was the now legendary caption: What an explosive grip!

The owner of that grip squared up to Gus — and it is evidence of the effect alcohol has on the eyesight that Gus still failed to recognize him. An excited crowd had gathered and were butting and shoving for a ringside view. Gus 'put up his dukes', as Rodwell Mazibuko of the *Black World*'s sports pages would have put it.

'Don't go for the kill just yet!' a voice from the crowd advised Gus.

'In fact, don't go at all,' shouted another.

'Circle the Bear,' a third voice suggested.

'Yes,' some wit agreed, 'in ever-widening circles.'

Gus heeded none of this. He went in for the kill.

The Bear neither bounced nor bobbed nor weaved. He just struck with one naked left upper-cut. Gus lifted off his feet and came toppling back to earth. I stepped forward, more out of honour than practical wisdom, and felt what must surely have been a brick in the shape of knuckles smash into my jaw. My lights went out before I crash-landed.

When I regained consciousness I saw Gus's face turning above me like one of those warped simanje-manje seven-singles miners jive to in hostels on Saturday nights.

'Are you okay, bra?' Gus asked.

'Just take me to my car. Please.'

'I'm afraid I can't. Lennie and Spotty have split with it.'

'At least they didn't try to commandeer me,' I said, licking salt off my lips.

'What are you talking about, Scara?' he asked me, slurring his words from drunkenness and the pain inflicted on his face by the Bouncing Bear.

'It's one helluva long story,' I said, holding onto my head to keep it from spinning off my shoulders.

Gus helped me to my feet. He wanted me to walk back to his caravan, but I insisted on going home, to intercept Khensani on her way to the divorce courts.

So my Volksie was in the hands of two very dubious coloureds and here I was on the train to Sofasonke with Gus, a ticket examiner with domestic problems that were mild compared to mine, and an army of women singing their praises to Jehovah and their taunts to me.

9

Bambi and the Censor

'Let me see if I've got this right. You're telling me you opened your door on Saturday morning and there was De Vries and his pal Ockert Viljoen, the Minister of Mines?'

'Yes!' I said, so annoyed at having to answer the question three times that I underlined the word with a blast on the hooter. (Gus and I had taken a train back to Riverlea this Monday morning to fetch my dear little bug, which we found remarkably intact.)

'And?' he coaxed me on. By now tears were streaming from his eyes and his shoulders bobbed up and down as he guffawed.

'He was with his pal Viljoen and . . .'

'You had no dagga the night before?'

'I did, Kinnear, I did okay? But that's beside the point.'

'Sorry,' he apologized mockingly. 'Dagga's beside the point. So?'

'They wanted to go to my father. I took them.'

'Ah!' Gus slapped his thigh in a sudden eureka. 'I know why they wanted you to take them to your Tata's.'

He was still fooling around but I decided to play along.

'Tell me?'

'They were on the run from this new bastard, whatsisname?'

'De Jong.'

'On the run from De Jong, right . . .?'

I neither answered nor nodded. But he needed no encouragement.

'He went to ask your Tata for asylum.'

'Ha! So my father's going to hide De Vries in the toilet in the backyard . . .'

'No, your father ain't no common or garden asylum-giver. He's 'gonna turn those guys into blacks . . .'

'Help them to blend in with the crowd?' I said, regaining my sense of humour despite my babalaas and Monday morning's bumper-to-bumper traffic.

'That's it,' he nodded.

'And then?'

'Well, as soon as we natives graduate from restless to revolutionary and take over the government, De Vries and Viljoen plan to make a comeback as black leaders.'

'Very interesting theory,' I mused as we drove past Croesus cemetery with its humps of raised soil, wilting flowers and scattered marble tombstones. 'I can see now that Mr Kinnear did not waste his money when he sent you to school.'

But Gus was not listening to me. He had rolled down his window, stuck out his head and shouted loud enough to wake the dead: 'Ciao, Uncle Marcus! Don't worry, where you're going the place is full of hot centre-spreads!'

Gus could be damn silly sometimes. But he looked sillier still this morning with his bruised jaw and black eye from our run-in with the Bear on Saturday night/Sunday morning.

'Listen here,' I said, 'have you done with your fond farewells to your ancestor?'

'It's cheaper than slaughtering a cow,' he said, rolling up his window.

'I'm going to write a story on De Vries and his crony for our paper.'

'You're not serious.' He sat up straight.

'Watch me.'

'Come off it, Scara. It will never get past the subs . . . it's a damn crazy story.'

'It's a damn crazy country!'

'Look,' he said with a sigh, 'Mahlatini will think we're — *you're* fucking around. For sure he'll tell you the dagga's gone to your head. See what we look like? black eyes and babalaas and now you want to write this "How I met De Vries" stuff. Mahlatini's gonna fire us, I bet you. We haven't had a story in weeks and he'll see this as an act of desperation.'

Even after I had stopped the car on the pavement outside our offices, we sat arguing for another five or ten minutes. I was determined to do the story, Gus was trying to convince me that our editor, Philemon Mahlatini, would take a more than cynical view of the whole thing. But I wasn't listening to advice today. I certainly wasn't going to take it from Baba Jakes, the night-watchman of the *Black World* offices, who passed us on his way home from his night shift. 'Too early to argue, boys,' he said, yawning.

We both ignored him.

Gus had to have the last word: 'And I don't think Mahlatini would like a repeat of those two posters over there.' He flicked his eyes at the *Black World* building.

As we got out of the car, Gus stared at me over the curved roof with a pleading look in his bloodshot eyes, imploring me not to write the article. I returned his beseeching gaze with a look that was just as bloodshot and determined. But the article about the white fugitive President waking me up in the wee hours was not to be: an intervention in the offices would see to that, and it was waiting for us inside.

In the lobby the two posters that Gus had referred to so ominously caught my eye. They were news bills which Mahlatini had had mounted on the wall under glass. One of them was from our own *Black World*, as you could tell by the masthead, and it read in bold black capitals:

CHIEFS GO DOWN 3-1 TO RANGERS IN SHOCK DEFEAT

The second poster was from the *Daily Star*, our white sister newspaper (if multiracial siblings were possible in the Republic). It read:

POLICE OPEN FIRE ON SOFASONKE STUDENTS

The date on the posters brought home the significance of these otherwise very commonplace news headlines: 16 June 1976. While black newshounds were sitting at Orlando Stadium, feverishly reporting on 'a controversial penalty', 'an unexpectedly powerful and dazzling combination of the Rangers forward line' and 'a record crowd of 12 000', white journalists were recording a massacre that made the world gasp and proved to be a watershed in the politics of the Republic.

But our white colleagues were not exactly the paragons of press virtue that we, to our shame, were led to believe: the famous schools uprising not only provoked a sharp increase in sales of firearms among whites, but also did much to boost the circulation of the *Daily*

Star. And several months into the uprising, after the umpteenth black victim had been buried, that paper held a huge party that was as raucous as Sofasonke was sombre. The *Black World*'s editor at the time pointed out their dubious ethics in an editorial, which turned out to be his swansong.

His successor, the baby-faced Philemon Mahlatini, hailed from Northern Natal and wore pants that ended about five centimetres above his fleshy ankles. But if we had come across him on this Monday morning in floral Bermudas and sandals it would not have surprised us more than what awaited us in the news room.

Next to my desk was a new desk. And perched on a chair was a newcomer. And the newcomer was a white man, a ruddy redhead in fact, who introduced himself as 'Sybrand Rautenbach, Government Censor'.

'What d'you mean?' I managed to ask while my jaw dropped open. I must have exhaled a blast of vile weekend air for Sybrand stepped back blinking uncomfortably. I remembered my encounter with Comrade Machel on Saturday morning.

'Well, you obviously know by now — or you're not a journalist,' he cocked his head as if awaiting a reply, 'that Dr De Jong has taken over as President. He has declared a state of emergency, effective immediately, and has appointed me as official government censor of this bantu newspaper, Mr . . .?'

'Nhlabatsi!' Gus shouted, aimed his Leica at me and the censor and clicked it two or three times.

'No no no no no no.' Sybrand waved a hand in Gus's face.

'Gustav Kinnear,' Gus said, grabbing the hand and pumping it vigorously. '*Black World* photographer.'

'Pleased to meet you, Mr Kinnear.' His voice was familiar, but not his face. Then I remembered. There was a cartoon programme for Afrikaner kids on state TV. One of the main characters was Meneer Slang, a snake of indeterminate species with a timorous, flattering, ingratiating voice and a talent for spoiling picnics and other outings.

'Aren't you Meneer Slang?' I asked.

'Oh, another fan,' he laughed, 'a bantu fan.'

I took no notice of this silly remark because something else amazed me even more. 'But De Jong took over on Friday evening . . . less than seventy-two hours ago.'

'We play fast,' he said with a reptilian wink. 'And now we can look forward to some stability in the Republic, don't you think —

with some guidance from the Lord Jesus Christ . . .' Another tilt of the head.

I mentally replayed the last argument I had had with Khensani. It happened that morning while I was shaving.

'You drink so much that things are happening in this place without you even knowing!' she screamed.

'If I wanted to keep up with the political machinations and massacres around here I'd have to be sober twenty-four hours a day,' I countered.

'. . . the Lord Jesus Christ,' Sybrand went on, 'whose representative here on earth is not the Pope, as some people like to believe, but . . .'

Gus started clicking away again.

'No no no no no,' he shouted, once more waving his hands in the air.

Gus was aiming his camera at the wall behind Sybrand, where a huge poster had been pinned up. It was a list of places one was no longer allowed to photograph, and it included everything from the Houses of Parliament to the local post office. There was no mention of posters though, and Gus was using that fact to be smart as usual: 'It doesn't say I can't take a picture of a poster which tells me what I can't take pictures of.'

Sybrand's head jerked back as he worked out what Gus was saying. 'Don't get clever now, Mr Kinnear, let's not get off on a bad foot.'

'Can I take a picture of your Bambi then?' Gus asked, pointing at a wall.

There was indeed a Bambi on the wall, a life-sized, pink, doe-eyed, polystyrene baby reindeer. While his brain did battle with the implications of giving Gus permission to take a photo of the lovable cartoon character, Sybrand explained how he had acquired it: he had rescued Bambi from certain death when Sybrand Junior's nursery school was closed down due to diminishing attendance, due in turn to a progressively decreasing white birth rate, due in turn to . . .

Eventually Sybrand agreed and Gus snapped away. He took several shots and even managed to cajole a supercilious Sybrand into posing with Bambi.

While garrulous Gus continued to chat to Sybrand, I strode over to the far end of the office, past the rest of the staffers who were discussing the weekend's turbulent political events and our resident censor in groups over cups of coffee and cans of Coke. I needed to make a phone call.

As I lifted the receiver, an inexplicable thing happened: for some reason I could not remember Khensani's number. This was crazy! I had dialled that number hundreds of times . . .? No! I reached for a dog-eared telephone directory on Mremi's desk and flipped through the pages, willing myself to recall the number before I found it. As I searched, my mind flipped back three years to a morning on the train . . .

10

Khensani

7.30 am . . . I'm standing on the train as it makes its way from Sofasonke to Johannesburg. As usual there is standing-room only. I am dressed in black pants, my Florsheim shoes and checked sports jacket, presentable enough for my interview at a factory as a wage clerk, but not too smart for the tsotsis on the train who have the habit of sticking their fingers into one's pockets as if they were theirs. An attractive young woman is sitting at the window, an arm's length from me. She is reading a novel and, as all lovers of literature will tell you, I want to know what it is. But there is no way of telling as her head is between me and the open book.

But a man sitting opposite her helps me out with this one. He asks her a question which I don't catch above the laughter and the chattering in Xhosa and Zulu and Tswana and Sotho and tsotsitaal. She answers politely and reads on. The man leans forward and speaks to her again and this time she closes the book and puts it on her lap while she talks to him. I recognize the cover and the title immediately: *The Beautyful Ones Are Not Yet Born* by the Ghanaian writer Ayi Kwei Armah. How can I ever forget the novel about an unnamed hero's sad and cynical wanderings through a bleak and filthy Ghana during Nkrumah's final years. And what a boring story! But even more memorable for me is proudly pointing out the misspelt 'Beautyful' to our English teacher, saying that I didn't think I wanted to read a book with a typo on the cover. 'Read it first,' Mrs Roberts said, 'and tell me afterwards what you think of the typo.'

As all this is going through my head, the sun glances fleetingly into the train and flashes onto the young woman's chest. A golden fish with an upswept tail. I've seen that somewhere before . . . It's the woman from the Jehovah's Witnesses! The one Mama chased from our door.

She reaches for her bag, takes out a pencil and a tiny writing-pad, the kind that looks like a toy. She scribbles on it, tears off the page and hands it to the persistent young gentleman. He reads it and looks pleased. He folds the note carefully and puts it in his top pocket. She goes back to her reading.

As the train pulls into Braamfontein station, they both get up to leave. This is one station before my stop in town but I decide to get off too: the three of us and a thousand other Sofasonke commuters. I lose her in the crowd! Don't ask me how, but I lose her. The fellow with her name and number on a piece of paper is still very much in evidence, looking very smug with his note in his top pocket as he slowly walks up the stairs into a sunny Braamfontein. I decide to extract the note from him. I go up to him without a plan.

'Hey, mfowethu,' I say, 'I need that sister's name and phone number.'

He stands still and looks at me bewildered.

'The sister you've been talking to on the train,' I explain as if I'm in a great hurry. 'I saw her give you her phone number and her name. I need to find her.'

'Why?' he asks.

'She left her child at the Centre.'

'The Centre?'

'Don't you even know what the Centre is?' I shake my head disbelievingly. 'Come, I don't have time to waste. Show me the note.'

He takes the note out of his pocket and hands it to me. It reads: 'Seek ye first the kingdom of God . . .' I look up at him. In a moment we have exchanged facial expressions: I'm a little bewildered now and he's the one with the smile on his face. He explains:

'I'm going to look for a job, my brother. I asked her for some funds. She told me to pray, to say these words to myself and then things will come right for me — in no time.'

As he tells me this I have already turned on my heel and am walking away.

'Hey!' he calls me. I turn around. 'She told me where she works.'

'Where?'

'You got something for me?'

I take out a fifty-cent coin and flip it towards him. He catches it easily, but it's far too little. He's disappointed.

'Gimme ten rand,' he says, tossing the coin back. 'Ten rand and I'll give you where she works *and* her name plus the surname.'

I take out five rand and hand it to him. 'That's all I have.'

'You have five rand fifty.'

I give him the coin too.

'Miss Theresa Madibane. And she works for the Help the Homeless.'

He was right. I found her number in the telephone directory and by ten that morning I was speaking to her on the phone.

'I phoned to apologize,' I said.

'What for?' Her voice sounded tired, squeaky.

'My mother's manners.' I explained how rudely my mother had got rid of her and her brother in Christ.

'Oh, I really can't remember,' she said, ignoring my little joke about her brother in Christ — or perhaps she did not regard it as a joke at all. 'Don't worry, that type of thing happens to us all the time.'

'Remember the woman who called your magazine "Watch the hour"?'

'Oh yes!' she laughed. 'You have a scary Mama.'

'May I take you out for lunch?'

'What for?'

'To eat.' Again she ignored my joke. But after some cajoling she promised to pray for guidance about going out with a total stranger.

'Look,' I said to her, 'how important is God to you?'

'He's my life,' she said without hesitation.

'And you were prepared to introduce Him to my mother, a total stranger.'

No response for a long time. Then: 'Let me think about it.'

Scara, I told myself when I put down the phone, you got style, sonny.

And the Almighty evidently did decide in my favour, because when I phoned her back after a few days she gave me a cautious yes. I took her out for lunch a week later, and three or four times over the next fortnight. By then she felt comfortable enough with me to invite me home. She did not live in Sofasonke but in a neatly kept flat in Johannesburg. She had managed to acquire the place with the help of a white colleague, who put the flat in her own name: it was illegal for a black person, even a Christian 'who had accepted the Lord Jesus

Christ as her own personal saviour', to live in the city centre where many a white sinner resided.

In the first weeks of our friendship Ms Madibane retained her serious, quiet disposition. She ate daintily, keeping her mouth closed and chewing slowly. Once she left an entire pork chop on her plate — without taking a single bite! Every time I think about it I salivate! She said grace before — and after! — every meal we ate at a restaurant. She combed her hair several times a day. She stepped over a perfectly paved sidewalk as if she were walking down a potholed Sofasonke street in the dark, blindfolded.

We had our first argument the fourth or fifth time we met. In a restaurant she got up in the middle of a meal to go to the loo. I was left to search the faces of other patrons, the red tablecloths and trolleys heaped with salads, the bustling waitresses weaving their way between tables. My eyes came to rest on our table. Theresa had taken her bag along with her, but she had left something behind. It was her passbook. But what was this . . .? I picked it up for a closer look. The passbook was encased in a stiff plastic cover the likes of which I had never, in all my thirty-one years as a black, set eyes on before. On the plastic cover, in black, embossed type, were the words PASSBOOK HOLDER repeated in Xhosa, Tswana and Sotho.

'What is this?' I asked her when she returned to the table. I waved the plastic cover, which I had removed from the book. She sensed anger rather than curiosity in my voice, only slightly tempered by the fact that we were in a public place and by my affection for her. She shifted into her chair, putting all the creases and folds of her elegant knee-length skirt where they belonged.

'You can see what it is,' she offered a weak subterfuge.

'Well, why did you buy it?'

'I didn't buy it.' She licked her lips nervously and took a deep breath. 'One of my white colleagues gave it to me for Christmas.'

I promptly took my steak-knife and slashed the offensive pouch into about fifty pieces, while Theresa took another trip to the loo to weep and the other patrons shrank from me as if I was a psychopath.

On the day she invited me to her flat she let me kiss her.

'I would like to make love to you,' I whispered in her ear.

She seemed mildly shocked and grew quiet. She asked me to leave earlier than expected, and for six days she would not see me or return my calls. Then on the seventh day the phone rang in my office. It was Theresa!

'Mandla' — she never called me by my nickname — 'I need a favour.'

'Anything for you, moratiwa.'

'A friend is coming to live with me . . .'

Aha! I understood now why she had been so reticent. There was a man in her life and he was moving in with her. She was phoning to ask me to stop pestering her.

'She's coming by train from Durban tomorrow night. Will you take me to fetch her from the station — please dear?'

'Of course, sweetie!' A woman, I noticed with relief.

She had another request. 'Will you wear your jeans and your red sweater?'

Very strange this. I was about to ask why, but then I decided I would just have to work it out for myself later. For the moment I said: 'Of course!' So she was still interested. I smiled to myself in my little office; when a worker came in to query a discrepancy in his pay-slip, he asked me if I found this lousy factory so wonderful to work in that I smiled all day. The woman liked me in blue and red, I decided. She was most certainly still interested. She could not come out and say so after giving me the cold shoulder for a few days. The coming to Jo'burg of some buddy of hers was a good excuse for her to say all is forgiven, come and get me.

The next day. Six o'clock. I arrived on her doorstep dressed in my red and blue as requested. I rang the doorbell. When she opened, I could not believe my eyes. She's dressed in blue jeans and a red sweater! The woman is lovely: a sexy bum and perfect breasts. Her eyes are sparkling as if she's just gulped down two glasses of champagne. But we're dressed like twins! Is she a little kinky maybe? No, I conclude, just her usual, innocent, childish self. I've seen this kind of thing before: lovers — black or white — sashaying down a Jo'burg street in their matching colours. But it's not for me. At any rate, I decided, there wouldn't be too many people who knew me at the station. Half of them would be white anyway, and they didn't count.

Deep in the background I could see that a table had been laid and the smell of roast chicken, potatoes and pumpkin drifted from the kitchen. We would have supper here this evening after we fetched Theresa's friend from the station.

'So tell me about your friend,' I said.

'She's a university room-mate of mine,' Theresa explained. 'We did Social Work together at the University of Natal. She's found a job in Jo'burg. I don't know why she's coming to work here. She'll tell us all about it tonight.'

'What's her name?'

'Khensani.'

'Khensani. That's neither Zulu nor Xhosa nor Tswana nor Pedi nor Shangaan nor . . .' But before I could finish all the language groups Theresa had given me a friendly shove out of the flat, her hands on the rump of my blue jeans! This was unheard-of a few days ago. Maybe God had told her what a great lover I was and how I always cleaned up afterwards.

As we walked onto Platform 16 to await the Durban train and Khensani, we passed a crowd of bubbling white people, happy to have a loved one home again, I could tell from the eagerness to carry luggage and the six or seven tales going at once. A kid gnawing on a toffee stuck a finger out of the crowd — at us — and quipped:

'Red-red, blue-blue.' Then he turned it into a chant which rhymed perfectly in his mother tongue:

Rooi, rooi
Jou hemp is mooi!
Blou, blou
Jou broek is nou!

White education was good, but not that good. One of the adults must have seen us approaching and made up the rhyme, and the kid had been tactful enough to blurt it out.

Red, red
Your shirt is pretty!
Blue, blue
Your pants are narrow!

If I were as white as the kid he would've seen my red, red blood in my face. So much for my theory that whites did not count.

At 7.30 the train pulled slowly onto the platform. First the length of whites-only first-class coaches, and then the second- and third-class coaches for the rest of us. Theresa hooked her arm into mine (another surprise) and quietly searched for her friend among the excited faces leaning out of the windows. Khensani spotted us before we could spot *her*.

'Hey, wena, stop making love and open you'lls eyes!' the voice from the train echoed in the subterranean station platform.

'That's her,' Theresa said with an apprehensive sigh rather than a burst of happiness. Almost as if she were pointing out a petty offender from a row of women at an identity parade. 'That's Khensani.'

I looked to where Theresa was pointing and saw a woman jump out of the carriage window and start running towards us. She looked bedraggled but stunningly beautiful and I half hoped that she was not quite as lovely as she looked from afar. But the closer she came the lovelier she seemed to get. I dragged Theresa towards her friend.

'Matching lovers!' Khensani said with some playful derision in her voice. She hugged and kissed Theresa.

What is she? I asked myself rather shamefully. I considered myself to be free of racist attitudes, but seeing Khensani on that first day suddenly brought home to my shamed conscience what my first reaction has always been upon meeting people.

She spoke Zulu with an Indian accent, spattered with the slang that flowed through the streets of Durban's coloured townships. Her hair was an alloy of dark Zulu curls and auburn Indian ringlets. Her smooth brown skin shimmered even in the sunless underground where I stood gazing at her. She was like one of those toy pictures that change colour in the light through some imperceptible movement of the hand.

She wore two or three coloured scarves around her neck. Every time she moved, gestured or rubbed her nose, bangles chimed and flashed.

She walked up to me and kissed me warmly on my lips, which went numb with surprise. I heard Theresa telling her my name. It sounded far away, as if I had just regained consciousness on a city street and was listening to a passer-by give the police some personal details: my name, address and whether I was an employed or indolent bantu.

'You have lovely hair,' I said, shaking her hand. It seemed rude not to acknowledge this simple and obvious fact.

'It always looks better when it's dirty,' she said. 'Ask Theresa.' She combed her fingers backwards through her hair and with one hand captured most of the tresses like the tail of a pony. Then she turned her back on me. 'Hold it for me,' she said, without a 'please' or a 'thank you'. Why? I wondered, long after she had slipped an elastic band from her wrist onto the spill of hair.

'Because it was a gift from you to me,' I told her, answering my own question several months later.

'Oh, you sentimental fool,' she replied immediately. 'It's called flirting, that's all: you know flirting?'

We drove home to the flat. I thought I saw Khensani winking at me from the back seat. But I had seen many women wink at me from there before, even when the seat was empty. The two women chatted about student days.

And continued chatting about student days when we were seated around the supper table, eating roast chicken, and avocado pears which Khensani had brought from tropical Durban, wrapped in news-paper to ripen.

'Why did you leave your job?' Theresa asked her.

Khensani burped, slapped her tummy for having taken in too much food, and began to tell us about her former employers: a liber-al, semi-governmental social services organization. She told us about the budgets, flagrantly fluttered from desk to desk, and the discrep-ancies they revealed in government allocations to the aged, infirm and poor of Durban's various communities. For every rand spent on a black pensioner, three hundred were spent on a white.

'I looked after seventeen white pensioners a week,' she explained. 'It used to be eighteen but . . .'

'One died,' I said, trying to display my skills in simple logic.

'Uh-uh,' she shook her head. 'Number eighteen was a blind woman. I used to help her to get dressed, take her shopping, that kind of thing. She complained to my bosses about me when she discover-ed that I was black. As if it was some kind of privilege to see her wrinkled old white bum twice a week.'

Theresa winced. I laughed so much that I swallowed a spoonful of avocado pear whole and was seized by a coughing convulsion. I had my back slapped by Khensani, who saw a lump of her velvet-smooth tropical fruit transformed into a missile and a statue of the most serene of holy mothers caught full in the eye!

After Theresa had baptized the statuette in a gentle lather of dish-washing liquid, it was time for me to go. Theresa took me to the door, walked me down to my little Volksie, and got into the passenger seat beside me. I waited for a tirade of invective about blasphemy and general bad manners. But before I knew it she was kissing me full on the mouth. A trembling exploration under her red sweater revealed the shocking absence of a brassière! — discarded some time between supper and washing up. Further reconnoitring revealed other wonderful carnal delights and we made love for the first time in the cramped space of the squeaky back seat of my car — all the more cramped for having our minds preoccupied with the girl newly arrived from Durban.

Theresa and I took Khensani out with us to restaurants, movies, the theatre. She feebly declined our offers sometimes, but always came along in the end. She hated staying in the flat alone and had not made many friends in Johannesburg yet — although men did begin to phone as the weeks went by. We also spent some Saturday nights at home, cooking, chatting or playing Scrabble. One of these nights was particularly memorable and exciting. I had to start the game but I was stuck with all those consonants that are tucked away at the end of the alphabet. All I could come up with as an opening word was:

SEX

The women waited for my usual ribald remarks, but I reserved them all and sat back. Khensani was next and she made:

Y
SEX
B
O

'A perfect cross,' Theresa said, tilting her head to read the word. 'But sorry, no Zulu words.'

Khensani gazed into my eyes, smiled seductively, and withdrew her word.

Yebo, I thought to myself. Yes. Did she mean it?

One afternoon a month later the phone rang on my desk, which was piled with more rubbish than a Sofasonke refuse dump. It was about the time that Theresa usually phoned and my buoyant mood tempted me to say, 'Hi Theresa.' But she had chided me for this childishness in the past, so I uttered a simple and restrained 'Hi' into the mouthpiece.

'Howzit?' Even in those two syllables I could hear the songs of the ghettos and the waterfronts and the suburbs of a subcontinent.

'Khensani.'

Before I could say anything else she launched into a story about a movie that she had seen, beginning at the end, and then moving on to a scathing review, the actors' names and lifestyles, and a jumbled beginning. But I didn't mind at all. I sat back listening and smiling, enjoying the music of her voice and her vivacity. But Khensani could go on for ever and eventually I had to ask her why she had called.

'Are you coming around after work?' she asked me.

'Not tonight,' I said. 'The Volksie's got mobility problems.'

'Ooh, posh, hey. Other cars they just get stuck and that.'

'Please be careful what you say about my Volksie.'

'Excuse me.' We both laughed, then she continued: 'Well, I've made some pancakes. I've got a little godchild in Durbs and his mother phoned and said Jabu's got his first tooth and I want to celebrate. I'm looking at a photo of him right now, the child's a looker. I tell you, on the day he was born I had to go for my driving test that same day, but his mother's sister and I, we finished a whole bottle of champagne one time and the instructor he failed me and said he knew about drunken drivers but I was the best. What a performance.'

'Celebrate with Theresa.'

'Aw, but you know she's gone off to some retreat or whatever she calls it . . . I'm alone and all.'

'Gimme half an hour,' I said, feeling my heart begin to pound in my chest, an African drumbeat the meaning of which was all too clear.

'Scara?' She never called me 'Scara' in Theresa's presence.

'Yes.'

'Bring chocolate but.'

Twenty minutes later I had emerged from the dark cage of the elevator and was knocking at Theresa's door — but waiting for Khensani to open.

When she did, we smiled at each other like two people who exchange secrets only to discover that their secrets are identical. We had spoken too recently to concern ourselves with pleasantries. Her feet were bare. I stared down at them, indulging a fetish I had never confided to anyone. She wore a loose-fitting, décolleté dress which seemed a size too big for her.

'Come,' she said, turned and walked into the dark interior of the tiny one-bedroom flat. Outside the sun went down contentedly behind a Jo'burg skyscraper as if it had seen me safely to my lover's abode.

Khensani had prepared for my visit: PP Arnold rose from the dead, and swathed in her long plaits and rainbow-coloured scarves, she sang a widow's lament to a lover she had left while he was labouring to put bread and light on their table at night. I sat on the bed while Khensani fetched hot tea and the pancakes. A sudden silly mood took hold of me and I recalled a childhood trick. Quickly I unwrapped the Bar One chocolate bar I had brought. I tore the dark-brown wrapping into tiny pieces and, with a dentist's precision, covered all my teeth except one incisor. When she returned to the room I was ready for her. I averted my face and announced: 'With all the powers vested in me I declare this teeth party open.' Then I turned around and gave her my one-toothed grin.

Khensani collapsed on the bed laughing, her dress flying above her knees, and I glimpsed chocolate-brown thighs and red panties. I regained my teeth and kissed her. I could see her brown eyes staring back at me, feel her breasts heaving against my chest. One of her arms found its way around my neck and she returned my kiss.

'Wait, wait,' she whispered. She jumped up and went to lock the bedroom door.

She returned to my arms and we made love, sweating both, gliding over and into each other. Later we lay in each other's arms.

'I love you,' I whispered, frightened and happy.

'I loved you long before I met you at the station that night,' Khensani said. 'We'll have a long long love affair and afterwards you can write about it.'

'Afterwards?'

'When you marry Theresa. Oh what have I done to my friend! But I love you, Scara. Make that toothless thing for me again, with the paper. Where's my chocolate? Make me laugh some more.'

Then we kissed again and I discovered a truth: that when love blows its beautiful flowers smack into your heart your lover's lips are truly sweet, not metaphorically but sweet as if the lips, the tongue, the saliva all produce their own honey.

The serene mother on the mantelpiece began to take up the song of the blues singer — the blues singer wept for a betrayed woman — in my briefcase I heard a new novel I had bought that day and not yet begun to read flutter its own pages and read itself — the curtains whispered in a sudden breeze — the police vans ten storeys below sang as they took black prisoners to a jail far away. I would've heard more insane things if a key in the front door had not jerked me and Khensani back into Theresa's room.

'Oh God!' one of us whispered. Theresa was back home.

'What do we do?'

'Hullo, Khensani! I'm back.'

'Oh yes.'

Khensani pointed to the wardrobe-to-me-to-the-wardrobe. Soft and quick, like a black somebody fleeing from the law, but with the sound turned off, I took my Florsheims, one in each hand, and jumped into the wardrobe. Khensani shut it, opened it —

'Oh yes? What do you mean oh yes?'

'I mean . . .' Khensani wavered.

— and shoved my briefcase in beside me.

The women's scent was as musty in here as their voices were muffled outside. Something, a shoe or the corner of a small box or a book, pressed into the base of my spine. A petticoat stroked my cheek, mohair chafed the nape of my neck. A cold buckle swayed against my forehead. I sat still, crouching next to my heart.

'You've locked the door?' That was Theresa's voice, with more question marks in it than there were hangers in the wardrobe.

'Oh yes, I feel safer but, with the door locked when you're not here.'

The bedroom door opened.

'Just pray. God will protect you.'

'Theresa, did you see . . .'

'What's that?'

I held my breath.

'Melted chocolate,' Khensani said. 'Theresa, there's someone on the twelfth floor who came looking for you.'

'When?'

'Just now.'

'Pearl?'

'I dunno, she said it was urgent. They godda sick child over there.'

'Pearl, it must be Pearl.'

'Hey!' Khensani shouted. 'What are you doing?'

Sweat began to flow down my face.

'I want a jersey, it's cold outside.'

'No!' I felt Khensani's body heaving up against the door of the wardrobe.

Exclamation marks of speechlessness hung in the room like stalactites.

'Are you okay, Khensani?'

'Yes.'

'Then let me take my jersey out the wardrobe . . .'

'No!' Khensani's voice was hysterical, laughing and crying all at once. 'Theresa, just go quickly, please.'

'Khensani, are you okay?'

'Yes!' shouting. 'Just go!'

Then, miraculously, Theresa relented. She turned on her heel and left. The wardrobe door opened. Khensani was crying and laughing at the same time.

'I love you,' I said. 'You're worth all this.' It was one of those silly things that I seem to spend my life saying.

She nodded and let me kiss her. She was too weak from shock to respond.

'Go now,' she said.

I gathered up my things and disappeared. If I ran I might just make the last Putco bus to Sofasonke.

11

Bewitched

Public Utility Transport Corporation. Or 'Putco' to the thousands of workers who squeeze into them each morning, city-bound, and then squeeze back into them at night to get home to their smoky stoves, their guttering candles, their bleak skull and crossbones.

I boarded one of these green buses, in love with Khensani and wondering how to call off my relationship with Theresa, for whom I felt pity, which in turn filled me with guilt. But the interior of a Putco bus at seven o'clock in winter will quickly wrench such emotions from one's heart.

The bus was filled with the anonymous silhouettes of rows of people sitting two deep and shrouded in scarves, hats and their own individual miseries. I paid my fare to a morose driver who had seen almost every black hand that made the city work push a coin through the window of his cage. He put my ticket in my sweaty palm that still had the faint bouquet of Khensani clinging to it like the sticky juice of a mango.

I walked down the aisle and found the last empty window-seat. I rubbed a giant asterisk out of the misted window and stared into the dirty darkness outside: a hobo in a long, greasy coat flinging rubbish out of a KEEP YOUR CITY CLEAN bin, cars sailing across the Queen Elizabeth Bridge in the distance, the glowing coals of a mbaula against the wall of a NON-WHITES toilet.

Someone took the place next to me. I smelt him, Vicks Vaporub commingled with warm factory sweat, and felt the corrugated rub of his corduroy lumber-jacket. We exchanged polite nods and concentrated on our silence. The lights in the ceiling shone despairingly through a decade of grime. I thought about the new novel in my case, but I needed more light to read by.

The bus began its steady journey to the townships. An empty beer bottle rolled on the floor from one end of the bus to the other, in long screeching arcs, its sound amplified by the collective awareness that no one was prepared to pick it up and prevent it from being smashed into dangerous shards. Good deeds at this hour might be seen as a weakness.

A group of male voices at the back of the bus rose above the murmur. A bottle was uncorked and the pungent aroma of brandy filled the air. Someone cracked a joke and they all laughed. For a while they continued like this — drinking, joking and laughing. Then one of them got up and strolled down the aisle.

'Hey you pigs from the zones,' he shouted, looking from side to side, just like one of the preachers who rode these buses in the mornings, 'I have something important to tell you, so listen carefully.' He reached the front of the bus and turned to face us. 'I want you all to open your purses, your wallets, your pockets. And when I make my way down this aisle, hand it over: your rands, your cents, your rent money, your furniture money, your fahfee money, your papgeld, zonke.'

The man beside me moved slowly and purposefully. I turned cautiously to see what he was doing. Without taking his eyes off the thug in front, he slowly pulled a long dagger from the folds of his jacket. He felt my body stiffen at the sight of the weapon.

'Don't worry, my bra,' he whispered, still looking ahead of him. 'This is not for you. This is for that fool over there who comes in the dark demanding money from people he don't even know and all.' The parlance and accent were the same as Khensani's. He was a Durban boy.

I said nothing. He continued talking to me. As he spoke, he slipped the knife, blade first, down the sleeve of his jacket, carefully, the way a circus sword-swallower might have eased it down his throat. And his words came out slowly, with spaces between each syllable.

'Me, my bra, I don't worry wit nobody. I go to work, I come back, I eat, I sleep, I watch TV. But now dis . . . dis cunt . . . he want to fuck wit me. Well let him come my way . . . me, I'm waiting. And . . .'

He flicked a glance at me.

'. . . last time he fuck wit a human being.'

Last time he fuck wit a human being. I looked at the youth in the front of the bus and thought what a cheap, senseless piece of filth he was. For a few cents from each of us he was about to lose his life. It angered me. And it angered me that he was prepared to walk down a dark aisle and accost people one by one. But it had been done before — with a one hundred per cent success rate — one punk bullying an entire busload of people — mostly hard-working mothers who were going home to cook and to worry about next month's rent. Well, the success rate was about to plummet.

The youth had taken off his frayed checked Ayers and he began to move forward. I heard the first dolorous clink as someone's measly coins dropped into the cap, like a poor man's alms into a velvet basket. He moved on and the coins dropped at five-second intervals.

I had taken out no coins for the tsotsi. Whatever happened after my companion struck, there would be no more money collected that evening.

'Come, come, come,' I heard his voice louder now: he was four seats from us. 'Don't tell me that's all you got.' Shaking the cap, he moved on again.

My friend's right hand travelled slowly to his left sleeve. I felt his body tense. He waited.

The tsotsi was one seat away from us, so close that his shadow threw another quilt of darkness on our black faces. He thrust out the cap to the woman sitting in front of me. The point of her scarf arrowed down her back as she looked up. I imagined her looking straight at him as I heard her say:

'My son, is this what I raised you to do?'

Without knowing it, she saved his life.

When I reached home, Mama had a pot of water on the stove waiting for me. I washed the sweat of fear and lovemaking from my loins while Mama berated me from her bedroom for coming home at such a late hour. Then she came to the kitchen, gazed into my face and declared, with shock in her eyes, 'You have been bewitched.'

12

Calling
7102211

'Hey, wena, Scara.' Mremi was trying to attract my attention. I closed the directory and looked up. He was sitting at his desk, waving a phone at me.

'The madam,' he whispered, and then, assuming that I was pondering the plight of the *Black World* and the future of the media, he waved a hand in Sybrand's direction and said, 'Hey, don't worry, this censorship business, it can't last . . .'

Sybrand was the furthest thing from my mind just then, but it would've been an indictment of my commitment to free speech if I'd told my colleague that. 'You think so?' I said, taking the phone from him.

'Sure.' He was the only reporter I knew who neither drank nor smoked. But I once took a bet with Gus that he would do both before the end of the year.

'Hallo.'

'Scara.'

'Yes, it's me. I suppose you have a censor too . . .?'

'Yes, everyone in the media, so don't feel unique and all.'

'These phones have probably been tapped too by now,' I warned.

'Ummm.'

'Good morning, Mr Tapper,' I said.

Khensani giggled.

'So, what kind of advice is verboten?'

'Well, my column is not affected. I can go on telling the people how to mend their broken hearts . . .'

'I'll speak to you this evening,' I said.

'Okay,' Khensani said with a sigh that had its source at the bottom of her heart and soughed through the telephone like a sad wind. 'Did you manage to get rid of the corn plaster?'

'Huh?' I said, momentarily caught off guard by this seemingly strange question, before I remembered this morning: as we were preparing for work, Gus struggling into his shoes in the lounge where he had slept, me with my head in a dish of water, Khensani came upon one of my used corn plasters lying on the kitchen dresser — a filthy habit which I seemed to have no success in conquering. I was ordered to throw it away immediately. So off I shuffled, bare-chested and mad at myself, to the dustbin in the yard. There the offending piece of plaster still retained some of its adhesive qualities and decided to remain attached to my thumb (probably mistaking it for my big toe). A slanging match ensued between me and the plaster right there at the bin. And now I know that Khensani must have been watching this ridiculous spectacle from the bedroom window.

She put the phone down before I could find something intelligent to say.

Later that morning we all crowded into the boardroom where Sybrand, with the chubby Mahlatini at his side, explained the many implications and ramifications of the new censorship laws. All the while Mahlatini stroked a phantom beard and looked perplexed and self-important: evidently the prospect of an empty newspaper was the most newsworthy event in his life.

'. . . And this is why I have been posted here by the new administration,' Sybrand said. 'So that the letter of the law can be carried out. And as soon as the violence in the country subsides to acceptable universal levels . . . I'm outta here!'

By way of some consolation he told us that coverage on sport would be unaffected. 'Which should please you all, as *Black World* allocates seventy per cent of its pages to soccer.'

'Can't this guy say anything without a cliché?' I muttered to Gus.

'You have a question for me?' Sybrand said, raising his eyebrows and looking at me from the other end of the boardroom.

'What has happened to De Vries?' I said impulsively.

'That is not relevant nor is it legal . . .'

'Some people claim they've spotted him in Sofasonke,' I said.

Mahlatini threw back his head and guffawed. This gave everybody in the room their cue and we all burst out laughing. Even Sybrand, after glaring at me for a long time.

'What are acceptable universal levels of violence?' Gus asked me as we were wetting our whistles at Sis Jessie's. She had a wart on her left ear lobe. And to achieve some equilibrium, she wore a ruby in her right ear lobe. She was a beautiful woman though.

'You should have asked ou Sybrand that,' I said, untying my shoelaces and admiring the condensation streaking down the two brown bottles on the table. 'What we have to ask ourselves is how you and I are going to get some publishable news.'

Sybrand was taking his job very seriously back in the office. While Bambi spent the day spreading his benign pink smile around, the censor was cutting telex messages to shreds, tearing his red pen through already heavily self-censored copy and poring over photographs for any hint of prohibited background.

But, in this race-conscious Republic, where the children's classic *Black Beauty* was once banned by an overzealous censor who thought it had something to do with African racial pride, Sybrand's work also had its more amusing moments. Peter de Vries, Wits Demons centre forward and national hero (meaning that he had a strong following even amongst blacks, who cheered for him from the small nook allocated to them in the white stadiums), had scored his second hat trick of the season.

DE VRIES UP TO HIS TRICKS AGAIN

our sneaky subs suggested. But it ended up on our sports page as a bland:

DEMONS MAN DOES IT AGAIN

Two other patrons sat in a far corner playing a sluggish game of draughts. Each of them had a litre of beer and was bugling it (which is what we say in Sofasonke when someone drinks straight from the bottle). A third, lone patron got up and belched loudly, asked for nobody's pardon and left the room, headed for the toilet or a more exciting shebeen.

I stood up in my socks, took my glass of beer and went to stand by the window, to stare at a drab township street.

'We're in shit if we don't get something quick, Scara,' Gus was saying. 'The last time you and I had a good story was . . .'

'Jesus,' I interrupted Gus, 'here comes the biggest crook, con artist, and teller of tall stories that ever walked the streets of Sofasonke.'

Gus got up eagerly, Leica at the ready, and came to take up a shooting position next to me.

'There's only one man there,' he said, lowering his camera. 'And not a very impressive-looking one at that.'

This was true. Nothing in the way Makaphela walked (a pigeon-toed hobble) or looked (below average height, sparse tufts of beard on sunken cheeks) or dressed (a frayed blue lumber-jacket far too small for his small frame, recently whisked off a washing-line) inspired awe, respect or admiration. But the felon had wit and imagination in abundance.

A bunch of schoolkids skipped past him as he swung open the shebeen's rickety gate.

'Seven-One-Oh-Two-Two-One-One,' they chanted at Makaphela, waving playfully.

Makaphela waved back, smiling like a monarch on walkabout.

'What's that the kids are saying?' Gus asked.

'No idea,' I shrugged.

One of the draughts players provided the answer. 'Makaps appears on Police File every week,' he said rather perfunctorily. 'Now you see at the bottom of the screen they always give his name and that number, 7102211, and they say, "If you see this man please call this number."'

'Sons of my mother,' Makaphela Moyane (Makaps to his friends, shebeen queens, gangsters and even his own mother) called out to Gus and me, stopping dead in the centre of the lounge and holding out his arms for an embrace which did not happen. His eyes darted to the bottles and he produced a twinkling smile. 'I am so happy to see you.'

I introduced him to Gus and told him to organize himself a glass and join us. Most drinkers would have called to Sis Jessie to bring a glass but Makaps thought it wise not to burden the woman with an extra chore for the day. Probably because his name featured prominently in the 'tick' book rather than out of consideration for her. When he went to fetch the glass I turned to Gus.

'The answer is to make our own news,' I said.

He must have seen the light in my eyes.

'You have a plan,' he said knowingly.

I nodded slowly, to indicate confidence. 'Mahlatini will not know what hit him,' I said.

'And Sybrand? Does he too get struck without knowing the origin of the blow?'

'Old Sybrand, well, I think he'll approve,' I nodded, even though I suspected some snide reference to the encounter between the Bear and my jaw, which still ached whenever I turned to look to my left.

'And Makaphela's got something to do with this?' He shoved a thumb at the door Makaps had disappeared through on his way to fetch a glass.

I nodded. Makaps went around the township, using everyone, exploiting every situation and making us all jump to his tune. It was time, I felt, to use him for my own ends.

In this silence we were able to hear an exchange between Makaps and Sis Jessie in the kitchen. It went thus:

'Makaps, if you don't pay me — at least one instalment soon — you are no longer welcome in this spot of mine.'

'My darling, give me the other ruby earring and I'll sell it for you at a good price . . .'

Sis Jessie clicked her tongue — or was it the sound of a kiss? — and then Makaps emerged, glass in hand, and helped himself to our beer.

'So the comrades gave you a hard time on Saturday, my learned friend?' he asked me, a mocking smile dancing on the corners of his mouth.

I should've known that Makaps would be in possession of such intelligence.

'Not at all,' I said. Me made to look the fool? No way. But he laughed and sipped away a head of foam.

Gus had a look of complete enchantment on his face. This did not go unnoticed by the scrawny tsotsi. He began regaling us with stories of his recent past. That very morning the police had arrived on the doorstep of 'Number One', as he preferred to call his house in Zone 16. Their intention, he explained, was to take him into custody for a crime they believed he had committed a day or two before.

'Stop being so mysterious, Makaps,' I reprimanded him. He was drinking our beer (at quite a pace too) and so I felt we were entitled to some details.

'Enterprise,' he said.

This was an old joke but Gus flattered him by pretending to look puzzled.

'I *prise* open a place and then I *enter*,' Makaps explained. 'Anyway, the police arrive to take me off to jail. They bang on my door and I roll along to it and open and look them over and wonder when I'll see my little old house again — or my little old skull and crossbones, as my learned friend here likes to put it.' He drank another glass of beer in three huge gulps while we waited.

'"We're looking for, er, Mackafella Mo-yarnee,"' Makaps mimicked the white cop.

'"Mackafella," I said, "what has my dear brother been up to this time?"'

'"Can you just tell us where he is please?"'

'"Gone to work, like most decent and peace-loving Sofasonke citizens did this morning," I told them. "The new President assured us that if we got on with our lives we would soon have the most stable and prosperous country in Africa. And Mackafella is just like Rockefeller in America. My brother's big on peace and prosperity."'

'They believed that?' Gus asked.

'I won't say one hundred per cent,' Makaps admitted proudly, 'but enough to go away and watch my house from across the road for a few hours.'

'But these guys usually come in with pistols blazing, kicking every black arse in sight,' I said, also a little suspicious of Makaps's latest story. 'Why didn't they arrest you?'

'Simple,' he explained. 'When I said I rolled over to the door that's what I meant, gents.' He put a cigarette that he had bummed from Gus into an ashtray and demonstrated in his chair with a rolling motion of his hands. 'You see, my mother she's in hospital and she's left behind her squeaky wheelchair, which I decided to put to good use: when they came knocking I threw a blanket over my legs and rolled over and opened the door.'

I told Makaps about the new government's invasion of our offices, about Sybrand and his Bambi and his scissors and our difficulty in getting some good, exciting, readable news. 'And you're just the man to help us make some of our own, special news,' I concluded.

Makaps looked puzzled. I took a swig of beer and leaned forward to explain his role. He listened carefully for a few minutes, nodding away and gulping down our beer.

'Tell me, my learned friends,' he said, 'I know all these whites, but who is this Bambi?'

I tried to resist a sidelong glance in Gus's direction, but these things are completely involuntary.

'Ag, that,' Gus explained, 'that's just a little deer from a children's story. This Sybrand guy got it from his lightie's crèche . . .'

'Ah,' Makaps pointed a triumphant finger in the air, 'like a sheep or something!'

'Ja, like that,' Gus nodded. He turned to me. 'So don't tell me you're proposing that . . .?'

'Look, our jobs are on the line here,' I began to explain quickly. 'These white people, man, they're not only censoring us in the office; what with curfews, detentions, roadblocks, they're censoring . . .'

'Life,' Gus found a word for me.

'Hey, wena!' Sis Jessie growled in the doorway, a damp dishcloth in one hand, a dripping saucepan in the other. 'You know the rules in this place: no politics.'

'No problem, sister,' Makaps assured her. 'Please guys,' turning to Gus and me, 'let's just discuss business, okay.'

Sis Jessie returned to her kitchen, driven back more by the smell of burning pap than by Makaphela's insincere reassurances.

But Sis Jessie had nothing to worry about. For the rest of the afternoon we would not use the words 'white' and 'police' or their derogatory equivalents.

'Desperate situations call for desperate measures,' Gus said, and so we spent our time planning Operation Bara. When we started the afternoon had the rich golden hue of the lager we were drinking, and when we finished the night was as dark as stout. I dropped Gus in Riverlea, driving off with a merry *poop-poop* on the hooter as the caravan door swung open, leaving my friend in a rectangle of light to face the wrath of his Charmaine with her slippers and her moon-shaped heels.

I had to face Khensani.

13

Severed Arms
and Soaring Sales

The next day Gus and I met at Baragwanath Hospital. It was a warm summer morning, if these things are important to you — bananas showed off their curves on the makeshift tables of street vendors, pumpkin slices wobbled like sloops on a slow river, people squeezed into minibus taxis, perfume escaped from under arms and mingled with sweat, cars sped down the highway, friends called out to friends — but all this did nothing to remove the tiny spikes of remorse that were stuck to my heart. Indeed it all made me feel worse. Drinking non-stop — through a change of Presidents, as my lifetime companion, Khensani, kept reminding me last night to the familiar tune of banging pots and slamming doors.

'Where were you all night?' she had asked.

I told her that Gus and I had been to visit Colin, an old friend and school buddy of mine who had been in intensive care after a car crash a few weeks ago.

I will never forget the look my wife gave me: so full of contempt and pity that it provoked extreme anger in me.

'What's your problem now?' I shouted. 'Is it a crime to go and visit a friend in hospital!'

'Colin died two days ago,' she hissed, shaking her head. 'If you had been sober when I told you, you would've known not to use him as an excuse.'

The memory of that moment was so humiliatingly painful even now in the light of day that I shut my eyes in shame. When I opened them again a blue minibus taxi had stopped across the road. The door slid open with a screech and Gus squeezed himself out, wriggling like a malalapipe sleeper emerging from a stormwater drain. His camera bag appeared first, slung over his shoulder. He saw me from across the road and began to fool around while he waited for a chance to cross the busy highway, doing a pantomime to show that he was suffering from a severe babalaas. I leaned against my Beetle, wishing that I could crawl back into bed and wake up long after whatever was going to happen to me, to the people around me, to the government, the police, the people in prisons, had happened. Like Rip van Winkle — that Afrikaner shopkeeper, as Makaps might have put it — who had taken a twenty-year kip.

Gus came weaving across the road. 'If you've got the aspirin,' he cried, 'I've got the headache.'

'Colin's dead,' I told him.

'St Christopher's Colin?' he asked.

I nodded. That was the only Colin we both knew.

'But I thought he'd make it.' He sighed, came to lean next to me against the Volksie, and took out a rumpled cigarette from his pocket. From the gold ring on the filter I could see that it was from his wife's packet.

'He died two days ago.'

'Shit!' he said, slapping his forehead with the palm of his hand. 'Who told you?'

I told him what had happened to me last night.

'Oh, shit!' he moaned, administering another couple of slaps to his forehead. 'Spare me the details, spare me the details.' After a long gloomy pause he produced a manila envelope, opened the flap and let five or six photographs slide into his hands. 'Check this out.'

There were three photographs of Sybrand the Censor and three of Makaphela the Conman. All six were head-and-shoulders portraits which Gus was adding to a collection for a possible exhibition. I knew that he wanted some captions from me and decided to tackle Sybrand first. The man looked ridiculous, beaming in his jacket and old-fashioned tie, with Bambi outbeaming its master in the background.

'The whites have entered the forest,' I said in a sudden burst of inspiration.

'The what?'

I explained the origin and meaning of the famous, ominous line from *Bambi*: 'The humans have entered the forest.'

'I like,' Gus said, managing a bleak smile despite his babalaas. He took out a notebook and scribbled it down.

'And him?' Gus held up one of the pictures of the formerly intrepid, currently feckless Makaphela, waving it close to my face.

Then I saw what Gus was trying to draw my attention to in the picture. Stuck to the shoulder of Makaps's lumber-jacket was a clothespeg! If ever there was proof that he had stolen the garment off the line of some unfortunate Sofasonke housewife!

'Yow!' I exclaimed. 'Look at that!'

'You see it now?' Gus burst into cackling laughter, causing a passer-by to change course abruptly and make a wide detour around the Volksie.

'Well,' I felt obliged to defend our co-conspirator, 'he used to be good, he used to be really clockwise.'

After a ponderous pause Gus said: 'We still going ahead with Operation Bara?'

'For sure,' I said. 'No turning back now.'

'If he comes.'

'He'll come.' I flicked my cigarette into the dust, hoping secretly that Makaphela had forgotten the entire, ridiculous plan, made in an alcoholic stupor.

'Tribute to Colin,' I said. 'He would've loved this.'

Colin — the late Colin — would most certainly have loved this. A jazz pianist of promise, he had been the only other Sofasonkan who attended St Christopher's with me. On his return to Sofasonke about a dozen or so years ago, he had begun a passionate love affair with a woman from Zone 9. But there was one snag: the woman, Thandeka was her name, was already attached to the leader of the Chicagos gang, a fellow known only by his nickname, Chippa. (The name was a clue to the dexterity he had shown on the football field a long time before he dropped the ball and took up the knife in pursuit of a sporting life.)

Colin, eccentric and flamboyant man that he was, went everywhere dressed in a white doctor's dustcoat (or should that be a doctor's white dustcoat?). He played jazz at night in a drunken nightclub where nobody paid much attention to the notes that he kneaded and twitched into music. But he put up with the abuse of the crowds, for in the mornings, his white coat flapping in the wind like the cape of a virginal superhero, he swept through the streets of Sofasonke to trysts with the beautiful, willowy Thandeka.

'You're taking a helluva chance, bra,' I told him. Chippa had killed for less.

'I'm careful and clockwise,' he assured me. But he did admit to some close encounters. Chippa had once knocked on the door of a house — where Colin and Thandeka were spending the day — in the mistaken belief that a fellow gangster and friend of his was living there. He bellowed out his friend's name in a drunken voice while the two lovers lay huddled and naked. Eventually Chippa cursed, spat into the dust, turned on his heel and staggered off.

There were other close shaves, but, as I once said to my friend, man cannot live by close shaves alone.

And matters did come to a head eventually. Tongues wagged all over the township, and the sounds those wagging tongues made were jeering and taunting the ears of the cuckolded Chippa. 'Thandeka is sleeping with the doctor,' people were saying. And everyone believed both these rumours: that Colin was a medical doctor and that he was having an affair with Thandeka.

Early one weekday morning Thandeka flew unexpectedly into the skull and crossbones where Colin lived with his widowed father. Several brothers were all in exile in neighbouring African states at the time, in training camps, and his father was at work in the city. Colin himself was still asleep. Thandeka ran into the bedroom, crashed into a tower of records, sending Dizzy Gillespie and Abdullah Ibrahim spinning, and collapsed on the bed, her breath gone.

'He's coming! He's coming!' she gasped as he sat up in bed reaching for his clothes. Despite the fuzz that still stuck to his early-morning brain he had a very good idea who was on his way. And as the angry stampede of Chippa grew louder outside and Colin reached for his white dustcoat, Thandeka cried out in terror, 'He's got a garden fork, he's been shouting all the way down here, "I'm gonna kill the doctor! Today I'm gonna kill the doctor!"'

Colin stretched and shook the sleep out of his system. Thandeka couldn't believe this indulgence.

'Colin, run!' she screamed desperately. 'The back door. Go!'

'No,' he said. And that was all, for the front door burst open and Chippa filled the house with the maniacal rage of the cuckold, perforating the stuffy air with the garden fork in a rehearsal of what he was about to do.

'Chippa!' Colin called. 'No noise in this house please! Sit down and I will attend to you now.'

'Awright, doctor,' Chippa said feebly. The fork could be heard dropping to the floor with a muffled twang, and Chippa could be heard sagging with sibilant disbelief into an old Ellerines easy-terms armchair.

Colin dressed slowly: immaculately ironed fawn pants, the all-important dustcoat, and as many pens as he could find around the house. He put these in a row in his top pocket so that the brightly coloured caps stuck out like military decorations.

When Colin made his grand entrance into the lounge, Chippa was staring at the tines of his weapon like a gardener caught between the thorns of his rose-bushes and the bouquets of the blooms.

'So what is your problem, young man?' Colin said in a sand-papery, Satchmo voice.

'De people dey say you, you making sex wit my girl . . . doctor.'

'Chippa!' Colin's voice boomed.

Chippa shifted back with a gasp. As did Thandeka in the adjoining room.

'Chippa, Thandeka happens to be a patient of mine. The woman is suffering from acute . . . passionitis . . . did you know that?'

'She tell me nothing, doctor.'

'Well, Chippa, I have a busy day ahead of me. If you make such ridiculous allegations hever ragain' — with this pronunciation Colin was mimicking the headmaster of St Christopher's — 'I will sue you down to your last underpants. Get the message?'

'Yes, doctor.'

'Now get out of here!'

Gus and I sat in the Casualty section of the hospital, smoking under a NO SMOKING sign. It was a few minutes past eight. Makaps had still not arrived.

As usual, Baragwanath Hospital had begun its morning business on a high note: sitting rather inertly on a bench opposite us was a huge Mama whose legs were the size of tree-trunks — trunks whose blighted bark was rapidly peeling away.

I turned away from this nauseous sight and focused my attention on a mother and her toddler son, who tugged fretfully at her dress.

'What's wrong with him, Mama?' I asked her.

'His pennis,' she said — rhyming the word with Dennis rather than Venus.

'What's that?' Gus asked, leaning forward.

The mother undid the kid's fly to expose a penis the size of a banana.

A car's brakes squealed outside. Two youths jumped out, both looking as if they had seen a vivid picture of hell. They swung open the back door and a body fell into their arms. What I saw brought vomit from my stomach swishing into my mouth. The man's left eye was dangling outside its socket, on his cheek — no, one couldn't say that, for there was no cheek there!

Gus grabbed his camera and leaped to his feet. They walked towards him, two young men dragging a third. Suddenly, somehow, the two knew that their friend had died, with his arms around their shoulders. 'The police killed him!' one of them screamed, his eyes suddenly drowning in whirlpools of rage, and he fell to his knees. The other made the clenched-fist salute of the liberation movement. The dead body fell to the floor.

Gus captured it all. But none of it could be published.

Makaphela arrived while the dead youth was being dragged away by two hospital orderlies.

'The comrades,' he said. Makaps, Gus and I sat on a long bench watching the stains of blood being douched from the tarred entrance with a familiar-smelling disinfectant, the bustle of nurses, the discordant voice on the intercom.

'D'you have the arm?' I asked Makaphela, eyeing the big plastic bag that he carried in one hand.

'Aw, Scara,' he said, giving me a supercilious look. 'You think I'm who?'

I turned to Gus. 'Is it loaded?' I asked him, pointing at his camera.

'Filled up with Fuji,' he assured me.

The next day the front page of the *Black World* screamed

MAN RUNS THROUGH BARA WITH SEVERED ARM

and my byline, the first in weeks, was on the story. The piece was accompanied by no less than three spectacular pictures of horrified patients shrieking and fleeing from a man who held aloft what appeared to be his own severed arm, dripping with gore and entrails, in the biggest hospital in Africa.

Mahlatini sent for us after the morning edition had hit the streets

— and been gobbled up like mealies thrown to starving chickens.

'Oh shit, he knows it's a bogus story,' Gus groaned, spitting his gum into a bin.

'Gus,' I said, 'don't act nervous: he knows zilch, man. A country boy from Natal? Just act normal and let me do the talking.'

But we didn't have to do any talking. As we entered the editor's office he began to read the first two paragraphs out loud:

There was chaos at Baragwanath Hospital yesterday morning when an unidentified man clutching a severed arm still dripping with blood ran through the crowded Casualty section.

Black World reporter Scara Nhlabatsi and photographer Gus Kinnear, who happened to be at the hospital on a private visit, recorded the gruesome event which has stunned people throughout the province . . .

Mahlatini stood up and darted around his desk to give us each a resounding slap on the back. He put his arms around our shoulders. I got a generous whiff of his sweet antiperspirant mixed in with his sweat.

'Now this is how I know you guys,' he said. 'Where the action is, on the ball.'

He seemed to be on some kind of ball himself, bouncing all over his office, his trousers showing off a little more of his white socks than usual.

It looked like he would go on for ever, and I was beginning to worry that Gus would break down under the welter of accolades and confess to our ghastly hoax. I knew exactly how my colleague was feeling just then: when I was a kid I played football for the under-thirteen Sofasonke Pumas. We lost a cup final through an own goal scored by none other than yours truly, Scara. When I reached home that afternoon my elated mother had already heard that I had scored a goal and was in the process of cooking my favourite meal.

The editor's telephone rang.

'Follow it up, boys,' Mahlatini clicked his fingers musically and waved us out.

In the news room a reporter shouted into his phone, 'Here he is now,' and handed it to me.

'Scara.'

'Hi.' It was Khensani. 'I see you've made the front page.' She sounded as pleased as if I had just won a year's supply of free beer and a sack of dagga in a competition.

'Yeah, what d'you think of the story?'

'Why don't you meet me at home tonight and I'll tell you exactly what I think. But on one condition . . .'

I had a good idea what that condition was, but I enquired anyway, 'What?'

'You have to be sober.'

I put the phone down, gently. And it rang again. I picked it up.

'*Black World*, good morning.'

Makaps chuckled on the other end. 'When do we celebrate?' he said.

'Meet us at Sis Jessie's. Fourish this afternoon.'

I was all for celebrations, of course, but there was also the question of forward planning. We would have to track down this unidentified man with the severed arm. Perhaps he would strike again? I could see him running through Park Station, sprinting across a football field, popping up at a stokvel.

He had potential, this guy. I could see him evolving into a sort of one-armed Black Pimpernel.

14

A Holiday
in Salisbury

I've been on leave for a month, and Khensani and I have just got back from Zimbabwe. I haven't had a drop of alcohol for, let's see, three weeks, five days, seven hours. What's more, I've promised Khensani that I'll bring this Black Pimpernel thing to an end as soon as I go back to work, that I'll go and see what my parents want from me, and that I might even see a doctor about this baby that she thinks is such a long time coming.

I began a bit of an exercise regime when I went on leave. I'd realized that my return to lovemaking was leaving Khensani quite breathless — not from the passion I was unleashing in her, but from the pressure I was exerting on her with my beer belly. I started by running on the spot for about five minutes. Then I began running around our block. That usually took at least twelve minutes and left me with no energy to do anything else but stare at the ground in our backyard and watch my own sweat moistening the earth.

I even considered getting a new job. Maybe the challenges at the *Black World* had long since come and gone, I thought. Maybe the learning curve had flattened out into a long straight line. Gus and I had done good work once, worthwhile work. We had risked our lives more than once to get stories and pictures the cops didn't want us to have. Now we spent our time chasing chimeras. Maybe I needed a change.

Khensani turned back into the cheerful, witty and caring woman she had always been but I had lost sight of in the blur of alcohol and the murky clouds of dagga smoke. I had also forgotten how beautiful my wife was, her unblemished face with its natural eye-shadow —

three white spots below her eyes, like tiny stars — her elegantly shaped eyebrows, her full lips, her charming smile, her playful flirtatiousness which stirred feelings in me of pride and jealousy at the same time. I received a reminder of this forgotten coquettishness when our telephone rang one evening in the middle of the week. I was busy drying the dishes which Khensani had just washed. She dried her hands and went to the lounge to answer the phone. The house was quiet and I had no choice but to eavesdrop.

I am careful these days not to use the word 'giggle' in describing the laughing sounds that women sometimes make. But there is no other word to describe Khensani's bantering laughter on the phone that evening.

'That was Khumbo,' she said when she returned to the kitchen to make a pot of tea. A mischievous smile still lingered around her mouth.

'What's her case?' I asked.

'Do we have to book our tickets on Saturday morning?' We were planning to go to Zimbabwe to visit her father who lived in exile, and Saturday had been set for booking the train tickets.

'Uhm . . .' I shrugged, feeling that I needed more explanation before I could answer. 'Why?'

She told me that her friends knew we were going away for a few weeks, so they wanted her to go shopping with them before we left. 'There's an Indian shop near the Koh-I-Noor record bar there. Help My Krap it's called . . .'

'I know the place.' It was a kind of bargain basement on the ground floor, with good-quality fabrics heaped in disarray from floor to ceiling. And as the name 'Help Me Scratch' implied, you could find whatever you needed if you just dug deep enough.

'And now Khumbo, Bontlhe and Tselane want to buy duvets and curtains there. The place is packed to the rafters with all kinds of stuff and the prices are cheap and that.'

'And why do *you* need to go with them?'

'Because if I go the prices are even cheaper.'

'How can that be?'

'You really are getting old,' Khensani teased me. 'The shopkeeper is Achmat and he's got the hots for me.'

I turned around to look at my wife. One hand held a steaming mug of tea. The pinkie of the other hand scratched daintily at the entrance to one nostril. She looked at me superciliously and I could tell what she was thinking: that life went on while I went shebeening and paying hospital visits to dead friends.

I left Khensani to go bargain hunting at Achmat's crazy shop while I went to buy the tickets alone, hoping that the ticket clerk at the railway station would be a charming woman who would suddenly have the hots for me. But all I got was an Afrikaner with a dribbling mouth who kept saying 'Stend in the queue' and 'One-way or return?'.

Later that day I found myself in the vicinity of Help My Krap. Khensani had described Achmat as tall, dark and handsome. I decided to pop in, just for fun, to see for myself. He was tall — but only if he stayed behind the counter where he could stomp up and down on the raised wooden planks in his socks and sandals. When he smiled at me he revealed a set of stained teeth. He had a beehive of a beard which hung like a baby's bib onto his khaki banyan and hid a pockmarked skin. 'Hah!' I said to his face, and strode out of his stifling shop, feeling more silly than satisfied.

We were holiday-makers at home and our house filled up with the familiar aromas of curried chicken, fried eggs, coffee and homemade ginger beer. I suspect that with this last Khensani was trying to wean me off the real stuff.

Children gravitated to our open door to visit, all unannounced, all attracted by the smell of food, by the new bonhomie that manifested itself in Khensani suddenly turning the hose-pipe on me, by Aunty Khensani whose picture appeared in their favourite magazine with stardust below her eyes, dispensing wonderful advice to the lovelorn and the broken-hearted.

From our neighbour at the 'back opposite' came a little pigtailed ten-year-old who jumped over split-pole fences to spend the evenings with Khensani and me, grating carrots, stirring a pot and gawking at the paintings on the walls, the floor carpeted with our books and magazines, the words from my fingers transmuted into regimented lines on my computer screen.

I remember her first visit. She knocked timidly one evening, incessant little taps that could have gone on for ages before I heard them above the noise of the radio. I opened the door and looked down on a crop of hair so dishevelled that I cringed.

'Yebo?'

She uttered a few incoherent words, trying all the while to turn her feet and her hands into knots, as unconfident or shy children tend to do.

I sat on my haunches and asked her to speak up, this time in Tswana. Again she mumbled. Then suddenly she looked over my shoulder and held her hand to her mouth, but too late to stifle a sharp gasp. She had spied Khensani who had come to the rescue and I can decipher her actions thus: she was simply struck by my wife's beauty or she recognized Khensani from her picture in the magazine.

'What does the little tinky-winky want?'

Khensani could compile a concise dictionary of silly terms of endearment — which she uses rather indiscriminately, I feel.

'I don't know,' I said.

'Usanana lwam. Tell me in my ear, moratiwa.' Khensani knelt down and cradled the child in her bosom, spiky, dirty mop and all. The girl whispered her request into Dear Khensani's ear. What would it be, I wondered: 'My lover left because he doesn't like lice.' 'When is a good time to move from a bug-infested house?' 'My best friend has suggested that I use soap as a daily cleanser. Is this good advice?'

'Scara, get the child a roll of toilet paper.'

'Oh, of course,' I said. 'How could I have failed to grasp such a simple, everyday request.'

After the girl had left with the toilet paper, Khensani turned to me. 'Don't practise your sarcasm on the child,' she warned me gravely.

'What does she know?' I countered. 'She doesn't even understand English.'

'She picked it up in your tone, you smart twit. In any case, she didn't ask for a whole toilet roll. She needs the cardboard tube for some project they're doing at school. They obviously don't have paper at home so . . .'

'I know, I know,' I said.

'She's an abused child,' Khensani told me later. Her father was in jail, her mother drank, slept around, was out of a job and neglected her household.

The little girl's name was Zodwa, but she soon changed it to Khensani, believing, in her preadolescent fantasies, that she and my wife shared a common destiny: 'Will you braid my hair, Aunty Khensani — just like yours.' 'I've asked my mother to buy me a dress like your blue one, with the bow at the back.' 'Aunty Khensani, I think I shall look like you when I grow up; I dreamt that it will be like that.' 'Aunty Khensani, you must begin to have your babies now because I want to hold them in my arms while you cook the food.'

And some surprising gossip too: 'Aunty Khensani, is Ntate Scara a comrade?'

'A *comrade*. Now why do you ask that?'

'I saw him with the comrades the other day, there near the shops. His friend had a big sore on his head and I told him where the hospital was.'

Ah! the girl with the choopa!

I dusted off my computer and began writing short stories again. I even decided on a different genre, dispensing with that fantastical, surreal nonsense. I revived my career with a story that was a tribute to old Colin: the dangerous and amusing love triangle between him, Thandeka and Chippa, put down exactly as the man had told it to me, with none of my usual embellishments of fantastic plots and idiosyncratic characters.

Khensani told Zodwa alias Khensani that we were going to Zimbabwe.

'I'll go with you,' she said innocently. 'If you and Ntate go for a swim in the sea then I'll look after your clothes.' This kid was plunking away at my wife's heartstrings.

'You're our friend,' Khensani told her, 'not our slave. There's no reason in the world why you should watch our clothes while we're having a good time. Maybe one day you and I will have a swim together and then we'll let Ntate watch our clothes for us.'

'Isn't she a sweetie?' Khensani asked me.

'Ja,' I nodded, 'but she really must brush up on her geography — even if she won't brush up on her hair.' I paid dearly for that remark. When we went to bid farewell to the folks down the road, my Mama asked us which part of Zimbabwe we would be visiting.

'Harare,' I said.

'Oh,' she said, disappointed. 'It's a pity you are not going to Salisbury. I have a second cousin who married a makwerekwere in 1967 and went to live there.'

On the way home, Khensani broke into that Sam Cooke evergreen:

Dunno much about history
Dunno much about geography . . .

The next day, the eve of our departure, did not end quite so happily, although we set out with philanthropic zeal to make it a satisfying one. We decided to buy Zodwa a dress with a bow at the back, or indeed any dress that took her fancy. This was consolation for not being able to come on holiday with us. We told her about this plan and drove her into town to choose.

Zodwa sat in the back of my Volksie playing the worldly-wise little lady. She had taken to emulating Khensani and so she sat with a scuffed black shoe dangling from one foot and a little finger scratching from time to time ever so gently at the entrance to one nostril. But as we entered the city she began to show signs of bewilderment and quickly lost her poise.

'Mlungu!' she gaped at the white people who drove by in their cars or sauntered across the road at pedestrian crossings. She had never been to Johannesburg — a mere thirty minutes' drive from Sofasonke!

We found a shop in Bree Street where dresses hung in row upon row of styles and colours and textures: swishing chiffon, crinkling crimplene, pleated cotton. Dresses with big buttons that sparkled, puffed up sleeves, sailor's collars. Shades of blue, pink, red, yellow; stripes, dots, flowers, motifs . . .

When Zodwa had to choose, she burst into tears. 'Too many nice ones,' she sobbed.

We travelled to Zimbabwe in a half-empty train, which meandered slowly through hundreds of kilometres of dense bush where the Chimurenga war had been fought hardly a decade ago. We made love, ate, and talked and talked for two days and nights.

A sign on the door of our compartment provided us with something to pass the time.

PLEASE DO NOT EXPECTORATE

'What does it mean?' Khensani asked me. I did not know, nor did we have a dictionary to look it up.

'Dunno,' I shrugged. 'But we've probably done it already without realizing it.'

'Ja, about six times since we left Jo'burg.'

We both stared hard at the word, until I suggested: 'Perhaps it's short for "Please do not expect to get to Harare before eight".'

'No,' Khensani shook her head with mock seriousness. 'It means "Please don't talk rubbish in the company of your wife".'

The game carried on throughout our holiday, and 'expectorate' became a ridiculous catchword for all kinds of amusing or absurd behaviour. Khensani's father joined in good-naturedly at a Harare restaurant on the evening of our arrival. Khensani and I ordered roast chicken and potatoes from a talkative waiter who stood no higher than the tabletop but boasted that, despite his size, he had seven wives and thirteen children — and two more on the way.

'Why more children?' Khensani wanted to know.

'Because thirteen is an unlucky number,' I quipped.

'You could've stopped at twelve,' she said, showing some of the 'Dear Khensani' skills that had made her a famous advice columnist, but the man was already on his way to the kitchen. He returned with our plates, each with a massive bird spread-eagled in a bed of rice and surrounded by a laager of roast potatoes.

'A whole chicken!' I exclaimed, staring at my plate. Khensani was speechless, holding her head in her hands and gaping in amused disbelief.

'Please do not expectorate,' Comrade Tau warned with a grin. The crow's-feet in the corners of his eyes reminded me of Tata.

Comrade Tau. That was my father-in-law's nom de guerre. But to refer to him as my father-in-law was strange. He seemed more like my friend, just as he was clearly a friend to the exiles and expatriates who came to visit him from time to time to see his daughter, to hold meetings or simply to chat.

I had expected probing stares and searching questions about my politics, my career, my devotion and loyalty to his beautiful, precious daughter and our childless marriage. But there was none of this. When he did question me it was to reveal a yearning to be home after a decade in exile, to breathe the tropical air of Durban spiced with the salt from the sea, to taste the pickled mango atjar and the fish curry. In the middle of a serious conversation about the evils of racism back home he would ask:

'Khensani, the restaurants in Durban, do they still have those handwritten signs on the wall?'

'What?' screwing up her nose.

'Please no combing hair in here.'

Comrade Tau had spent his life in exile hopping between the Frontline States to escape assassination by the Republic's death squads. 'But now I can relax for a while,' he told us. 'The boers think that I am dead.'

'How come?' Khensani asked.

'In a cemetery in Maputo there is a grave which bears my name,' he explained. 'How it got there I do not know — but I am obviously not in it.'

Comrade Tau was brimful of stories of his life in exile. He had seen many deaths, many betrayals and many long days and nights of hankering after home, a family life, a nine-to-five job. But with his daughter and me he showed a brave front, and a grin that revealed yellowing teeth came readily to his bearded face. One of his most memorable stories was about the time he fled the Republic and went to seek asylum in Zambia.

One of the first Zambians he met was the President himself, a personable man with a disconcerting stammer, who had proudly led his country from independence to bankruptcy in a couple of decades. The President held a banquet in honour of the young men and women from down south who had begun to take up arms against the oppressive boers.

Twenty homesick and bedraggled young Republicans sat in a government house in Lusaka trying to twist their ears into the shape of this new accent, and trying to stop their stomachs from rumbling over the chicken and pap, while the President stammered on about 'these-er young men-ah who are prepared-er to give up-ah their lives'.

The President uttered a few more words and waved his famous white handkerchief as if he was about to surrender to the flies that hovered around his huge, sweaty face.

'I think he's asked one of us to pray,' someone said.

All twenty young men, without exception, had given up Christianity; having been evicted from God's house and hounded in His name for being black in the Calvinist Republic, they had grown wary of religion. Now a Christian African leader was calling on one of them to lead them in prayer. No one wanted to do it. Tau was nudged in the ribs so persistently that he finally stood up, cleared his throat and explained: 'Mr President, I would like to pray in Afrikaans, the language of the oppressor at home, so that his God will hear our pleas for peace and justice . . .'

'Yessa, yess, go ahead,' the President nodded.

Tau proceeded to recite all twenty stanzas of 'Dapper Joris en sy

Perd', an Afrikaans version of 'How They Brought the Good News from Ghent to Aix', while the President, his eyes shut tightly, wove passionate amens through the rhyming couplets.

Before we left Zimbabwe yet another man was smitten by my wife's beauty. His name was Comrade Joe and he was an exiled cadre of the Pure African Revolutionary Movement. He was a pimply, undernourished fellow with red eyes which he lasered in on her throughout our two-week holiday. One evening we attended a cultural gathering in honour of Republican women of all races who had marched on parliament to reject the carrying of passes by black women. Comrade Joe would not leave Khensani's side. She smiled warmly at his overtures. She even held his hand as she listened to his life story and his racing pulse. Eventually, when she explained that she was really in love with me, the spurned guerrilla flew into a raging tantrum.

'You are not a black woman,' the outraged fighter told her. 'Therefore you are not entitled to the fruits of our suffering which will come soon.'

'Well, I'll just have this then,' Khensani said, choosing an apple from a bowl in the centre of the table and taking huge bites.

'What is she then?' I asked, feeling the anger rise in me.

'Just a coloured, a mulatto with some Indian blood who has learned to speak Zulu.'

'A mulatto who has tormented your soul all week,' I spluttered.

'Ah,' Tau said, joining us at the table, 'Comrade Joe is at it again. Comrade Joe, tell these people how you pure Africans have been conducting the revolution so far. Tell them how your leader wrote letters to all your comrades in the country on his Unisa exam pad, telling them all to be at a certain place at a certain time to take up arms against the boers. Tell us how the boers intercepted those letters one by one and rounded up seventy-four comrades in one night . . .'

Comrade Tau turned to us. 'The figure would have been much higher if the bungling fool had not run out of paper.'

'You are a reactionary!' Comrade Joe snarled.

And as he got up to leave the table, Tau called after him: 'Tell them how I found you in the snow in Switzerland, drunk, frostbitten and blue, and how I rubbed your ugly face until you came to life again.' Tau chuckled. He would not go into more detail than that, but promised that we would get more in his memoirs, 'when this whole messy struggle is over and done with'.

127

Hearing Khensani being called a mulatto with Indian blood did not bother any of us. But it did inspire a story from Tau that she herself had never told me.

Khensani's mother was as beautiful as her daughter. She was the offspring of a white sugar-cane farmer of British extraction and an Indian woman whose grandparents had come to Natal as indentured labourers and joined Gandhi's satyagraha campaigns and marches against racial oppression. Tau had married her and lived happily in Hammarsdale, a slum near Durban. Six months after the wedding, on Christmas Eve, Tau and his pregnant wife found themselves shopping in Durban when her water broke. Tau laid his wife down on a pavement, her head resting on his canvas bag. He ran through the droves of holiday-makers, flew into an Indian fast-food shop and telephoned an ambulance.

Within minutes the ambulance siren was heard screaming up the road. Two men in berets leaped out of the van and dragged out their stretcher. They were about to put the woman on the stretcher when they noticed that she was not white. 'Sorry,' they said, without looking sorry at all, and raced off, leaving her gasping in pain on the pavement.

There was no time to be angry then. A rickshaw man, a tall bare-chested Zulu with beads on his ankles and an ostentatious headgear of horns and feathers, drew up like a stallion. Without a word he helped the woman into his rickshaw and made for the hospital. Khensani was born in the rickshaw, and her mother drew her final breath there too.

Grief-stricken and angry, Tau joined the Movement, took his daughter and went to live in Swaziland where he trained secretly in guerrilla warfare. Khensani attended school there, but when she was sixteen she had to flee once more. The young Swazi king insisted that she attend the annual reed dance where he could pick and choose from all the nubile beauties who paraded their bare breasts before him. UmKhosi Womhlanga was the name of the dance — the Dance of the Kingdom. Tau himself had witnessed this ceremony many times in his native KwaZulu, with his distaste growing each year. Each maiden picked a reed from a river bank and danced before his majesty, who ogled each one with serious intent, from smiling top to wiggling bottom. From the bevy the monarch chose only one beauty — for the year. The reeds were then used to build the king's newest connubial hut.

Tau had always disapproved of this ancient, sexist ritual. But now his very own daughter would be involved!

Tau explained to the king's representatives that his daughter was not a Swazi maiden but was living with him in exile in that kingdom. The representatives dutifully took this message to the young monarch, but he would have none of it. Khensani had been living in the Kingdom of Swaziland for sixteen years, he said. She spoke the language, which was similar to Zulu, understood the culture and should now be prepared to give back to Swaziland some of the hospitality she had received.

'Give me a few days to think about this,' Tau said. But no sooner had the representatives turned their backs than he had packed up and left his flat in Mbabane. A few days later Khensani was back in Durban, without her father, where she stayed with an aunt.

'Why did you never tell me that story before?' I asked Khensani on the train back to the Republic.

'You would never have believed me but,' she said.

'Imagine, Khensani, you could have had a king, with all the comforts that go with it.'

'Yes,' she sighed, appraising me with a mocking smile. 'Don't think I haven't thought about it a million times.'

15

A Diary
in the Sofa

I went to see Mama and Tata a whole three days after Khensani had gone over to say hello, when we returned from Zimbabwe. I tried to put it off for as long as I could, but Khensani began to nag.

'What do they want to see me for?' I asked her.

'Do they need a reason?' she asked me.

'No, but they usually do have one.' I didn't tell her that Tata wanted to treat me to cure our childless marriage, but she must surely have made this discovery for herself by now.

'Well, it's about that Pimpernel stuff you and Gus have been doing. The paper has been full of it.'

Two more stories on the Pimpernel, filed in advance, had been due to appear while I was on leave, but I had no intention of writing more. 'As far as I'm concerned, that's over,' I assured Khensani.

'The whole of Sofasonke is still abuzz with it, and one or two of your father's patients have been having nightmares about it.'

'Shit!' We were back in Sofasonke.

I parked the Volksie exactly where I parked it on that day when I brought De Vries and his henchman to my father's house a few months ago. I resolved to ask no questions about the day in question. It was a figment of my wild marijuana imagination, I decided, and I would make no reference to it at all — although I suspected that my parents would not be so reticent.

I was about to knock on the front door when I heard my father and another man filling the backyard with their laughter.

Tata and a grey-bearded neighbour, Ntate Ngwenya, were having lunch under our old mulberry tree. As kids my buddies and I used to call the old man Ntate Magwinya because of his thick, oily lips which he liked to smack at intervals. I rounded the corner of the house in time to hear Tata, a spoon poised over a cooked sheep's head, declare, 'One eye for you and one for me.' Then the spoon plunged into the head and came away with the glutinous eye dancing in it as if trying frantically to catch a glimpse of — me!

'Aha!' Tata exclaimed, looking up at me with a glint of pleasure in his eyes. 'On the same day that my appetite returns my son appears.'

Ntate Ngwenya grinned at me slyly before burying his face in a Tupperware bucket of frothy home-brewed beer. When he emerged again, smacking his lips, Tata spoke.

'Usually when he comes to see his parents, it is with two or three sticks . . .'

'Yebo,' said Ngwenya, finding a comfortable grip on his own stick.

Tata spent his childhood in Bizana in the Transkei. Before the mealie harvests, boys were sent in among the mealies to kill the hundreds of rats that used to invade the fields and devour the crops. For this annual rodent massacre each boy would be armed with a stick. Then there were the stick fights. On a whim a boy could be challenged to a fight and would have to defend his honour without a second thought. For this he needed two sticks. And whenever a boy was journeying on an errand or a visit from one village to another, he would arm himself with three sticks. There was always the possibility of being attacked by dogs and a stick could be thrown as a missile and lost when defending oneself against these village mongrels.

Tata had converted these prosaic rural experiences into an urban metaphor to describe the moods that people displayed when they called upon him. Mild irritation was a one-stick mood, aggression was two sticks, violence was three. I compared this, in a Standard Eight essay entitled 'My Father's Work', to a thermometer which a doctor pops in a patient's mouth to take his temperature.

'. . . But today he comes to me with one stick,' Tata diagnosed.

'Uhmmm,' Ngwenya nodded, anxiously eyeing the brew which was now in my father's hands and which, evidently, he was taking too long to drink before passing it back.

He confuses sticks of wood with sticks of dagga, I thought, but warned myself against thinking such snide thoughts lest they reveal themselves on my face as a sneer.

'Take the spade there and loosen the soil,' Tata instructed me, pointing along the wall of the house where he had a small herb garden. 'Be careful that you don't dig up my little plants.'

I hesitated, considered refusing. After all, I was thirty-four years old and I hadn't come all the way here for a spot of gardening. But I had come — eventually — to make peace with my parents and to be put on the right road. I looked down at my immaculate Florsheims, pretending that these tony red size nines were the reason for my hesitation. I gripped the spade and began to dig like a man preparing his own grave.

'MaScara!' Tata called to my mother. Somewhere in the skull and crossbones she responded with an enthusiastic 'Yes!' for she knew by the name she had been called that I was here.

'Bring that paper on the cupboard here, please MaScara.'

My mother came out with a copy of the *Black World*, slapped me on the shoulder with it as she passed me and handed it to Tata.

'You don't forget to come inside and see me,' she said as she went back in.

'Yes,' Tata said, pleased that the inquisition was going exactly as planned. 'Listen to this, my friend.'

His friend was once more gulping away at the beer, but Tata glanced my way to make sure that I was paying attention. He read:

Yesterday the Pimpernel struck again. He hijacked a bus and caused hysterical passengers to scream and faint when he sped down Jan Smuts Avenue holding one bloody severed arm aloft. Daisy Sibeko (22) and Sarah Mazibuko (30) became hysterical and flung themselves from the speeding bus. The two women were rushed to hospital by our reporter Scara Nhlabatsi and photographer Gus Kinnear. Both women are in a stable condition . . .

Tata flung the paper into the dust and glared at me. Not knowing what to say, I leaned on the spade and waited for the scolding.

'Is this what I sent you to an expensive school in Swaziland for?'

Ntate Magwinya smacked his lips to show whose side he was on.

'Now what does Tata mean?' I was beginning to sweat, from the exertion of digging my father's stupid herb patch, which probably yielded nothing more than a clove of garlic every second year.

Tata breathed heavily and took the bucket of beer from his friend by force. 'Do you think this thing that you are doing is a kind thing to be doing to people? People who have spent too much money and many years to read the white man's language? And fifty cents every day to buy this white man's paper?'

'No, Tata.'

'Then why are you doing it?'

I told him about Sybrand the Censor and how he was cutting to shreds every piece of truth that reached the office: deaths in detention, the kicking to death of a black gardener for daring to pee in front of a white woman, the stoning of a black boy from a bakkie full of drunken rugby supporters . . .

'And if you cannot write about these ugly things does it now mean that you have to make up ugly things for your own people?'

'No, Tata.'

'Then why, Mandla?'

The toilet door creaked in a slight, sudden breeze. Somewhere a mother called a child. But from me there was silence. Nothing in the world would get me to tell Tata about profits and about using cunning methods to hang onto one's job.

Tata realized that he would get nothing more out of his stubborn son. He made me promise that I would not write lies again, then he got up to pay a short visit to the toilet.

Old Magwinya waited until Tata closed the toilet door. Then he turned to me and in a conspiratorial whisper, he asked: 'But, Scara, who is this Pimpernel?'

Mama was cleaning the cabinet when I walked in to greet her.

She could see that I had just received a tongue-lashing; perhaps she had eavesdropped on the scolding from behind one of her lace curtains.

'How's the job, Scara?' This was Mama's way of consoling me.

I answered this and several other questions in monosyllables.

'I saw Khensani at the station on Saturday.'

'She told me, Mama.'

'And she told me the good news.' She fluttered the cloth in my face to convey her delight and let ten thousand dust mites loose in my nostrils.

'What news, Mama?' I coughed out the question.

'About you.'

'What about me?'

'Aw, Scara, that you have agreed to go to the baby doctor.'

What crudity! I picked up a soapstone ornament lying on the couch and explored all its bumps and ridges. How could Khensani go and blurt out my bloody private affairs in the middle of a station concourse surrounded by thousands of strangers. Why doesn't she just publish my sperm count in that stupid column of hers . . .!

'And you are giving up the drinking, I hear?'

. . . And the number of days I've been on the wagon!

Suddenly Mama held a book under my downcast face.

'What's this, Mama?'

'Those white men that you brought here, the one who calls himself our President but he can't even come out and speak to the women, he is the one who left it here, there between the cushions on the sofa.'

On the cover of the book was an ornately embossed crest: an ox and a springbok about to lock horns but prevented from doing so by a huge protea flower that bloomed radiantly between them. Underneath this was the motto: Unity Is Strength.

I opened it and found, to my dumbstruck amazement, that it was the personal diary and appointment book of no less a personage than Willem Adriaan de Vries!

Mama stood back to gaze upon her elated, trembling son.

'Now you can copy down all his dirty secrets in your paper,' she said.

I looked up at her. I couldn't publish any of his secrets. But I was too excited to explain the censorship laws all over again.

'Don't let your Tata see what I've given you.'

'I won't, Mama, I won't,' I promised, shoving the diary inside my cardigan and making for the door.

My dear mother called after me: 'Hey, Scara, my lightie.'

A mother who uses slang when addressing her son has joy in her heart. I turned around, struggling to hide my eagerness to get going. 'Yes, Mama.'

'Your father has been reading to me all your reports about Mr Pimpernel and I am definitely sure I know who he is.'

'Who is he, Mama?' That damn Makaphela has been singing from shebeen to shebeen.

'He is a white man who paints his face black to commit these ugly sins against our people.'

'Awu, Mama, how do you know such a thing?'

'I'm telling you.' She folded her arms smugly. 'That surname Nel, it's a white man's surname. I worked for the Nel family there in Kensington.'

First name Pimper, surname Nel. Elementary, my dear Scara.

'Mama,' I said, hugging her, 'you're the best.' I took a fifty-rand note from my pocket and pressed it into her hand.

The diary was written in a clumsy, uncomfortable longhand. A few of the entries were smudged and almost totally illegible (I imagined him sometimes hiding the diary under a moist armpit). They were all in the language which he revered so much that he built a mammoth shrine to it: an obelisk three storeys high which had cost the country millions of rands.

It was unfortunate, I thought, that the year had been only three weeks old when De Vries lost his diary. Yet there was enough in those pages for a dozen stories and profiles. I lapped up and digested every word with relish. The entries ranged from the humorous:

2 January MONDAY
Meet with Olivier, Intelligence. Olivier in intelligence is like Father Christmas in a black belt. The intelligence this man provides I can get from my bantu gardener for a rand. Maybe it's time for a shake-up here. Possibly Botha, or DG in Internal Affairs.

To the innocent:

8 January SUNDAY
Invited to do television broadcast on the role of the white man in spreading Christianity and Civilization in Africa: anniversary of death of seven missionaries at hands of bantu pagans. Thornton to brief me in the morning. Thornton advised me not to use the phrase 'missionary position' in my broadcast as last year. Don't know why. Must ask Thornton.

To the beguiling:

12 January THURSDAY
The Americans are insisting on putting black workers in executive positions in their Apache food outlets: their bantu [deleted] negroes are giving them headaches. Van Jaarsveld says we can do without these outlets (677 country-wide). I think we need to

capitulate otherwise we get more negative news wherever the communists are.

To the personal (and the entry which interested me most):

13 January FRIDAY
Dr Van Tonder tells me that the tapeworm problem is not serious. But what does he know? Why is it that my last six predecessors have all had tapeworms and have acted strangely as a result of this affliction? Whenever I mention this to Dr he gives me that cynical smile and tells me that it is the prostate I should be worrying about at my age. 'And stay away from the braais,' he says.

There was also an entry relating to the visit to Tata. It read:

18 January WEDNESDAY
The political situation is getting out of hand. Africans crossing the border to those camps in the north where the communists train them. Then coming back loaded with weapons: AK 47s, grenades, limpet mines. The more we kill the more they multiply. Nhlabatsi may be able to give some advice here.

And later:

The scheming behind my back is dividing us right down the middle between verlig and verkramp. The chaos is upon us and I believe that the time has come for action. The detention of Sibisi and his fellow terrorists is in a sense detaining progress of the entire subcontinent. I say we release them without making a public song and dance about it and we quietly tell the world that we've let them go. De Jong (chief whip, chief conniver if you ask me) says to hell with the West. Sibisi and Co. are dangerous and they stay on the Island.

The rest of the diary was blank, except for appointments scattered over the coming months. The one regular weekly appointment that struck me was: haircut. Now De Vries — as you have probably seen countless times on this country's currency — did not have much going for him in the way of hair. But he did possess a few streaks above his ears and in the nape of his neck, and he seemed to think they needed regular tonsorial attention. I turned to today's date — 23 March THURSDAY — and there it was again: haircut.

My own little appointment book carried a much more humiliating entry for this day:

Dr Farquharson, Obstetrician and Gynaecologist, 4th floor, Medical Towers, Bree Street

Yes, I would finally make my merry way to have my balls weighed, my sperm counted and whatever else they do to a black man whose body knows that it is not a good idea to father a child in the epoch of white rule. But when your partner insists that her biological clock is ticking away, you have to do what a man sometimes should not do.

On the spur of the moment I decided to combine this appointment with something more pleasant, something presidential: a haircut. I needed one too.

The barber-shop was a tiny, run-down room on the edge of town: two high chairs with men perched on them, mummified in white sheets, two Indian barbers — Naidoo and Dadoo — gossiping away rather perfunctorily and probably sick to death of each other's voices, vacillating between Gujarati and English.

Yellowing and torn issues of magazines robbed of their centre-spreads, which tried to cheer up the walls. An old two-bar heater hibernating on a sagging armchair since last winter.

I took a seat and began to page through a magazine. That was use-less: De Vries occupied fifty per cent of my mind, and a certain Dr Farquharson the other fifty per cent (not necessarily in that order, ha ha ha).

There were no medical schools for blacks in the Republic. These days a small quota of black students were being accepted at the white universities, but these were graduating as vets and GPs. There had been one paediatrician, a certain Dr Enos Dlamini, whom the *Black World* had made a huge fuss about before he left the country to marry a white girl and to attend to the medical needs of London kids. Farquharson was still here, in the land of the strikes, the riots, the bombs, and the devalued currency. Maybe he was a brother after all (only joking).

'Oh, to be white and free and twenty-one/Now that the jacarandas are in bloom,' a familiar voice recited with a hearty chuckle.

I looked up and there, in one of the swivel chairs, was Gustav Kinnear. He was trussed up in a frayed, discoloured white sheet and a dark ginger wreath of shorn hair had formed around his shoulders.

'No bolidicks, blease,' Dadoo bleated, snipping away musically in the air above Gus's head and pointing to a crudely pencilled sign on the door: NO POLITICS IN HERE. Gus ignored him and the sign.

'You following me around?' I asked him.

'Who was here first?'

Dadoo swivelled him around and I spoke to his reflection in the mirror. 'I've got something to show you that's gonna make you believe the things I tell you.'

'What things?'

'About my father's illustrious visitors.'

'Such as?'

'Deepfreeze.'

He arched his eyebrows as if to say, 'Here we go again.'

He asked about Zimbabwe, Khensani, her father, and even about little Zodwa who he had met at our house once or twice.

'She's there almost permanent now,' I told him. 'Making up for lost time.'

'How's work?' I asked.

'You've got a nerve to ask me that,' he said without any resentment. 'Mahlatini has teamed me up with Miya. The man is determined to track down the Pimpernel before you get back.'

At the mention of the word 'Pimpernel' the two barbers exchanged glances and simultaneously fired off a volley of words at each other, one in Gujarati, the other in English.

'That story's closed as far as I'm concerned,' I said.

'That's what you think. It's taken on a life of its own. The Pimpernel has been spotted in Dobsonville, wrestling with a ghost, who also had one arm, in the middle of the night, in Mdantsane, dancing at a stokvel, even playing the machines at Sun City . . .'

'One one-armed bandit challenging the other,' I said.

'Hey,' Gus said, laughing, 'why don't we get hold of Maka . . .'

'No,' I said. 'Enough is enough.'

'Blease keep head still.'

'I know someone who thinks he's a white man whose first name is Pimper, surname Nel.'

'That's the best,' Gus roared, 'that is so stupid!'

Serves me right for not disclosing my source.

Gus was not as discreet as me when it came to divulging such personal details: 'That stupid wife of mine didn't want to spread those legs for me the other night because she thought the Pimpernel was watching.'

That made me laugh so much that the two barbers stopped and looked at me uneasily. I imagined that Charmaine doll of Gus's (not that I would call her that in public) saying, 'Not tonight, Gussie lovey, the Pimpernel is watching.'

Gus and I changed seats and Dadoo began shearing me without asking what I wanted.

'Read any good stories lately?' I asked Gus's reflection.

He knew I was waiting for his assessment of 'Dear Gwen' but he kept talking about something else.

In the end I had to ask: 'So what did you think about it?'

'About what?'

I gritted my teeth.

'Don't greet your teeth at me,' he said, exaggerating my accent. 'The story's great, it's a damn good read, there's nothing wrong with it.'

'Then what did you want to say about it?'

'It's all wrong . . .'

'Gus! Make up your mind!'

'Keep still,' Dadoo warned me, 'udderwise I cut off hear.'

'Gimme a chance,' Gus said. 'The soap rep — Jerry — and his girlfriend, it was not like that at all in the fifties. Neither was Percy Sledge around back then. Otis Redding maybe. Also check on the Vauxhall. And I don't think there's a Prince Edward Drive in Northcliff. And there weren't highways then, or supermarkets. I mean the whole story's riddled with anachronisms.'

'I know all that, but I couldn't go and research the thing when these bastards have obliterated our entire history . . .'

'No bolidicks . . .'

'This isn't fucking politics, man!'

Dadoo stepped back in alarm. 'Keep it cool, my friend,' he said. 'Not so much hanger.'

This time it was Gus's turn to laugh, shaking and sniggering and looking like a mischievous little township brat with his short back and sides. The two barbers and I both joined in.

'Do you remember the poet George Cupido?' Gus asked.

Who didn't know the revolutionary coloured poet from Cape Town.

'I shall spill the beans of my bondage
and snare you with the chains that bind me
while you count your white lies that shrivel and blacken
in the African sun . . .'

Gus and I stared in amazement at Naidoo and Dadoo as they came to the end of their barber-shop duet.

'He's on the Island,' Naidoo said.

'Well not any more,' Gus said. 'He's in Jo'burg and I'm seeing him —' he glanced at his watch '— in half an hour's time. For lunch.'

Gus looked at me in the mirror. He was meeting someone who could tell us something about the man Sibisi. Someone who had spoken with Sibisi and broken bread with him, not to mention rock. He winked and nodded. Here was a chance to recover some of that obliterated history. Farquharson would have to wait. I nodded back.

We went off, rubbing our itching necks like twin comedians, to meet a poet who had spent eight years on the Island for inciting people to take up arms. I could not believe how exciting my visit to the barber was turning out to be.

We walked two blocks up into Diagonal Street, through a vista of Indian women swathed in saris, sitting behind their hillocks of curry-powder, pyramids of tomatoes, bags bulging with potatoes. And jazz breezing stridently through the air from the lips and the fingers of black Americans and South African exiles yearning for home and freedom. And crowds, pickpockets, beggars, lovers coming and going. Gus stopped dead in his tracks in the midst of all this.

'Where are we meeting him?' I asked, beginning to believe that this was a ploy to get me back onto that tornado of carousing I've been trying to recover from.

'Right here.'

'And where are we taking him?'

'Right here.'

Right here was the pavement outside the restaurant of a Chinese gentleman called Why, whose entire menu consisted of pap and steak with cartons of maheu to wash it down.

Why also provided twenty steel chairs and tables for his customers — about one thousand sweating, unfastidious, hungry blue-collar workers who elbowed and butted their way up to his counter every lunch-time, filling the diner with their calling and shouting and the sweat of their brows and their armpits. As a result of this popularity, two per cent of Why's customers sat down to their pap and steak at a table while the rest squatted in the sun on the pavement outside, listening to the music from the record bar across the road.

After about five minutes a man appeared from between the legs of the bustling masses and stood before us. His many years on this earth had not endowed him with much vertical growth. I recognized him from a photo I had once seen in a roneoed copy of a banned poetry magazine. His hair was grey, and his face seemed to have succumbed to the sandstorms that bombarded the quarries of the penal island.

He wore Lee jeans, still blue and crisp, fresh from the racks of the boys' department of an outfitter, and a green T-shirt with a fat red exclamation mark emblazoned on its front.

He stepped forward, grinning and pumping his puny legs luxuriously as if he had been cramped up in a very tiny place for hours. He gave old Gus a bear-hug which ended up as a grapple with my friend's bum.

'Mr Cupido,' I said, stepping forward with my hand extended, 'I am pleased to meet an elder statesman of revolutionary literature.'

'Hey, Gus ou pal, tell me, who's dis fucker?' he said with a contemptuous guffaw.

I was dumbfounded. And in that speechless instant I knew that I was not going to like the man. I had never dreamt that I would ever meet Georgie Cupido, simply because he had been stored away on the Island for almost a decade. But if I were to have imagined such a moment, it would certainly have been a meeting of two writers, two imaginations, two sensitive souls. Instead, he insults me!

Gus, too, was embarrassed and muttering something about his 'best friend . . . smart writer . . . good journalist . . . we come a long way . . .'

'Well, I'm not an elder statesman, my pellie,' he said imperiously in his singsong Cape Coloured accent, 'I lead de way from generation to generation. I will be more radical in my rage against oppression den de generation of tomorrow.'

'I hope we're free by then,' I said, 'so that you can save yourself the trouble.'

Gus sighed as deeply as if he had just stepped into a turd, and stamped his foot.

In the background an exiled jazz pianist laced an African jazz tune with the words:

'You can go to New York if you like
We're sticking around here in Manenberg.'

Together with the Island, Manenberg was the place that had bred the likes of Cupido. But the jazz pianist was far away in New York, while I was stuck with Manenberg.

'Three pap and steaks!' Gus shouted the moment Why deigned to cast a narrow, Oriental eye his way.

'Tlee pap and steak!' Why echoed to the little window behind him, losing some of the consonants in the process — but I wasn't complaining; Why had a communications system that worked impeccably between himself and the four black women in the kitchen, whose chattering could be heard above the sizzle of steak and the bedlam this side of the counter.

'One rare!' Cupido added.

'What?' Why asked, his eyes flashing in a scornful frown.

'I said one steak rare,' Cupido repeated.

'You blelly mad!' Why shouted. 'What you tink dis place, Kelton Lestulant? Fuck off!'

'But did you really think you were going to get a rare steak?' I asked the poet on the pavement as we tore into our well-done, mass-produced wads of beef.

'Of course not.' He licked his fingers, his eyes fixed on his enamel plate.

'So?'

'So I was just exercising my right as a citizen to *ask* for a rare steak.' His laughter sent spurts of animal fat onto the pavement to make little blotches.

I could find neither mirth nor logic in this; instead I heard in the distance the voice of a receptionist calling, 'Mr Nyalabutsey, the doctor will see you now, Mr Nyalabutsey . . . oh dear.'

'Tell Scara what you told me yesterday,' Gus was saying, lowering his voice. 'Describe Sibisi . . .'

'One step at a time,' Cupido said, holding up one little paw. 'They fetched him and the six from the Treason Trial and took them away.

They told the rest of us to shut up about it or they'd bring us back to die there.' He guffawed. 'But I've been out fourteen days today and I've told about a thousand people so far.'

'Where have they taken them?' I asked, expecting another rude remark.

Instead, he shrugged. 'You know the rumours. De Vries released them and they crossed the border before the right-wing could reverse his decision.'

I asked a string of questions. What was it like to be with Sibisi for so many years? Is he really the powerful leader that legend has made him out to be? What does he look like? Did he have anything to do with selling soap before he took up arms and went to jail? Did he have a girlfriend who was an agony aunt for a newspaper?

Cupido gave me a long, ponderous look. 'Have you met him?'

'I drove somebody to the Botswana border a couple of months ago,' I shrugged. 'Maybe it was him, maybe it was one of the others.'

'Sibisi once advertised Lifeguard soap. In the fifties and early sixties. His picture appeared larger-than-life on hoardings all over the country, above the slogan: LET'S GET OUT ALL THE DIRT. When Sibisi became General Secretary of the Movement they used this slogan as an ingenious and ready-made advertisement to further their cause. Then the bastards rounded them all up after they took up arms. Sibisi, Karim, Bhengu, they were all given life sentences and every scrap the Movement ever published was banned for possession. Obviously those hoardings were taken off in no time, from Cape Town to Pietersburg.'

Around us, laughter, the scraping of enamel plates against concrete paving, hundreds of tales, anecdotes and gossip about mlungu, weddings, funerals, the violence in the townships. But for me there was only one story — as long as this unpredictable tokoloshe kept it up.

'What about a photo of Sibisi. Don't tell me there isn't a single photo around today,' Gus said.

'Don't tell me there isn't a shebeen around here somewhere,' the poet said with a burp.

There was, down an alley, less than two minutes away. Another barber-shop, which had started out as a genuine enterprise but soon graduated/deteriorated (depending on which way the fly on the pate looks at it) into a den where a drink could be had in the company of friends and a bet placed on fahfee, the numbers game, run by the very same Why of pap and steak fame. Gus and I ordered beer, the poet ordered a glass of some sickly sweet wine which he drank without wincing, despite the long years of enforced abstinence, and which brought a squadron of green flies happily winging their way to our corner.

'There's one hoarding left,' Cupido said.

'Where?'

'Where?'

'Kingsley Carmichael.'

Kingsley Carmichael, affectionately known as KC, magazine magnate. His name was synonymous with black journalism and there was probably not a black journalist on the continent who was not familiar with it.

KC's story was legend. He had been brought to the Republic as a kid in the thirties and had made his fortune in the motor trade. When he saw that there was not a single newspaper or magazine produced specifically for the black reader which captured the exciting buzz of black politics, culture and sport, he saw possibilities of increasing his fortune while giving some of his money back to those who, because they were black, did not have the opportunity to make fortunes themselves. If this sounds too philanthropic for you, then it's because I'm sort of quoting straight from the last KC interview I read. *Black Gold* was launched in the fifties and this vibrant magazine soon became a household name for its racy style and its boldness in confronting political issues relevant to black people.

Meanwhile, Cupido was enjoying the suspense while we waited to hear about the KC connection. He took another swig of wine, leaned forward (the fat man lying prostrate on a couch in the corner, muttering to himself, might be a member of the Secret Police for all we knew) and said: 'Kingsley, he's got an eye for what's going to be priceless tomorrow. When the government arrested Sibisi, Kingsley got a truck, drove out to a rural area with some men and took off an entire hoarding. He's got that Sibisi hoarding mounted on a wall in his basement.'

'That I have to see,' I said, jumping up and spilling beer over Gus's Leica in my excitement.

'Why not?' the poet replied. 'He's a buddy of mine. Let's go.'

I changed my mind about Cupido. He wasn't so bad once you got used to his rudeness. Or once you'd had a couple of beers.

In no time we were in my Volksie and on our way to the northern suburbs. Now, take my description of Northcliff from my 'Dear Gwen' story — the swimming-pools, the shady, dappled avenues, the nannies in their white aprons — and you have the domicile of the eminent Kingsley Carmichael.

Cupido pressed the button at the wrought-iron security gate and a voice bristling with static and impatience sputtered out of it: 'Yes.'

'Kingsley!'

'Yesss, who's that?' I could almost hear him wanting to hazard a guess.

'Open up, fucker!'

'Cupido! Aren't you supposed to be under house arrest or something?'

'Not any more, fucker!'

'Oh dear, I told my connections at the Ministry to slap another ban on you, but they must have overlooked you.'

There was a click and the voice was gone. Cupido turned around to face us and asked with his impish eyes whether we had noticed the familiarity.

Gus offered a patronizing, 'Wow!'

KC himself came to the gate, flanked by two very athletic-looking boxers (of the canine variety).

'Look how my "Dear Gwen" story has grown,' I whispered to Gus.

'And check what has happened to the maid,' Gus said. 'Turned into an old white male.'

'What about these fuckers?' Cupido asked KC, pointing at the dogs.

'They are very particular about who they bite,' KC said. He managed another chuckle at his own joke despite the cigar that was stuck between his teeth.

His hair was white, his smile was broad and cheerful, his seventy-year-old body was wrapped in a shimmering green gown with gold edging, his feet nestled in thick, fluffy slippers.

'If you were black,' Cupido said, 'you could be arrested for promoting a banned organization.' The Movement's colours were black, green and gold.

'Cupido, Cupido, Cupido,' KC clucked. He introduced himself to us, put his arms around me and Gus and ushered us into the grounds of his mansion. Picture fountains, statues, a swimming-pool glinting in the sun and a trio of gardeners dextrously guiding Flymoes over rambling lawns.

We sat in a lounge which had more statuettes and carelessly discarded sandals and pot plants and bowls of fruit in it than *Ben Hur*. We all looked conspicuously scruffy in those plush surroundings, Cupido more so than Gus and me.

'Who do you work for?'

I was looking down at the rich red carpet but I knew KC was speaking to me or Gus: there was none of the good-natured, half-irritated tone in his voice reserved for Cupido.

'*Black World*,' Gus told him.

'Aha,' he said, 'Mahlatini.'

Cupido got up and made for the liquor cabinet, where he promptly smashed a glass. KC was unperturbed by this clumsy accident. He gazed intently at us and a light came into his eyes.

'Are you two the Pimpernel hounds?' he asked.

I nodded.

'Nice little hoax,' he said approvingly. 'If the government doesn't allow you any news, you make up your own. That's what life's all about.'

'Sure,' I nodded, wishing Tata were present to hear an intelligent mlungu singing our praises because of our stories.

An ugly grey cat materialized and leaped onto his lap.

'Hey, Kingsley, where's Queensley?' Cupido shouted from the bar. 'I hear she gets younger every five years.'

I started to laugh but stopped abruptly when I noticed that Kingsley was not amused.

'I've brought them to have a look at Sibisi,' Cupido said, bringing us each a drink: beer for Gus and me, whisky for the two of them.

The cat arched its back at the mention of Sibisi.

'Tell your cat they're my buddies,' Cupido said, throwing himself into a chair and gulping down his drink.

'Later, later,' KC said. 'Where's the manuscript, Cupido?'

'It's coming. I've finished the second draft and I'll send it up to you next week.'

'That's not what you said the last time we spoke.' KC sighed and wet his lips with some whisky. He looked at Gus and me. 'I've offered this fellow an overseas publisher for his autobiography — an offer any writer in the Republic would jump at . . . wouldn't you?'

He was asking me to take sides against Cupido and I happily did, saying, 'Definitely.'

'Except that you haven't lived yet, fucker,' Cupido reminded me.

'True,' I agreed, 'I've still got all my teeth.'

KC laughed so much that he spilled his drink. And Cupido smiled at the joke: he seemed to take it as well as he dished it out. He fetched us another round of drinks.

'Hey, Cupido,' KC called across the room, 'have you remembered to include that story about the time we worked together at *Black Gold* and some fellow came in to complain about an article you had written?'

'I've given it a whole chapter,' Cupido said.

'Come and tell us the story then,' KC said.

Cupido did not need to be persuaded. But he did first check the level of his drink to see if it would sustain him through his tale.

'One lazy afternoon, we're all trying to get through the day, putting copy together . . .'

'More likely trying to work through a haze of alcohol,' KC said.

'Suddenly there's a tall, bearded white fellow at the door. I'm the first to spot him. I greet him, but the fucker he's in no mood to wish me a good afternoon. He's got a copy of the latest issue of our magazine in his hands and he's come to see KC to complain about one of the stories we published. We all freeze — which story? It's some story written by none other than George Cupido. I'm determined to know what's his case so I tell him to please have a seat while I go and see if KC's around. I go and tell Carmichael there's a fellow here to see him. As I walk across to his office' — he points a thumb at Carmichael — 'I get this plan in my head. I go into his office and I tell him there's a fucker out there to see him. KC says what about, I say he won't say, but I say to KC, I say I've been trying to talk to the guy but he's as deaf as a doornail . . .'

'Dumb as a doornail,' KC says, 'but go on.'

'I tell KC the guy can't hear a thing and that he'll have to talk loud. KC says no problem. Then I go to the guy who's sitting there and I tell him that KC will see him but I tell him KC is hard of hearing. The man says no problem, he'll talk loud. As soon as the man goes into KC's office they start shouting at each other and the whole office can hear exactly what they're saying.'

After the laughter had died down, Gus asked KC if he could take a few photos. The amenable old man agreed and Gus got some good 'cat on the lap' shots.

The drinks flowed on and on — every man for himself now, since Cupido had broken another glass and disappeared to the loo. The talk flowed too: politics, culture, literature, photography.

'Look at a couple of back numbers of *Black Gold*,' KC told Gus. 'You'll see what those old guys used to produce, despite the fact that none of them ever had the opportunities to learn the trade. On-the-job training, that's what it was.'

'Did you ever meet Sibisi?' I asked him.

He shook his head. 'Bhengu and the other lads, yes. Bhengu when we, *Black Gold*, published the potato convicts scandal. Bhengu was an activist who worked for the Movement in the rural areas. And when we exposed the fact that black pass offenders — so-called offenders I should say — who had been convicted were being forced to work on potato farms as slaves, Bhengu came to our offices to tell us where these guilty farms were. He even pointed them out to our reporter and later he came to thank me for printing that story and I said any time, and we chatted and so on.'

KC took a sip of whisky, stroked the cat and smiled mysteriously.

'But you do know the rumour about Sibisi being friendly with our "Dear Gwen" of course?'

Gus and I exchanged glances. Then it must've been Sibisi in my car that night! My heart began to pound. I had to see that hoarding now. I was onto something really big here. The very second the government lifts the state of emergency and the censor leaves our office, I file the scoop of the century. In the meantime, maybe Gus and I can somehow track down Sibisi in a neighbouring state some-where and get an exclusive.

'Is Gwen still alive?' I asked KC.

He shrugged. 'There was a time when one was told these things: you know, so-and-so has left the country, that one has died in London, this one has given up the struggle and joined the Salvation Army. But lately no one tells you nothing about the old times and those old comrades.' He sighed, rather too dramatically, I thought. 'But there is someone who can assist you.' He clicked his fingers: 'Jacob Khoza. He worked for us. He knew all about this close friend-ship . . .'

'Jacob Khoza. Where do we find him?'

'He went on to work for *Fighting Words*. A tabloid that closed down, aah let me see now, when you fellows were little toddlers. A workers' socialist paper, badly run by Bolsheviks . . . but full of good intentions, the right to form trade unions, that kind of thing.'

KC on politics:

'There was something about the fifties that made the battle for liberation in this country more imperative than ever before. I was fortunate to travel in Africa and Europe in the early fifties. This gave me a perspective on the country that the white minority government and its blind followers refused to see. What was it I saw? That all over Africa the fight against colonialism was intensifying and countries were becoming free — Kenya, Ghana. 'And why not us?' a young Bhengu, Sibeko and Sibisi were saying . . . And when whites had a referendum to cast off the shadow of the British crown and turn the place into a Republican shambles, Sibisi turned to the armed struggle . . .'

KC on literature:

'Despite having no written literary heritage, despite the banning of all black writing that showed so much as a hint of social responsibility, black literature will triumph and white writing will not matter. Why? Because it is not by, for and about the people who matter.'

I named two famous white writers, challenging him to show me how irrelevant they were.

'Oh, bollocks,' he said, 'bollocks. Show me one person in your street who reads them and I'll personally — what shall I do?' He swirled his glass. 'I'll confer on those writers a prize of great monetary value. The KC Award for Relevance in the Townships.'

'The KARIT Award,' I said.

KC smiled politely, but I don't think he understood the witticism.

KC on Cupido:

'He's got enough potential to become a writer of world renown, if he can be weaned off the bottle. I was rather hoping his spell in jail would do the trick.'

KC on the present whereabouts of Cupido:

'But where is the little leprechaun? He's been gone for a very long time.' Meaning more time than he needs to satisfy even the most demanding of nature's calls.

KC put down his glass and headed for one of his many bathrooms.

'I hope we can get to see that hoarding now,' I said to Gus.

'Good idea,' Gus said, but my poor friend was beginning to drag his vowels and stumble over his consonants.

I looked at the empty bottles packed onto the coffee-tables. And a fleeting thought of Khensani and Dr Farquharson, who I had yet to meet, made me wince. But a good look at that hoarding and that presidential diary hidden in my car would make it all worthwhile, I managed to convince myself.

'Cupido, you bastard!' KC's voice echoed loud and angry through the house.

Gus and I stumbled out of the lounge and down a passage. A bathroom door stood wide open and we made our way inside. KC was standing and cursing, his hands flying in all directions. And the reason for his fury was Cupido, who was lying naked in a bath of foamy water, a whisky within reach of his short right arm, a cigar in an ashtray in his left hand. Despite KC's red-faced rage, the poet appeared calm, almost half-asleep, while tiny little rainbow-coloured bubbles popped all around him.

Eventually, he opened his eyes, looked up at us, slid into a sitting position and asked his former boss: 'What's your problem, fucker?'

'Okay, all of you, that's it,' KC said, yanking the skinny, foam-flecked poet out of the water. 'Out of my house. Now!'

'But what about the hoarding . . .?'

'To hell with the hoarding!'

Within five minutes we were back in the car.

'Where would you like to be dropped?' I snarled at the offensive little tokoloshe dripping on my back seat. Unfazed by the whole incident, he was still sucking at his damp cigar.

'Hey, fucker,' he started, but before he could finish his curse, I swung around and slapped him.

On Jan Smuts Avenue I stopped the car, dragged him out and drove off.

'Wait, wait, wait,' Gus said looking back, 'reverse.'

'I'm not picking him up again . . .'

'Reverse.'

I reversed until we were alongside Cupido.

Gus stuck his head out of the car. 'Hey, Cups,' he said, 'walk all the way down here. Bree Street is up ahead. Get a taxi there to Mafika's place. You'll be okay.' He turned to me. 'He told me Jo'burg's changed since the last time he was here. I thought I should help him out there.'

When we were on our way again Gus turned his head slowly and looked at me.

'What?' I said.

'I should've taken a picture of him back there. He looked so, so *tender,* the fucker.'

16

Flowers
for Gwen

We shouldn't have needed to search high and low for one Jacob Khoza, but we did. I know I should be ashamed of this. But it is more amusing than embarrassing. This is how the hunt happened:

Friday, am: Gus and I decide to phone KC and, before he slams down the phone, ask him to please tell us who the editor of *Fighting Words* used to be, and whether he is still alive. The rest is easy. But first we have to look up Carmichael's number in the telephone directory. This takes us two hours. Gus phones. Carmichael's maid answers (or, in this case, one of the maids). He asks for KC. She tells him that Mr Carmichael has just left for America. Gus tells her that he said nothing about going to America yesterday when we were sitting and having 'a coupla drinks with him'. She asks if there is any reason why he should have told us his plans. Gus admits that there isn't. Goodbye. Gus thinks that maids are getting cleverer and cheekier by the day. He reckons that if the whites want to remain in power for another couple of decades they should seriously consider closing down all those literacy groups in the suburbs.

Friday, noon: I have an idea. I phone our sister newspaper and speak to a friend of mine, Sipho Ndabeni, who covers township news for their extra edition — identifiable by its logo: a dark map of Africa — full of soccer, music reviews and the death toll in Sofasonke and other townships.

'How's the news in the black townships?' I asked him.

'Black townships,' he said, 'that's a tautology.'

'It's what?'

'Tautology. Like "reverse backwards", "tree-lined avenue" and "black townships".'

Sipho is such an arrogant bastard, I told Gus afterwards. 'There's some whitey sub-editor teaching him the language and he's showing off to his black brothers . . .'

'Black brothers,' Gus said. 'Tautology.'

'Fuck you, Gustav,' I said. But I couldn't swear at Sipho.

'Thanks for the lesson,' I said to Sipho, 'you got a helluva lot out of Bantu Education.'

He laughed. 'What you wanna know?'

'Ask your white comrades there who was editor of *Fighting Words*, a newspaper, some Commie thing that was around in the fifties.'

'Why should I ask them?'

'Because they might know.'

'It was Tommy Philips. Born in Mauritius in 1919. Came to the Republic in 1925 with his parents. Classified coloured. Joined the Communist Party in 1949. Founded *Fighting Words* in 1953. Placed under house arrest from '53 to '62. Fled to the UK . . .'

'. . .!'

'You want me to go on?'

'No, thanks. How d'you know all this?'

I could hear him laughing up his sleeve. 'I did a feature on the man in the Extra just before the censors came.'

Saturday and Sunday: Another lost weekend.

Monday, am: Gus and I are both hung-over and so we can't think what we should do to track down this Jacob fellow.

Monday, pm, Interlude: I've spent I'm not sure how long staring at Sybrand the Censor, watching him pore over photos and copy with a self-important air of responsibility, as if he was part of some exclusive white team that was saving the world from the devastation we writers and photographers (Blacks, Jews and Communists, according to Sybrand) wanted to wreak on it.

Tuesday, am: We have a breakthrough. Gus has found a neighbour, a woman who lives in Riverlea, who used to work for *Fighting Words*. We visit her. She is as huge as my own mother and wears glasses as thick as a Coke bottle. She tells us about three thousand times that she is not a communist any more and that is the first thing we should say underneath her name when we put her story in our paper. Gus winks at me and we do a quick mock interview while Gus takes a couple of shots of her. Then I ask her about Comrade Jacob Khoza. She can't remember anyone by that name. Are you sure? I'm sure. Then, as we're about to leave she tells us that there was a man called Jacob who used to be a messenger. Where is he now? He went to work at Waterman's Outfitters when the paper was banned.

Waterman's Outfitters. About two blocks from where we met that tokoloshe poet from Cape Town and where I sometimes bought the odd cardigan and pants. Indeed, I think Khensani bought me two shirts there for my last birthday — large.

We find a young brother working there with a tape-measure slung around his neck like a doctor's stethoscope. We tell him we're from the *Black World* and ask him about Jacob Khóza. The name brings a huge grin to his face.

Yes, he worked here for a long time. He was fired. So what's happened to the old-timer, he wants to know.

Gus and I look at each other — askance — as they used to say in our old English set-works.

'Well, that's what we came to ask you, mfo.'

'How can you ask me that when he works with you?'

'Works with us?'

'Yes, man. Jacob is Jakes! Your night-watchman.'

'Jakes, how long have you been working here?' I didn't really want to know the answer: it was a rhetorical question, a little preface to 'such a long time and you don't breathe a word about *Black Gold*'. But Jakes licked his lips, leaned back in his chair and stared into the humid African night. Everyone had gone home and Gus and I had joined him in his tiny night-watchman's office with a bottle of brandy. His head was covered in grey curls, except for a shiny bald spot, which he scratched as he thought about my question.

'Six years.'

'You worked for *Black Gold*?' Gus asked him.

He sat up, startled. And before he could recover, I asked if he remembered Sibisi. He looked at us suspiciously.

'Jakes, don't worry, we're doing a story on Sibisi.'

'But the boers they say no politics in the paper no more.'

'Have we ever listened to the boers?'

In answer to my question he picked up the afternoon edition of the *Black World* and swept it under our noses, to smell the rubbish, it seemed, rather than read it:

was the story of a Sofasonke bride who had warned her groom that the day preceding their marriage would be his last as a drinking man. While they were taking their vows she had smelt a mint-flavoured liqueur on his breath. Instead of saying 'I do' she had been heard to say 'What did I tell you?' before all hell broke loose.

COPS PUT SPOKE IN WHEEL OF BICYCLE THIEF

was a self-evident little pun from our court reporter, and

DOMESTIC NABS BURGLAR

was a tribute to one Dora Mofokeng, a 'buxom' domestic worker who had cornered and beaten up a burglar who tried to make off with her 'madam's' jewellery.

Baba Jakes threw the paper down on the table.

'You rest your case?' Gus said with a friendly smile. The smile on my face was sheepish.

'Huh?'

'Okay, well,' I said, coming to my own rescue, 'was there ever a time when you didn't listen to the boers?'

Baba Jakes's eyes flashed with indignation. 'The fifties,' he said, 'the Defiance Campaign. We burnt the passes, stayed away from their factories and their mines. We sat on their benches . . .'

'And the papers, like *Fighting Words*?'

'We wrote it all down, everything: who was in jail, who died there, who got kicked to death by the boers. And when the police came and raided the office we went out and threw the papers on the streets so that people could read them.'

'What about the fighters? Sibisi, did you ever meet him?'

But Baba Jakes would not be taken for granted. He glared at us with disdain.

'You boys,' he said, 'every day you walk past me, up and down, up and down. Maybe once a week you say, "Heita, Baba." But mostly it's just up and down, up and down past me as if I'm . . . I'm . . . nobody. Now you bring brandy . . .'

'Because we want to learn now, Baba,' Gus said in an appeasing tone.

He considered this but remained unconvinced. 'How did you find out about me?' he asked.

'Waterman's,' I said.

'Awu, you know about that?' He poured himself another shot of brandy. This time he was the one with the sheepish look on his face.

'Give me a cigarette,' he said, even though he had a full pack of Lexingtons on the table. We were paying for our news, it seems. He dragged deeply on the smoke and went on, 'Waterman is crazy. I wear his clothes, but I don't steal anything. Still he tells me to go.'

What did he mean?

Before he downed his brandy he had told us the story.

Baba Jakes worked for Waterman's as a night-watchman. Night after night he huddled over a brazier, clutching a knobkierie to fend off would-be burglars with an eye on the outfitter's stocks of smart clothes.

Night after night and season after season of staring into glowing embers must surely give rise to many a hypnotic illusion and Baba Jakes decided, on one fateful night, to indulge in his fantasies. And having yielded once, it became a compulsion.

At around four in the morning, just before daybreak, when the coals in his mbaula faded to grey embers, and with them the likelihood of a break-in, Baba Jakes would rise, his joints cracking loudly in the quiet night, and steal his way into his own employer's shop.

There he would don the very latest in sartorial elegance from the fashion capitals of the world. And decked out in genuine leather from Boston, hugged in flannels from France, buttoned-down in shirts from Germany and swirled in gaudy scarves from Spain, he would parade down the carpeted aisles singing his own praises, colonizing for forty-five minutes the wonderful world of the white man. Coats would sway on their hangers as he brushed past them, as if bowing in admiration, while stony-faced pink dummies stared out of the window, mutely indifferent to his transformation.

This early-morning session on the catwalk continued happily for months until customers began to complain that the clothes smelled faintly of woodsmoke and sweat. A spy camera was installed and captured Baba Jakes's nocturnal promenades on film.

Because he had not actually stolen any of the clothes, no charges were laid. But he was fired.

'Waterman is crazy,' he concluded again.

Frankly, I thought Baba Jakes was the one who had lost his mind, along with his teeth, but for a change I followed Gus's example and kept these thoughts to myself. Instead, I asked him again, 'Did you know Sibisi?'

Baba Jakes paused for such a long time that I thought he had gone to sleep. I was about to repeat the question when he said with a deep sigh, which seemed to blow away the cobwebs from ancient memories: 'Sibisi and me, we worked together at Western Deep Levels.'

'What?'

'That time already, Sibisi he was fighting the white man. He was a clerk, me, I was a real miner. Then they fire Sibisi, and me I follow in his footsteps.'

'Why did they fire him?' I wanted to know. And was I glad I asked! You see, Baba Jakes was not the most forthcoming of interviewees — but not because he was stingy with the facts. This gem of a story was for him banal stuff, not worth repeating.

'Well, the miners, once in a while the doctor, the white doctor, he comes to give us check-up. We stand six six six, one behind the other behind the other in long rows. Now the doctor come and he must check us one by one. But the doctor he is lazy. He keeps the stetiskop on the first man's chest.' Baba Jakes pressed a thumb against Gus's chest in demonstration of a stethoscope. 'And then he asks all six men to cough.

'Sibisi, he said this was no good. So they fire him.'

That was the story.

'And Gwen?'

Baba Jakes smiled and nodded. We waited another eternity before he began to talk again.

'They were very close friends,' he said, 'Sibisi and Gwen.'

'Like Scara and Dear Khensani?' Gus asked with a wink, and a wince: he was not used to drinking brandy with government dash (the Coke had run out).

'Dear Khensani,' Baba Jakes said, startled, 'she's your girlfriend?'

'My wife,' I said with a feeling of extreme pride, although, as matters stood now, that status was growing more and more tenuous by the day.

'She advises good, that one,' he said, raising his eyebrows in obvious admiration. 'Look after her, young man.'

I nodded, once more feeling like a fake in Baba Jakes's presence, with a brandy in my hand and about six in my bloodstream, not forgetting the two beers Gus and I had gulped down for lunch.

'Tell us about them,' I goaded.

'I thought they would get married,' Baba Jakes said, 'but he was always running away from the police and hiding somewhere. He came to the offices of *Black Gold* a few times, there at the bottom end of Bree Street, and Gwen and himself they used to go to a small restaurant to have lunch. But when the campaigns got hot, that was the time he stopped coming. The Movement began the armed struggle. So now the government they banned the Movement and started picking up the leaders everywhere. For a long time they searched for Sibisi but he was always a step ahead of them, you know why?'

Gus and I shook our heads.

'Because Gwen was sending messages to the Movement in the magazine. A spy in the police was giving her information about the police's plans. Now what she would do, she would write these plans in her column, in codes. But in the end Sibisi was arrested and the boers tried to make her to testify against him. She said no. They put her in jail for a few months, they beat her up. But that Gwen, she's a tough somebody that one. She never gave in. Sibisi heard what was happening to her. He sent a message to her in prison. He said testify, you won't be able to tell them anything new. But she refused still. They hurt her, those boers. They made her blind in one eye and now she walks with a limp.'

'She's alive?' I asked.

'She's alive,' Baba Jakes said. 'She's a tough one that. You want to meet her?'

'Yes!' we nodded eagerly.

He gave us directions to her house in Zone 17, Sofasonke.

'Tell her Comrade Jacob sent you, Secretary of the Sofasonke branch of the Movement.'

'Do you mean you were or you still are?'

'I think that needs another night of deep discussion,' he said, 'and another bottle of this.'

As we stumbled out of his warm office into the night, he called after us: 'Don't be surprised by what you see there!'

'Baba,' I said, 'do you know Nhlabatsi the doctor?'

'Of course I do.'

'Well, I am his son. I have seen men and women from the north and the south, with problems of the body and the soul, presidents

158

of countries, yes presidents of countries, ministers of mines, rain queens, impotent policemen and oversexed priests, all of them. And you tell me don't be surprised . . .'

Gus blew the hooter of my car outside.

'That's all I say,' Baba Jakes said.

Saturday evening, April Fool's Day. I fetched Gus from home, hooting outside 213 Colorado Drive and waiting for him to appear; I didn't want to get into an embarrassing exchange of words with that Charmaine of his. He appeared with his thin tie dangling like a pendulum and his camera slung over his shoulder. I had insisted that we look decent for this meeting: I too had polished my Florsheims, wore a cream-coloured shirt, a checked jacket that was getting a little tight for me, and because I wasn't living at home I had asked Gus to bring one of his ties.

'The tie,' I said as he got into the seat that had become his over the past couple of years.

'Got it,' he said proudly, pulling what looked like the old skin shed by a moulting mamba out of his pocket.

'Why did you bother?' I grabbed at the tie but he yanked it out of my reach.

'Now, now,' he said, 'don't bite the hand that clothes you. I had to shove the blooming thing somewhere otherwise Charmaine would've asked all sorts of questions again.'

'Okay, okay,' I said half apologetically. I hadn't been at home in over five days.

'So you're also sleeping malalapipe,' Gus joked but cut short his laughter when I did not join in. 'Where d'you sleep?'

'Right here in the car, in my own backyard.'

After staring at me for a while he said: 'I think you're missing Khensani.' And sniffing the old fish-and-chips odour that had become part of the Volksie's interior, he added, 'And her cooking.'

In answer to that, I said: 'We're early, how about a shot?' I didn't tell him that I wanted to steel my nerves in case there was indeed a surprise awaiting us at the House of Gwen, as Baba Jakes had warned.

'We can't go drunk,' he said.

'A nip and two,' I said, which translated into two singles brandy and a litre of beer each.

During the fortification at the Black Widow's, Gus introduced the Sibisi topic again.

'Hey,' I said, looking at my watch, 'that reminds me: flowers!'

'What d'you mean?'

'Sibisi asked me to take her a bunch of flowers on his behalf.'

'What a time to remember.'

I had an idea. I told Gus what it was.

'Jesus,' he groaned, sitting back in his chair, 'can't we sometimes do things like normal people?'

We walked amongst the headstones, searching for fresh graves. They weren't hard to find: mounds of earth, plastic wreaths, and what we were looking for — fresh flowers. Anthony Ramaite, dearly beloved husband of Lebohang and father of six Ramaites, provided the daisies. Petros Santu Mabandla, a posthumously generous soul who lived for fifty-four years, parted with a huge bunch of carnations, and little Selina Africa, who sadly lived for only five, gave up her posy of dahlias.

Gus and I drew up outside the house in Zone 17, the back seat piled with our floral booty.

'I've been here before,' I said.

'You talking previous life, hallucinations, dagga . . .?'

'This is where I picked up Sibisi, when I was commandeered.'

'So why didn't you tell Jakes that?'

'Because I didn't realize it was the same place. And besides, I haven't been inside.'

The house was third from the corner, and stood out from the rest of the skull and crossbones in the dark street, distinguished by nothing more than two rooms that had been added on to the original, tiny structure, a coat of light-brown paint, and a low, darker-brown precast wall. The kind of abode that elicited the remark, 'Poor but proud' from passers-by.

We walked up a garden path hardly five metres long, which cut the yard into two squares of lawn.

Before we could knock the door swung open.

'Good evening, boys,' said the silhouette, a male voice, an old man's voice . . . Jakes's voice!

'You've come to the funeral?' Baba Jakes asked.

The huge bunch of flowers in my hands was dripping water onto my Florsheims. I held the bunch aside.

'What do you mean, Jakes?' I whispered.

I heard Gus swinging around behind me, fiddling with his clothes as if he were suffocating.

'Gwen's dead,' Jakes croaked.

'Jakes,' I said, 'Jakes Khoza, is this what you mean by a surprise?'

'She died this morning, you fool,' he snarled, exposing a scattering of teeth as sparse and crooked as the headstones we had recently been wandering among. 'Come inside.'

Gus and I followed Baba Jakes and we walked in Indian file through a small lounge from which the chairs had been removed: the nightwatchman leading the way, a journalist in a checked jacket bearing flowers in the middle, a muttering photographer bringing up the rear.

We entered a room full of people. There were men and women of all races — Africans, whites, coloureds, Indians — but nearly all of them were old. A simple pine coffin stood in the centre of the room, covered in an array of flowers, white, yellow, pink, red. A black priest stood at the head of the coffin. It was his voice we heard as we came into the room, but now he stopped talking and looked at *me*.

'Please,' he said, smiling, waving his palms at the coffin.

I stood transfixed, gazing at him.

Gus whispered in my ear: 'Put the flowers on the coffin.'

I stepped forward and laid down the bouquet. I wanted a drink. I stepped back against the wall and squeezed in between Gus and a tall white woman whose black mantilla cast a criss-cross of gloomy shadows on her face.

'Our sister has brought us together here tonight,' the priest continued, 'in a manner which we all know is illegal in this Republic. But in death she has defied these racist laws as she defied them throughout her life. We all knew her and were inspired by her courage and her commitment. The man she loved cannot be with her tonight, but we all know that he will be with us soon. Many centuries of suffering under the madness of racism are finally coming to an end. But now is the time for the biggest fight of all because the closer we get to liberation, the tighter the madmen cling to their power.'

He caught the eye of one of the mourners and a wan smile of recognition flickered across his face.

'Brothers and sisters,' he said, speaking faster now, 'this is an illegal gathering: mass funerals have been banned under the latest state of emergency. We could not simply hand our sister over to the authorities, nor could we notify all the women's groups, the youth, the civic organizations. We could, however, have a quick, quiet funeral and invite just a few of the close friends Gwen knew.' He swept his palms in the air in an all-encompassing gesture.

'There will be memorial services in the near future. In the meantime, the longer we wait, the more chance of danger from the police . . . or of the community turning this into a rally in which we would risk losing many lives. Would anyone who wants to view the body of our sister please step forward now.'

I stepped forward and cast my eyes on Comrade Gwen. I could swear Jakes chuckled as I did so — although Gus said afterwards he was just stifling a sob. The dead woman in the coffin was *white*! Not white as in deathly pale, but white as in European! What was she doing here? In a coffin in the middle of Sofasonke? How had she managed to die in this place? To live in it?

Someone touched my hand. It was the priest.

'Move on please, brother,' he said, indicating again with his clerical gesture that a patient queue had begun to form behind me.

And then, for the second time that evening, Gus and I found ourselves in the cemetery, laying to rest our sister: a woman we had almost met, who had gone about her life in the segregated black township of Sofasonke, who had resisted racism, fallen in love with a black leader, and fought campaigns and done things which I have yet to learn about, which many millions may never learn about — millions whose struggles she fought.

'What do you think?' I asked Gus when we were sitting in a shebeen washing down the grave-dust that still stuck to our throats.

'About the whole episode this evening I have only this to say: never steal from the dead; you'll be returning the stolen property — eventually.' He was very drunk.

So we had missed Gwen by a day. And Sibisi had slipped through my fingers. But where was De Vries in the great scheme of things? I wanted to know because, as far as I was concerned, he was a central figure in all of this. Events in the country were drawing to some climax and De Vries was as much a player as Sibisi was.

That night, when I settled down on the back seat of my car in my yard, I paged again through the presidential diary. It seemed that there was nothing out of the ordinary. But something made me sit up, an appointment dated

4 April TUESDAY

Inauguration of new President in KwaVindaba — if security sorts out the mess between that stooge Phadi and that terrorist Nkadimeng.

I never thought that I would agree with De Vries on anything, but on the question of Phadi we agreed one hundred per cent: that stooge, Phadi, was indeed a stooge. He was a former clerk in a rural clinic who had been enticed into becoming the President of the homeland of KwaVindaba. The enticements included an astronomical salary, a palatial home and a Mercedes Benz, a car he had fallen in love with while washing one that belonged to some petty official in the white government.

KwaVindaba was the latest milestone in the government's pursuit of Separate Development: settling black people in the most infertile dust bowls of the country in order to make space for Germans, Italians, Greeks and white fugitives from liberated Angola, Zimbabwe and Namibia.

Before the coming of Sybrand the Censor, Phadi-isms had been a daily feature of our newspaper.

When Bophuthatswana, another independent homeland, boastfully unveiled its own television station, Bop TV, Phadi remarked enviously at a press conference: 'I also want a TV Bop.'

And when he was taken up in a helicopter to survey all of KwaVindaba, he gazed wide-eyed at the helicopter's control panel and exclaimed: 'Good God! So many clocks!'

Nkadimeng, on the other hand, was a traditional chief who openly supported the Movement and its struggle for national liberation and was resisting independence.

This was all old news that hardly raised an eyebrow any more. All over the country patches of land were being turned into 'independent states' run by feckless government stooges who were building palaces and television studios and airports — even when they did not have any planes.

But there was a reason why this entry in the diary had made me sit up and think. According to a report in our paper, De Jong, the present President of the Republic, was going to be in KwaVindaba on Tuesday to preside at the inauguration of one Wilberforce Phadi.

'And you and I are going to be there,' I told Gus as we drove to work that Monday morning.

'Two hundred kilometres away, up there on the border,' Gus reminded me.

'I've thought about that . . .'

'And . . .?'

'We reopen the file on the Pimpernel.'

'Whatever will Tata say?'

'If Tata had told me what became of De Vries then maybe I wouldn't be doing this. Besides, I think I'm old enough to make my own decisions.'

Old Mahlatini was overjoyed when we told him about our plans to go for the Pimpernel. And as further encouragement, he took out of his drawer some pre- and post-Pimpernel sales figures which we already knew. They showed how sales during the hunt for the Pimpernel had more than doubled.

'If we can only know who he is that would make one helluva story.'

'We'll try our best,' I said solemnly.

'Yeah,' vowed Gus, punching the air with a left jab.

'Hey, guys!' the editor fidgeted with his crotch. 'Look carefully at your cheques this month, I think you will be pleasantly surprised.'

'Ah, Phil,' I said, 'you really shouldn't have.'

'What's all the pally-pally laughing about?' Sybrand asked, looking up from his desk. 'You guys get a raise?'

'No,' I quipped, 'Mr Mahlatini told us you're leaving today.'

'Oh no, I'm not,' he said, looking quite alarmed.

'Well,' Gus said, pointing a thumb in the direction of the editor's office, 'maybe you should go and talk to Phil about this.'

Sybrand jumped up so quickly he sent his scissors flying like a silver bird.

17

The Green
and the Yerrow

'Stop stop stop stop stop,' Gus said as we drove under a huge aluminium hoarding that read:

WELCOME TO KWAVINDABA
Independence Day 4 April

I braked hard and Gus stumbled out of the Volksie. To take a photo of the friendly new sign, I thought. But instead he retched and vomited, hurling the contents of his churning stomach onto the dusty ground of a soon-to-be independent KwaVindaba.

'Oh shit!' I shouted from the car and broke into peals of laughter that echoed over the expanse of dry veld, sending birds squawking and flapping their wings across the blue sky.

'Fuck you, Scara,' he groaned, bent double over his discarded pizza.

I know that it is impolite to describe somebody's regurgitated lunch in lavish detail, but KwaVindaba is a bleak, desolate place: ravaged veld, derelict villages full of widows whose husbands work in the deep mines of the far-away cities, bare-bottomed kids staring aimlessly at the horizon. The brightest spot in KwaVindaba at that moment was Gus's vomit.

Two cars zoomed past, their occupants pulling disgusted faces.

'And fuck you too,' poor Gus groaned.

A third car stopped. The driver got out; a beautiful woman in the passenger seat preferred to stay where she was and avert her eyes from Gus.

'Can't you wait until they build the casinos before you hit the jackpot?' the driver asked, striding towards the Volksie. It was none other than the erudite Sipho Ndabeni, reporter on the *Daily Star*, extra edition. He introduced us to his girlfriend, Nomsa. I gave her a friendly wave, which Gus duplicated limply, and she managed a smile.

'You've also come to see the white man's magic?' I said.

'Wouldn't miss it for anything.' We lit cigarettes, and Sipho took out a clean handkerchief, strode over to our suffering friend and gallantly handed it to him. Gus accepted the hanky with tears in his bloodshot eyes.

'What happened?' Sipho wanted to know.

'Off the record?'

He nodded, cleaning the dust from his sun-glasses with the end of his shirt.

I told Sipho all about it. Gus and I had spent all night at the Airport, a shebeen in Kliptown. I didn't have to tell Sipho about the Airport. It was frequented by the doctors, businessmen and other rich people of Sofasonke and its black surrounds.

The Airport owed its uniqueness partly to the fact that it sold whisky and rum, and partly to the ingenuity of its shebeen queen, Ma Spaza. She had a tape recorder attached to her telephone. On the tape were different sound effects from Jan Smuts Airport, Baragwanath Hospital and the Johannesburg railway station. If, say, a doctor phoned his wife from the shebeen and lied that he was still at the hospital, Ma Spaza would play the hospital tape and his wife would hear in the background such familiar sounds as: 'Dr Dlamini, Dr Dlamini, please come to Intensive Care immediately.'

I didn't tell Sipho this part, but I phoned Khensani from the Airport.

ding dong deeng, Flight 717 for Durban is . . .

'It's me.'

'Scara?' Her voice was sleepy.

'Yes.'

. . . for take-off. Will passengers please . . .

'Are you at the airport?'

'Ja, Gus and I we've got this assignment, we're leaving this evening.'

. . . to Gate 8B immediately.

'What assignment?'

'Top secret, but I'll tell you everything when I get back.'

She sighed. She had heard that one before.

This is a final call . . .

'I mean it this time,' I said.

'Dr Farquharson says you've never been there.'

'There's a good reason for everything.'

Flight 314 from Cape Town . . .

'I bumped into Khumbo day before yesterday. She was excited about some TV thing. What was she talking about?'

'The TV people phoned me last week. They want me to do a TV version of Dear Khensani.'

'You serious?'

'Yes, they're starting a black channel soon.'

'You'll be famous,' I said.

. . . please come to the enquiries counter . . .

'Make that "more famous",' I said.

'Scara,' she said, 'remember that I love you.'

'Me too,' I said. I had a feeling that she was warning me about something.

This is a final call . . .

I got off the phone to find Gus involved in a heated argument with a bunch of Sofasonke businessmen. Gus had asked them about ubuntu, and now he was arguing that it was racist for African people to claim that they possessed a kind of humanism that no other race possessed.

'Why are we slaughtering each other in the streets if we have this ubuntu?' Gus asked. While they were deliberating, he posed another question: 'How does ubuntu work in a black business?'

A handsome young tycoon from Tembisa, Themba Malefane, volunteered an answer: 'You see, my brother, a white man might give his employee a raise after that employee strikes or threatens, but we black businessmen, we go beyond a simple thing as a raise.'

'Pray tell,' Gus said sarcastically. He was very drunk and swaying in his chair.

'If my employee's mother dies, I attend the funeral. And that is ubuntu. That is something far, far better than a raise.'

'The biggest shit I've ever heard,' Gus sneered. That was the point at which all hell broke loose. Gus and I woke up drunk and in pain when the sun came up.

'Watch out for Themba Malefane,' Sipho said.

'What do you mean?'

'Just keep your eyes open, Scara.' Sipho put his sun-glasses back on and drove off.

After Gus had taken enough doses of clean KwaVindaba air to get back into the car, we continued towards the capital, Vindaba.

He asked me please not to speak to him again until he said I could. I left my friend alone as I drove the Volksie through the hot, dusty, treeless expanse cut into two semicircles by a half-tarred, completely potholed road.

At daybreak the next morning people began to descend on the newly built Wilberforce Phadi Stadium. Some came by horse and cart, one or two came by car, but the majority came on callused foot. I joined the crowds. Most were reluctant to talk to me but the little boys and girls, always less taciturn and suspicious than their parents and grandparents, told me they had come for the mahala Coke and chips.

Gus and I sat on the grandstand, in the shade, together with Sipho and other journalists.

This time Gus was clean enough to meet Nomsa, but he spoilt it again by calling her Numsa, the acronym of the National Union of Metalworkers, for which she worked. She glared at him with acrimony (or is it acronymy?) and ignored him throughout the proceedings.

'You've come so far to make a fool of yourself, bra,' I whispered in mock sympathy.

'Well, so has Phadi,' Gus said, checking his camera.

And he was right too.

The best 'curtain-raiser', we all agreed afterwards, featured the Alsatian, the cop and the bottle-thrower. The action began when a one-litre Coke bottle went whistling over our heads and flew straight towards a white policeman who was controlling the crowds (us). The cop had his back towards us, but the vigilant Alsatian saw the bottle coming and dived its unsuspecting master down to the dusty KwaVindaba ground. The missile sailed through the space which the cop's head had occupied only a second earlier.

Visibly shaken, the cop got up and slapped the dust out of his blue uniform. He picked up his cap and issued an instruction to his dog. The dog sniffed at the bottle a few times. Another instruction and the dog ascended the steps of the grandstand. I froze, as the animal seemed to be making its way straight towards me! But it brushed past me, snarling accusingly, and made for a man a few rows back.

The cop, his face red with anger and the scorching heat, hauled the culprit down onto the field, where he administered a few hefty slaps that sent a mixture of cheers and jeers echoing around the stadium. The luckless fellow was led away — possibly to earn the dubious distinction of being KwaVindaba's first criminal.

'An Independence Day that one KwaVindaban will never forget,' Gus said wryly.

For the next forty-five minutes we waited for the action to begin, shifting restlessly in our seats, making snide and smart little comments about Independence Days we had known, watching a scuffle between a few barefoot youths. Then a brass band that had been glinting patiently in a corner of the stadium screeched into action with a clash of cymbals and parched trombones.

This was our cue to stand up and be silent while the Republican national anthem was played. Then a military choir stood to attention and solemnly sang the new anthem. The KwaVindaban tongue does not possess the facility to pronounce the English consonant 'L'. But this did not appear to have bothered the composer, for we were regaled with a chorus that went:

We fighting our country
The green and the yerrow
The green and the yerrow

De Jong, surrounded by an army of bodyguards, emerged from a black, American car. Wilberforce Phadi emerged similarly. The two men, neither of whom had ever run for office in a democratic election, strode solemnly up a red carpet (pink to me, but maybe it was the harsh sunlight playing tricks) to a shady podium, their long-tailed monkey-suits giving them the appearance of a duo of multiracial devils ascending the heights of their nefarious careers.

Then came what a corpulent MC proudly referred to as 'the youngest army in Africa'. This consisted of one hundred and twenty men in shocking-green fatigues and pink berets marching in a column three men deep. They stomped past the two presidents, saluting, and the two men doffed their hats with exaggerated solemnity and held them against their hearts. A commander walked beside the column, barking out commands.

The men were made to march around the stadium. The spectators burst into loud whistles and applause as they passed. But just as they reached our side of the turf, things began to go horribly wrong: they got out of step and stumbled into each other and in the end fell into a heap, raising yet another cloud of KwaVindaba dust.

'Oh my dear God!' the MC's voice boomed plaintively over the speakers. 'Things are not going according to plan!'

Gus was snapping away at the flailing arms and boots of the youngest heap in Africa.

'What the hell happened there?' I called out to him.

Gus took a picture of me, shrugged, and turned back to the heap.

But the explanation soon came buzzing along the talking, laughing heads: it seems that the soldiers had been rehearsing all week, with all the commands given in English. But today the commander, swept up in the mood of patriotism and pride, had decided to surprise his troops with some commands in the vernacular. The word for 'left' in Vindaba was 'phul', and that presented no problem. Unfortunately, the word for 'right' was 'ephulomendaya'.

This was proving to be better than I had imagined. I had come here to the homeland in the ridiculous belief that I would solve the mystery of the missing President and the Minister of Mines. In fact, I was no closer to tracking them down. But I was enjoying my investigations immensely. And the fun was not over yet!

The orange, white and blue flag was lowered and, to the strains of the new national anthem, the KwaVindaba flag was hoisted. At first the flag was quite coy about showing off its colours and emblems, keeping everybody guessing.

'Must be a blazing sun there somewhere,' an old man said. He himself looked like an emblem of ancient sagacity: callused hands on gnarled stick and weather-beaten chin on gnarled hands.

'Assegais embracing a calabash.'

'I think it's a chicken!'

But soon enough a good gust of wind came up to put an end to the speculation that had Africa's youngest nation buzzing. The entire flag had been designed to look like a hessian sack, while a mealie took pride of place in the centre. The green leaves of the mealie had been partially peeled away to reveal the rows of yerrow kernels. The excited buzzing was immediately replaced by a palpable perplexity. What could this mean?

Suddenly a child's voice, the voice of an adolescent boy, blared loud and clear from the giant loudspeakers; the voice had that shy breathlessness that is usually brought about by nervousness or excitement, made even worse by the shock of hearing one's own voice amplified. I attended many an eisteddfod with Mama and was an expert on these things.

The boy began to speak in halting gasps. On the dusty turf down below, Gus was turning around like an insect in a bottle trying to locate the source of the voice. And the two presidents on the podium were sharing this perplexity with as much dignity as the heat and the surprise would allow.

'Mr Presidents,' the invisible boy began, 'on behalf of myself . . .'

'. . . and your friends, and your friends . . .' two or three voices urged excitedly over the loudspeakers.

'. . . and my schoo-oolfriends,' he threw in a few extra vowels to appease those he had overlooked. 'I thank you for teashing me English and for giving me a good land . . .'

'. . . country, country,' his friends urged again like seconds in a boxing ring.

'. . . er country . . . and for giving me a flag that looks like a mealie-meal sack. Now I can wear my flag proudly on my buttocks . . .'

18

Star Wars
and Cattle Cries

The situation looked very bleak indeed for me now. *Clack clack clack*, Gus's queen had jumped dramatically over my queen, a horse and another queen. It was the third time Gus had trounced me that day and possibly the thirtieth game he had won for the week. He was definitely the undisputed champion in Block C of the Johannesburg Prison, also known as 'Sun City'.

This was not my idea of spending a leisurely Saturday afternoon. But I was in prison 'at the pleasure of the President of the Republic' and so was Gus and so was an old acquaintance, a certain Comrade Wounded, who was playing Monopoly in a corner of the communal cell and complaining about the irony of having to go directly to jail and not collect two hundred rand as he read out his fate on a Community Chest Monopoly card.

Comrade Wounded and his youthful comrades had marked their arrival in prison with a marathon toyi-toyi and chant in praise of Sibisi that carried on throughout the night. Once, when he got his breath back, he shouted to me: 'Ah, Mr Reporter, so you've joined the struggle!'

Under the state of emergency we could be held indefinitely — 'De Jong is obviously hard to please,' I remarked to an unamused Gus.

The games that I had been playing here included Monopoly — a South African version, which meant that you could saunter in a silver hat down Jan Smuts Avenue or President Street, and even own property on these expensive Johannesburg thoroughfares no matter the colour of your skin. We also had draughts, snakes and ladders, chess (although this game and draughts could not be enjoyed at the same time by two different groups of prisoners as there was only one board), Chinese checkers, and ludo (also not possible to play when snakes and ladders was in progress as it was on the reverse side of the board).

This Compendium of Games (distributed by Arlenco, PO Box 9162, Roggebaai, 8012) had been presented to us by Justice Raymond Goldberg after the government had reluctantly agreed to a judicial inquiry into the conditions of detainees. The Minister of Police, after much deliberation, had decided that we could have these little amusements. And for his kind efforts we had dubbed the judge 'Father Christmas'.

Of the twenty or so cellmates, I had been one of the first to be detained — at about two o'clock in the morning, in my Volksie, in my own yard, where I had been sleeping to escape the wrath of Khensani and to relieve her of the odours that emanated from me. Well, I had passed out there.

Banging on the windscreen.

I struggled to open my eyes. Figures everywhere, cursing at me and at the mud, they were squelching about in the mud; it had been raining. My heart leapt. Robbers! Hijackers! Come to slit my throat, to kill me for my Volksie.

'Take it!' I shouted at them.

'He's awake,' one of them said.

'Open up.' Another indicated that I should roll down my window. I did and a gust of brisk early-morning air blew into my face.

There were about eight of them, like gigantic ants around a dung-beetle: kicking at the tyres, shining torches underneath, trying to prise open the bonnet. Then I was outside and two of them were in. They found a notebook, a crumpled tie that Gus had once lent me, three empty liquor bottles.

'If jail doesn't kill you, this stuff will,' a white cop warned me.

About thirty township dogs were barking through all this. But my 'friends' were unperturbed.

'What about the house, sergeant?'

The sergeant assured us all that he had not forgotten about the house. They knocked up a frightened and shivering and bewildered Khensani, who clutched at the front of her nightgown and stared at me while they searched the house.

They pulled out drawers, frisked the hems of curtains, felt the floor for loose tiles, shook out a stack of folded newspapers.

When they took me away, I looked hopelessly at my wife while the most ridiculous thought crossed my mind. Dear Khensani, I thought, I won't even be here to help you clear up the mess.

Then followed a ride to John Vorster Square, a few slaps and a few questions and many threats, another ride in a kwela-kwela to Sun City.

Gus was Guest Number Two. The cops had tracked him down to Uncle Joe's, a 'Coloured and Asiatic Bar' where he had spent a long, drunken evening shooting pool on one of those rare occasions when he and I had not gone shebeening together.

A few psychopathic cops had laid into him with fists, boots and rifle butts. One of them had even burst into tears, Gus told me, and continuously spat in my friend's face as he cried out, 'You kaffirs and bushmen want to take away my country, my fatherland!'

They had confiscated Gus's camera and brought him here, groggy and bleeding.

I do not wish to repeat the procedure of interrogation and torture that I had to bear. If you really have to know, find one of those torture stories in a pre-censorship copy of the *Black World*. Any copy. At the end of it all I was given an A4 Croxley Cambric writing-pad and a Bic pen and told to write down my version of the events that led to my detention.

'He is after all a journalist,' one of my interrogators said. 'Maybe the kaffir writes better than he talks.'

Ha ha ha.

Before I was left alone in the 'interview chamber' I pulled the plastic tube out of its yellow casing and checked the level of the ink. I didn't want to be beaten up again all because of an uncooperative pen.

I wrote the following (including what's in the brackets):

My colleague Gus and I were sent on an assignment by my editor, Mr Mahlatini, to cover the Independence Day ceremony and celebrations of that so-called country KwaVindaba. The celebrations proved to be so damn funny that Gus took an immense number (meaning a lot of) photos. He took some pictures of that stupid bantu Wilberforce in his penguin-suit; he took a few shots of a white South African cop and his Alsatian laying into (om te moer of op te fok) a KwaVindaban national; he took some pics of KwaVindaban soldiers tumbling into one another and then falling into the dust; he took a few pics of the new KwaVindaban flag which looks like a

mealie-meal sack; and a few of the President of KwaEtc giving some innocent kid a few warme klappe all because the kid announced, through a
microphone that some fool had left dangling (om los te hang) in the grand-
stands somewhere (probably a stupid security policeman from the Republic
who left it there because he wanted to hear what we all thought about this
big circus where whites hand over the driest, most infertile (waar fokol
groei) bits of black land to black stooges in the name of Grand Apartheid.
Why is it that your most pleasant dreams are always our biggest nightmares?) that this flag was grand enough to wear on his arse.

After the circus Gus and I made for the nearest pub, feeling the need to
turn the arid (droë) KwaEtc dust in our throats into mud. In Vindaba, the
capital city, we popped into the Fountains Bar but were immediately
repulsed by three grotesque (lelike) Afrikaner giants who told us to fuck
off. Gus and I tried to protest. We told them that this was no longer
Republican territory and that apartheid laws no longer applied. The two
giants invited all the other white men to come and listen to the 'kaffir shit'
that these two (meaning Gus and me) were talking. We repeated what we
had said with all these beer- and brandy-breaths around us. They all burst
into raucous laughter and told us to go and fetch old Wilberforce himself so
that they could throw out three kaffirs instead of just two. However, said
one of them, Wilberforce was a sensible kaffir who knew his place, not a
cheeky bastard like the two of us. Then they punched us both and told us to
fuck off.

We walked out of the bar to the Volksie across the road. I got into the
driver's seat. Gus walked around to the passenger seat. He kept his hand on
the door-handle, waiting for me to pull up the little knob to unlock the
door. I shouted at him, as I have been doing for years now, to take his fucking hand off the handle otherwise the door won't open. I was feeling quite
angry and humiliated, and so was Gus, at being chased out of a bar.
Looking through the window of my Volksie I could see Gus chewing on his
bottom lip, which he does when he's angry.

Then it happened.

All of a sudden we heard a helluva bang. Gus ducked behind the
Volksie and I thought he had been shot by those fat guys in the bar. I
looked around towards the bar and saw about two or three of those giants
flying through smoke and glass. It was quite something to see. One of them
had been flung into the street. He tried to get up but he couldn't because he
was minus a leg and an arm. When he realized this he began to scream like
a little baby and two fountains of blood spurted out of him. Gus was shouting from behind the Volksie, 'Oh shit! No more film. Oh God no more
film! No more fucking film!' After the bits of glass stopped raining down
and the cries turned into moans, the police arrived, about four vans with
their dogs.

I never thought that I would be so happy to be thrown out of a bar. And

I swear that Gus and I had nothing to do with the above-mentioned bang. And I swear that Gus did not take a single picture of the whole thing; no suspicious characters anywhere or cars racing away from the scene.

Gus and I drove all the way to the Republic without a single drink, although we've never needed one as badly as we did on that Independence Day.

As soon as we reached Johannesburg we bought ourselves a whole litre of brandy. We just drank and drank until we were both very drunk. I dropped him off in Riverlea and went to the backyard of my own house where I passed out right there in the Volksie.

Believe it or not, that is what I wrote. And it's probably the most liberating piece of writing I've ever done. Written under pressure, no indulgent editing, no lies, no exaggeration, no sensationalism, no fantasy and imagination, and lots of discerning literary judges in boots who eagerly read every word long before the ink was dry.

I was quite certain by now that this detention had nothing to do with my attempts to track down De Vries nor with my being in possession of his diary.

I knew that I was going to get beaten up at least one more time. But, reading over my 'statement', I decided that it was worth it. I had written this thing in a rage and it all came out as a kind of catharsis, angry, sarcastic and insulting.

I wondered later whether this was not the result of my frustration: over the last few months of the state of emergency, every newsworthy fact that Gus and I dug up had been censored. Or maybe it was just the result of being slapped around and humiliated by some white thugs who went about beating up black people with impunity.

If ever you are arrested and thrown into a Republican prison there are a few things for which you have to be prepared: one of them is to be beaten up. The other is to go on a diet of pork. I'm not talking about crispy rashers of bacon in the mornings served up with slices of hot buttered toast and Farmer Brown eggs. Nor am I suggesting choice slices of gammon laid out alongside your favourite veggies.

The stuff we were given every day was boiled, stringy, studded with worms and bulging with fat.

Nobody ever finished his rations of pig fat. Nobody, that is, except Star Wars, so named because of his underpants which were spattered with a galaxy of red, blue and yellow stars, meteors and, after a few months in jail, a couple of black holes here and there. Star Wars had found himself in the tight and vicious clutches of the law after he and an angry band of the Marxist Students for Democracy had burnt a truckload of racist history textbooks destined for Sofasonke high schools.

I gave Star Wars two bits of advice, both of which he ignored.

The first concerned the zest with which he played Monopoly. One day when he was fighting over ownership of Roeland Street, I remarked that it went against his Marxist political beliefs to be fighting so furiously over private property.

He told me to fuck off.

The other piece of advice was more serious as it concerned his health. Star Wars always cleaned up the huge heap of pork on his plate. Then he collected all our uneaten pork and shoved that down too. I warned him about the dangers of eating pig in abundance. 'You could pick up a tapeworm from this pork,' I said. 'It lives in your body, it can even get to your brain . . .'

He told me to fuck off.

Then one night after supper one of the young comrades banged an enamel plate on the steel bars and shouted to the warders: 'uStar Wars uyafa!'

Star Wars is dying! We all ran to have a look-see. And it was true: about a week's worth of pig fat was flowing out of Star Wars, top and bottom. The youth looked up at all of us, his bulging eyes streaming with tears, snot flowing down his cheeks. The warders came and took Star Wars away to the prison hospital, leaving us to clean up the mess! After being hospitalized for a day or two, Star Wars was set free: the State, it seemed, was happier to risk his Molotov cocktails in the cities and townships than to have him soil their prisons.

A few days later I had cause to see the prison doctor too. My reason was far less controversial, but it made for a memorable visit anyway.

After taking a piss early one morning I pulled up my zip and got my penis caught in it. I yelped at the searing pain and, looking down, saw two bright streaks of red travelling down the length of my member. Very painfully I managed to get my poor tool unstuck. But the bleeding would not stop. I told Gus my problem.

'You have to go and get it seen to,' Gus said. 'You never know what shit you might pick up from this filthy place.'

A disturbing memory flashed into my mind: the kid with the pennis the size of a banana at Baragwanath Hospital.

So I called the warder and the next day I was marched off to the prison doctor. My visit to Dr Scheepers was itself not worth writing home about. He was a small, rotund, red-headed and morose white man. When he had studied medicine thirty-odd years ago at one of their tribal universities and afterwards taken the Hypocritical Oath, examining the guts of Star Wars and the penis of Scara Nhlabatsi must have been as far away from his mind as Black Power.

But here he was giving me a thorough examination — by means of a brief interrogation.

'Do you sleep arr-yound?' He thought I had picked up the clap somewhere.

'No.'

He gave me a tube of ointment, some tablets, and told me to 'take it easy'.

Case closed.

But it was the sitting around in the waiting-room that I will never forget. It was his nurse, you see, Mev. Groenewald.

She was a two-metre-high hulk with a fleshy face topped by a nest of mousy hair streaked with grey. Her legs, a pair of stumps, were ribbed with varicose veins. One podgy cheek sported a black mole from which sprouted a long hair; it reminded me of the neglected pot plants I sometimes saw in the kitchen windows of township skull and crossbones. She wheezed as she went about her duties in an unadorned room, intermittently removing her ancient spectacles to blow mist over their lenses and then to rub them on her dirty white smock. She also seemed to be faster from the waist up than she was from expansive hips to ankles covered in rugby socks. It probably had something to do with an unequal distribution of motor neurons. When she blew mist over her lenses the action was executed with alacrity: blow-blow-blow, rub-rub-rub on dirty cuff, then flick back onto bridge of nose. But the walking was executed with protracted slothfulness: a shambling gait from filing cabinet to wash-basin to medicine dispensary.

But she was the first woman I had caught sight of in two months. And I felt a passion for her that caught me unawares. My heartbeat quickened, a wave of adrenalin surged through my body, my breath came out in short, sharp gasps. My thoughts raced with ideas about how we could do it: under the table, with her spread out squarely and me humping away on top of her. And even if the doctor came into the room from his adjoining chamber he would see nobody. Or she could tell him that she had to go to the toilet. The two of us could go together, quickly. We could do it standing up in the ladies', me going down low like a circus performer or poised over her while she perched on the toilet seat, holding onto me in her favourite rugby tackle.

Better still, better still — a brainwave hit me — we could let Dr Scheepers in on our secret. He could keep watch at the door while we did it with all the foreplay the Amazon needed. In return for doc's co-operation and his sentry duty I could do his garden for him as soon as I got out of here, for about six months of weekends. White people seem to like that kind of thing very much.

When I got back to the cell Ngidi called me aside with a knowing grin on his face. Ngidi was a student leader from Tembisa who had been detained three days after me. He was a fat, jovial youth who was forced to retell, for the amusement of every newcomer, the tragi-comic tale of his capture. He had been on the run for several weeks while the police searched tirelessly for him. He was enjoying the fugitive lifestyle tremendously, he told us, the excitement of organiz-ing student meetings and consumer boycotts, as well as taking part in the odd stoning of police.

But one day, slinking along behind a low wall at the Tembisa municipal offices, he saw the cops and, worse, they spotted him! They gave chase, running along one side of the wall. He took to his heels on the other side. When they caught him they hunted around as if for something he had quickly discarded. Then one of them said, 'Where is the bicycle?' So speedy was my chubby activist friend that, looking at the visible top half of his body as he tried desperately to make his getaway, they were convinced he was on two wheels!

Ngidi had also been to see the doctor. He had to be patched up after his captors had shown him how much they had missed him. Now he called me aside and asked conspiratorially, 'Did you also fall in love with her, com?'

June, July and August. The coldest months of the year. By now I was sharing the cell with thirty-nine other people. We had all been brought together because we had committed or were suspected of having committed certain crimes against the state. And, in some cases, because the law had reason to believe that we were *thinking about* committing crimes against the state. The one thing we had in common is that we were all black.

The worst of it was that we never knew when we would be

released. In two weeks, the next day, a year, ten years. Never. 'Charge or release us!' was the silent plea that quivered on our lips throughout those ice-cold months.

Even though the country's newspapers were heavily censored, we were prohibited from reading them. But somehow we managed. Newspapers were smuggled into our cells and we shared them, reading every word, from the latest fads and fashions in Europe and America to the comic adventures of Andy Capp, Hi and Lois, Modesty Blaise, the Lockhorns, Garfield. But about us, the most important people in the world, there was nothing. Even in my own newspaper. Sybrand and his censor friends were doing their work with assiduous enthusiasm.

· We could feel the winter in our bones, where the cold set in and caused a daylong itch as we sat huddled more closely together, absorbing the meagre rays of the short days that filtered through the tiny cell window. We could taste the winter on our chapped lips made worse by constant licking. We could hear it in the cough that seemed to flit from one throat to the other. We could hear it as cellmates hallucinated about coats, blankets, women.

At night we slept beside each other, shoulder to shoulder, woven together tightly like a bamboo mat, inhaling stale breath, sour feet, the stench of shit in the corner toilet. Three times during the cold night someone, a groggy voice, would shout, 'Right!' and we would all roll over onto our right sides. Fitful sleep for another hour or two and then, 'Left!' and we would all roll over again . . . 'Right!'. . . and then morning.

But one night, in the heart of winter, one of our number decided that he had had enough. Comrade Wounded woke us up with a piercing, primeval wail. Gabriel, a fair-skinned coloured from Natal who spoke perfect Zulu, sat up next to me as if in a trance, called out plaintively, 'Yakhal'inkomo!' — the cattle cry at the slaughterhouse — then fell flat on his back and, with a deep sigh, went back to sleep. But the rest of us sat up, frightened. Those nearest to Comrade Wounded tried to comfort him and asked him what was the matter, as if there was no reason in the world for his pitiful moaning. But the cries persisted throughout the night, tirelessly. Eventually the light in the cell was put on and a warder appeared at the door.

The warder asked us what was happening. Several among us had made their own diagnoses.

'He's mad.'

'It's acute depression.'

In the morning the warder brought two security policemen, white men with moustaches.

The moaning persisted.

'What's wrong?' one asked.

'. . . ooooohhhhhaaaaahhhhhhhhhh . . .'

'Mthethwa, what's the problem?'

'. . . eeeyyyaaaggghhh . . .'

'Look, Mthethwa, we know you have gone mad. But here's what we'll do: if you stop your moaning, we'll see to it that you're out of here before tonight.'

Wounded stopped crying immediately. And so he remained in prison with the rest of us for eleven months. He also became the source of whatever mirth was possible in that place for his failed, solo attempt at freedom.

Throughout our eleven months in Sun City we were allowed not a single visitor apart from Judge Goldberg, who was neither a friend nor a relative of any of the inmates.

My only contact with Khensani, if it could be called that, was by reading her advice column in the *Calabash*, which the prison authorities had decided to issue to us together with the *Farmer's Weekly*, a magazine for white farmers, and *Rooi Rose*, for their wives. I read Khensani's column with renewed interest, searching for words, phrases and expressions that were characteristic as if sniffing the air for her perfume long after she had left a room. 'Dear Aunty Khensani', a lovelorn lady from Nelspruit wrote:

My boyfriend, Duma, works in Johannesburg. He comes back only once a month to be with me. Kenneth is Duma's friend. Kenneth lives in Nelspruit. Kenneth wants to be my lover, he says if Duma loved me he wouldn't go and work in Johannesburg. Must I accept Kenneth's kind offer of love?

Khensani's reply was predictable:

No, Dorcas, follow your heart. Kenneth is trying to make you his own. But there is no reason in the world why you shouldn't be faithful to Duma. Is it his fault that he has to work so far from you, but? Surely not?

'No reason in the world', 'surely not', and sentences ending in 'but'. These were Khensani's phrases and I could recall them being used in conversations with me:

'Scara, there is no reason in the world why we cannot be happy together. No matter what these white people do to us, let them not take away our ability . . . and our right, to be happy together but.' Then I'd cringed at the sentimentality of it. But now the recollection brought tears to my eyes.

'Surely not' dredged up less sentimental memories. I stagger out of the Volksie and up to the door of my skull and crossbones. I knock, I hear her footfalls as she makes her way to the door. She opens it, stares at me with sleepy, sad eyes and says: 'Surely not, Scara.'

'Follow your heart' was a new one. And this unsettled me.

One night I dreamed of Khensani: I was walking aimlessly down a busy city street, winding my way through the vendors who were taking up more and more pavement space. I lifted my eyes high enough to look into a shop window I was passing. In a whites-only restaurant I saw the legs at the tables nearest the window. There, among all the white children's legs swinging happily, the legs crossed over each other, the legs stretched out in flannels, was a pair of brown legs in stockings. And on one of those legs was a mole, a dark spot which I knew. I looked up into Khensani's eyes. She was looking at me, smiling. I stared at her. She was speaking to me. I could not hear her behind the thick, bulletproof, plateglass window. But her lips moved and formed the words: 'Come, Scara, it's you I've been waiting for, what took you so long? Surely you know it's okay now, come inside . . . follow your heart.' I rushed towards the door — and found myself stumbling up the steps into Gus's caravan.

With every day that cast its shadows on the concrete prison I grew more and more desperate to speak to my wife, to tell her that I loved her. To convey a few words to her. Late one night, while everyone was sleeping, a plan came to me.

I woke Gus and explained it to him.

'You would need the cooperation of Visagie,' he said.

'But it doesn't mean he would know what was going on,' I said. Who was warder Visagie?

A few weeks after I was detained, the Young Lions — Comrade Wounded and his fellow fighters — were brought in, breathless, kicking and screaming. From the moment they arrived they showed their belligerence and uncompromising radicalism. They screamed out their wrath every night, cursing the 'System' and swearing revenge. All this noisy anger achieved nothing but only served to make life unpleasant for their cellmates who were not involved in this form of protest.

There was also heavy fighting among them. There were the Pan Africanists, who seemed to be bereft of any worthwhile ideology beyond their chants of 'Kill the Whites'. And there were the non-racialists or Charterists, as they called themselves, after a charter in which they promised the earth to everyone: houses, cars, jobs, the works. There shall be, there shall be, there shall be went the charter's biblical decrees.

These young firebrands showed very little understanding of the ideologies which they claimed to follow. A third ideology, that of white racism, had deprived them of an education that could make at least some of the simpler aspects of their beliefs understandable to them.

But what they lacked in education they made up for in their hatred of whites, their intolerance of opposing views and their inexhaustible energy.

We would be walking in single file down a corridor to fetch our food or to exercise. The Young Lions would sing a freedom song, their hands held in the clenched-fist salute. Then suddenly screams and the pounding of fists against a skull. One group had spotted a lone member of the other group. The line would collapse into chaos as bodies piled onto each other, enamel plates were turned into weapons and blood spurted.

Enter Visagie and his men with teargas, quirts and rubber truncheons.

The Young Lions also had a habit of flinging their enamel plates from our second-storey cell windows to the cement courtyard down below. It needed only for one youth's mind to snap, for one dish to go sailing down to the courtyard, and scores would follow, in an ear-shattering clash of metal on concrete.

Enter Visagie and his men to announce that none of those who threw away their plates would be fed until they fetched them from the yard and apologized to the prison authorities.

This would be followed by a two-day hunger strike, half planned and half imposed, until one by one they went down to fetch their plates.

After one of these episodes Visagie tried another tack. He called a few of the older inmates, including me and Gus, into his office and asked us what we thought about the rowdy element.

This was dangerous ground and Visagie knew it. None of the six or seven of us present in his office wanted to cooperate in any way with the authorities, even if it was against the 'rowdy element' who were making life unbearable for everyone else.

'What do you say, Chief?' He was looking at me.

'Well, Voortrekker, I say nothing.'

'Who told you to call me Voortrekker?'

'The same person who told you to call me Chief.'

He nodded, smiling.

'Look,' he said, 'I haven't called you here to ask you to spy on your people. But no amount of shit from them is going to lead to anyone's release.' Visagie was not a man who said very much. In his line of work he probably never needed to: a slap in the face calmed down a loud-mouth, a German shepherd had the same effect on a crowd, a bullet silenced a stone-throwing youth for ever. This time he pushed a typed sheet across the table for us to read. I began to read it in silence but Visagie suggested that I read it out loud. It was a memo from a Captain Joubert:

> You have my permission to take extreme measures to contain the unruly behaviour in Blocks B and C at the prison. If solitary confinement and beatings do not solve the problem then you must resort to removing the perpetrators from the cell altogether.

Visagie read my thoughts and nodded. 'Of course, it could have been written by me,' he said. 'But there is only one way of finding out, isn't there?'

None of us said a word.

'You are the responsible ones here. Do something.'

He had a point. We agreed to go back and speak to the Young Lions. So I saw Gus's persuasive tongue in action once again. Behind the lens he had become an almost silent recorder of events, and I had forgotten what he was capable of.

'Look, you bastards,' he told them, 'we are all here for some political reason or other. We are steeped in Marxism, Communism, Africanism, you name it. But let's take a leaf from the book of the great Che Guevara. To those who are tortured in the dirty cells of El Salvador, Nicaragua, Cuba, he says, and I quote: "Give voice to your outrage in the campaigns in the ghettos and show your mettle in the streets. But in the clutches of your oppressor, keep your anger hidden deep in your heart. For to reveal your rage to the enemy shows weakness of the extreme kind." Now I know that there is not a man amongst us who has not read these inspiring words. But we do not live by them. Why not?'

This seemed to do the trick. They quietened into a sulking pact. The fighting, swearing at the warders and throwing down of enamel plates stopped.

'I didn't know you were an expert on the writings of Comrade Che?' I said to my friend.

'What writings?' he said. 'I just hope these hotheads never ask me to repeat that quote.'

Enter Visagie.

'I see there have been some changes, Scara.'

I had no desire to exchange ideas on prison reform with him. I nodded. But as he walked away I called: 'Voortrekker?'

He still liked the joke and grinned. 'Ja.'

'I'm in love.'

This achieved the expected reaction.

'Don't talk shit to me, Scara,' he said.

'Not with you, man, your lips are too thin.'

He smiled. 'And my bum is too small, I suppose. Why do you blecks like your women to have such massive arses, Chief?'

'If I told you you would want one and then you'd get into trouble with your government.'

'Look, Chief, I'm not here to help you with your love problems . . .' He began to walk away.

'Visagie,' I called out to him. 'I don't want your advice, I just want you to post a letter for me.'

He turned around to show me a stern face. 'You're in jail, jong, not in some kaffir hotel in Nairobi. No visits, no phone calls, no letters.'

'Look, this is a letter to an advice column in a magazine. Just to ask advice about how to get back the woman I'm in love with when I get out of here.'

'Give it to me, let me see.'

I fetched the letter which I had written to 'Dear Khensani'. Visagie put it in his pocket without even glancing at it and glared at me. 'What are you trying, Scara?' he said, and swaggered away in his lazy gait, his keys jangling at his waist.

When I saw him the next day he simply wagged a finger at me and walked past the cell.

'It was worth a try,' I told Gus.

Three weeks later, we opened the *Calabash* and there it was:

Dear Khensani,

I need your help. I am deeply in love with a woman but I have not seen her for a long time now due to difficult circumstances. But my problem is that even when I did have the time to be with her, I wasted it. I once went with her to visit her father in a far-away country. We were truly in love then and ate whole chickens and learned new words such as 'expectorate'. But later I just spent my time drinking and chasing dreams that are still to be dreamt. As soon as I have the opportunity again to be with her I want to go straight to her and be with her for ever. Do you think she will be waiting for me?

Dreamer
Sofasonke

The reply:

Dear Dreamer

Something tells me this woman has loved you for a very long time and all. She seems to me to be a woman I know down to the bottom of my own heart. But she stopped crying and stopped hoping long before you left. Now she cries and hopes again, but her tears are not the same, her sadness is a different kind and her hopes are different. And now she has what she has always wanted; it is what she wanted with you but which you refused to give her. When you see her again there will be joy, but mostly sadness because a part of your lives has come to an end.

Among the illustrious company I kept in my first letter to an agony aunt was a young miner who signed himself 'Non-believer' from Denver. He did not believe that women menstruated and was convinced that his girlfriend padded herself up for six days a month to rest from his insatiable appetites. Then there was 'Soraya' from

Lenasia whose husband neglected to comb out and wash his luxuriant beard so that, during lovemaking, her nose was forever buried in unpleasant smells, among which she numbered masala, chilli, dhunia and ginger. 'Worried' of Carletonville came straight to the point: 'I am pitch-black and fat as a pig. What must I do?'

And if that was not enough, there was also a PS at the end of the column: Khensani will be on two months' maternity leave, but she will leave you in the very capable hands of Khumbo.

The next time I heard Visagie coming along with his keys jangling, I stood by the cell door. As he passed I called out softly:

'Thanks.'

'Don't mention it,' he said.

SECRET TALKS BREAKTHROUGH

Those were the words that greeted us one morning when the *Daily Star* was hoisted up to our cell from the courtyard below. After the whistling and the toyi-toying and the freedom songs had died down, I was elected to read the main story, and probably the biggest story in the history of the Republic since the Dutch landed on these shores three and a half centuries ago 'for refreshment and to stay a while'.

The contents of the story were summed up in five points alongside big blobs:

- Sibisi to return
- Armed struggle to be suspended
- Government of National Unity to be formed
- All political prisoners to be released
- Negotiations to start immediately

I looked up and saw Visagie standing at the cell door. I walked over to him, my journalist's instinct suddenly rekindled in the excitement and euphoria.

'How do you feel about it?' I asked him.

'Relieved,' he said. 'Now you can look after yourselves or kill yourselves, whatever you plan to do with this freedom.'

19

Freedom

We were released on a Tuesday morning in the month of February. We went to a huge waiting-room where we were given back our belongings: keys, jackets, ties, belts, shoelaces. We signed a document declaring that we were alive and in good health at the time of our release.

'And then what happens if you shoot me after I sign?' Gus asked Visagie.

He was in no mood to answer my friend's frivolous question. He handed each prisoner five rands, a gift from the State, to catch a taxi home.

There was a child on the taxi, a little girl on her mother's lap. I stared at the child: I had not seen one of those in many months. Gus stared too and could not help tweaking her sticky cheeks.

An elderly coloured couple, both drunk, stumbled into the taxi after us. The woman wore a red scarf which was tied underneath her chin. The man was a scrawny skeleton in a dirty white shirt and even dirtier grey flannels. They both brought with them a miasma of stale liquor, and shapeless packets of stuff that crackled and creased on their laps.

The driver called for all fares. We paid. It had doubled since I had last been on a taxi.

'Pay the driver,' the man ordered his wife.

'Me?' the woman said indignantly. 'Not me, you.' She jabbed a finger in his face.

'Rebecca, don't be silly,' the man said, 'you got the housekeeping so you pay.'

'Housekeeping, ha! What housekeeping? If there's housekeeping there's gotta be a house. Where's the house? That money is gone, like a bird.' She fluttered her hands, stuck her face derisively in his and went, '*Kiep-kiep-kiep.*'

'Rebecca jou moer man!'

Such vile language Rebecca would not accept. She retaliated with a smack that landed squarely across the man's eyes. He flew back against the seat and let go of his packets, which fell to the floor between the legs of the other passengers.

'Try that again,' he warned feebly, 'just try that again and you've had it.'

'Hey!' The driver slammed his hands on the steering-wheel. 'Hey hey hey hey hey! There's people here who want to get home. Take out your fares and pay — or fuck out of the taxi.'

'Okay, okay,' Rebecca said, 'don't get a baby here.'

Gus and I grinned at each other. Oh, it was good to be back in the world again, with the drunks and the taxis and the foul language and the thugs.

And the children! Dirty ones with snot running down their faces. Little boys pissing arcs into the air. Babies adding to the noise with their wails and their laughter. I stared at them as if I were a lunatic, watching their every move: the way their fingers disappeared into their noses and scratched away contentedly, the way little girls stepped about in their mothers' high-heeled shoes, pretending to be women until they fell down and reverted to being little girls again, crying their hearts out. But by far the best was to watch the little ones walking about with mummy or granny, gripping a tuft of the adult's clothing with one hand, sucking the thumb of the other hand, and so secure that they could be led to the ends of the earth.

Gus got off at Afcol, a huge furniture factory on the edge of Riverlea. He waved to the mine dump, the yellow mountain in the distance that cast a veil of dust over his township. He was home. He waved to me, punched the air and was gone, skipping down the road like a child.

The taxi took me all the way into Sofasonke. I got off three blocks from my parents' skull and crossbones. A small group of boys, barefoot in the street, kicked around a tennis ball. A little girl clung to a fence like an insect, chanting something in her baby language. A woman on her knees applied red polish to her stoep. I walked up Mapetla Street trying to make myself invisible, like a schoolboy with shit running down his legs: the last thing I wanted now was to bump into old friends and be forced to exchange courtesies before seeing my parents.

My plan worked — up to a point. Ntate Ngwenya, my parents' friend and neighbour, was surveying the street from his gate. His ancient eyes fell upon me and he gaped. His mouth opened up like a sink-hole. He stumbled out of his gate and into my parents' yard. He turned to me and gestured with a finger against his oily lips that I should wait exactly where I was.

'Let me break this news to your father and mother first so that the shock will not shock them.'

I nodded and watched him run up the little path. Then he shouted, 'MaScara!' and fainted, falling flat and raising a cloud of dust: to use a football metaphor, here was a goal and an injury at the same time, and the grandstand came alive with a cacophony of cheers and groans. Mama came running from the backyard. She saw me, stopped dead in her tracks and ran back. In no time she reappeared with a broom and rushed forward to sweep a path for me, ululating and bringing neighbours streaming into the streets, laughing, whistling and dancing.

Tata grinned like a child when he saw me and left immediately, in search of a beast to be slaughtered. 'We must thank our ancestors for this day,' he said. 'Come, Ngwenya. Let us go and find something nice and fat.'

Ntate Ngwenya slapped the dust out of his old clothes. His fainting spell had lasted less than a minute, but a jubilant Tata teased that he had been out for hours and had missed a great home-coming.

I watched Tata walk out of the yard and down the street with his friend. I realized then that my father was an old man. All the way down the street people were still coming out of their yards to see what the commotion was all about. Like a child Tata called out to them, 'My son Mandla, he's back. Go and see!'

After a bath and a hot meal, Mama told me about Khensani, repeating what I already knew. She was pregnant. The father of the child was from Tembisa on the East Rand. She lived there now, but came regularly to visit my parents. She had come to tell them about the baby one Sunday morning while her new man waited outside in his car. Khensani had cried and said that she had wanted so much to live with me, but that I had refused to make a life with her, drinking and chasing ghosts and old men for a living. Our house had been sold.

'Things are not so good, my son. But at least you are home. This tonight I am going to a save us,' Mama promised herself, unwittingly presenting me with another gift from her store of malapropisms: she was going to a church service. The March of Africa to Zion Church would thank God on my behalf for my safe return.

Mama took me into the tiny bedroom which had been mine a long, long time ago when catapults dangled from the wall and caterpillars crawled in jars. Long before my obsession with men with guns in their hands and tapeworms in their arses. There was a bed in the room again, and my computer and clothes in a cupboard.

Mama left me alone to touch my things and unpack my thoughts. Solitary confinement, I said to myself, and heard my voice croaking all around me. Gus, as soon as possible, I would go and find Gus, and drink.

But I would never drink with Gus again.

20

. . . And Death

Gus was murdered. Just a couple of days after we were released from jail. Gus, who had survived so many encounters with the police, from our schooldays in Swaziland to our days as journalists in the Republic.

We swaggered down dark alleys in Sofasonke, blind drunk, past thugs who had killed for ten cents. And he survived. We found ourselves diving for cover and dodging fists, flying glass and bottles. He survived. We stumbled into gun battles in war zones between cops and comrades. We were ordered away from a field where police had just killed children too young to know about all the things they had been deprived of. We walked off, in the cross-hairs of three or four rifles, rounded a corner. And as I took a deep breath of air, Gus aimed his camera at the cops and their bloody backdrop, clicked the shutter several times and shouted, 'Move, Scara, move!' And move we did. We survived that one too.

We even came through eleven months in Sun City. Then three days after our release I get a phone call from Riverlea. Gus is dead.

'No no no don't talk shit whoever you are,' I said. I was back behind my desk at the *Black World*.

'He was murdered, my bra,' he said sympathetically. 'You know me. I'm Spotty. Remember that night in the caravan, telling jokes and watching that thing about De Vries on TV . . .'

I cast my mind back more than a year to a night when I called on Gus to tell him about my travels with De Vries and Comrade Wounded and a man who went by the name of Jerry. Now I remembered Spotty, sipping beer through his moustache and laughing.

'Where was he murdered?'

'Right there in his caravan.'

'Who did it?'

'Remember Lennie . . .?'

Gus's killer was that slovenly little bastard with the scarred face. To think that we had sat there drinking together!

I heard for the first time that Lennie and Gus's wife had been having an affair and that they were equally disdainful of Gus's friendship with me and disgusted that he worked for a 'kaffir newspaper'.

At the funeral I got the details of my buddy's death.

Gus died telling a joke.

It was the Thursday evening after our release. Gus, Lennie and Charmaine were sitting and enjoying a few drinks. Apparently Gus was not at all suspicious of Lennie and his wife. He was in the same jovial mood he was in when I last saw him, skipping off to his house on wheels.

Lennie had just finished telling a joke which reminded Gus of another. I knew this joke, as did our editor and our once-resident censor, who had both begged to hear it several times, laughing at the way Gus mimicked the singsong Cape coloured accent and the slight drool that trickled from the corner of his mouth, all part of the joke which lasted a full five minutes.

'One night the Southeaaster blows Gammat into a bar there in Athlone. The guys in the bar look up and they see Gammat, the old skollie, shaking his head and muttering to himself. What's he saying? They they hear it: "I don't believe it, I don't believe it. Can that man park a car, Jesus, can that man park a car!" still muttering, and spitting on the floor. One of the guys says to him, "Sis man, Gammat! Stop spitting like that. This is a respectable place!" But Gammat he just goes on spitting and muttering and wiping his mouth as if he's heard nothing. Eventually the barman goes up to him. "Hey Gammat ol' pellie," the barman says, "what's 'e matter wit' you today man. Why you messing in de bar like dis." But Gammat, he doesn't even look up. He jus' go on spitting and shaking his head and saying to himself, "Jesus that man know how to park a car . . ." Then he orders a glass of wine and mutters again . . .'

Well, the one thing Lennie did not like about the joke was its length.

'Hurry up with this stupid joke!' he demanded.

'Since it's my house I think I'll take as long as I damn please.'

But he never did get to the punchline. Lennie got up calmly, went to the drawer, took out a bread knife, came up behind Gus and slit his throat.

A few weeks later I found good news for Gustav waiting at the office. An American magazine had published half a dozen of Gus's photographs in an issue focusing on Southern Africa. Six complimentary copies of the magazine were on my desk together with a cheque for five hundred dollars and a letter expressing interest in seeing more of his work. I had to take this news and the cheque — which would turn into quite a handsome amount in Republican currency — to Charmaine in Riverlea. There were a million places that I would rather have been, but I thought about it long and hard and decided that I owed it to my dead comrade.

When I pulled up outside the house, Gus's little boy, Derek, was playing in the sand near the gate. He looked up inquisitively and gave me a friendly smile when I stepped out of the car, the same smile that used to light up Gus's face whenever he greeted someone — especially a shebeen queen.

'Hallo uncle,' he said, slapping a stick against fawn corduroy pants that were far too big for him and surely too hot for the summer weather.

I went down on my haunches and ruffled his hair, sandy from the headlong games in the dust.

'Where's your mummy, my lightie?'

'In there,' he told me, pointing to the caravan.

'Will you go and call her for me?'

He nodded and ran up towards the caravan, choosing a route along a fence so that he could rattle his stick against it, and called out to his mother.

She emerged from the caravan and walked down towards me. When she was close enough to recognize her unexpected visitor, a sneer spread across her face.

'Hallo, Charmaine,' I said, extending my hand. I had rehearsed this courtesy on my way here.

She shook my hand once, limply.

A stocking covered her head, she wore a nightie even though it was well past noon, and her feet were lost in a pair of Gus's old shoes which had been cut open in front and cut away at the heels to turn them into slippers.

'What d'you want?' she asked curtly while little Derek stood between us, watching us both with wide-eyed curiosity. She did not invite me into the caravan.

'Gus's photographs . . .'

'I burnt up all that rubbish,' she said, cutting me short.

I was hardly surprised by this revelation, which was delivered with triumphant rudeness while she took hold of her son and held him up against her thigh as if it had suddenly become clear that I was some kind of bogeyman. The boy received this message clearly and his body stiffened as he looked up at me.

'That's a pity,' I said, sighing deeply while I waited for some curious reaction. It came soon enough.

'What d'you want with his things?'

'There are people in America who want to publish his photos. They wanted to give you lots of money — about three thousand rand for them . . .'

'Don't lie to me!'

This threat triggered off a response from Derek. 'Don't lie for my mummy,' he said, waving a grimy finger at me. 'My mummy's gonna burn your mouth with chillies.'

'I won't lie to your mummy about your daddy,' I told him. 'And to prove it I've even got a cheque for five hundred dollars for your daddy. That's one thousand five hundred rand.'

'My daddy's in heaven,' he said boastfully.

'Where? Where's the cheque?' Charmaine dared me to prove my claim with the same impudence as her son. I walked over to the car to get it. I sat in the driver's seat and took it out of the cubby-hole. Stapled to the cheque was a letter from the editor thanking Gustav Kinnear for his photos, requesting more of the same and hoping that 'your country's terrible problems are solved before you are all killed'.

'Here it is,' I called from the car, and would have given it to my friend's widow if she hadn't sent Derek to fetch it from me. But that is what she did, so I drove off. A little bit of courtesy was all she had to show — not so much for me as for the work which her late husband was so committed to. I think that as I drove off I saw a face peering at me from behind the curtains in the caravan. Someone's murderer was possibly out on bail. But I could have been mistaken.

21

Umshado weZinkawu

When I got back to the office after seeing Charmaine there were two sensational pieces of news waiting for me. The first was for the consumption of the country and the world: Sibisi would be arriving at Jan Smuts Airport late that afternoon, and a press conference would be held there and broadcast live on television. The second was personal: Phone Khumbo. Urgent.

'Scara,' Khumbo said, 'Scara . . . Scara . . . Khensani's in hospital.'

'What happened?' Did things always happen this fast or had I slowed down since I came out of prison?

'I don't know, we've just received the news — oh.God, what're we going to do? I think Themba was killed.'

'The child?'

'No, the child's father.'

'I mean is the child okay?' I said.

'Yes. It's a little girl . . .' She was sobbing, stumbling over her words.

'Who, who, who killed Themba?' My colleagues within earshot hardly looked up. Telephone conversations like these were an everyday occurrence.

'The comrades. At a roadblock.'

'So what am I supposed to do?' That must rank very high on the list of the stupidest things I've ever said in my life on the planet Earth. It was a remark which for a long time changed the way Khumbo looked at me.

'Ask yourself that, Scara, not me,' and she slammed down the phone. It rang almost immediately. Khumbo wasn't finished with me yet. 'Please, Scara,' she said, and then her voice rose suddenly to a shout: 'Go and see your wife or are you too busy chasing Presidents? The black President or the white President, it's all the same to you, you useless bantu!'

'Okay, okay,' I said, 'let's be rational about this. I have also lost a friend. Gus is dead. My best friend is dead.'

'You think I don't know that, Scara? You think Khensani doesn't know? She phoned me in tears when she heard about Gus. She wanted to get hold of you, to be with you.'

I took the rest of the afternoon off and went to Ma Two-Tone's. I chose the place because it was usually deserted in the afternoons. I ordered half a bottle of brandy, the first since I was out of prison, and a litre of beer. Ma Two-Tone put some jazz on her crumbling record-player.

'When are you getting CD technology, Ma Two-Tone?'

'Is that a new kind of beer?'

'Never mind,' I said, blowing smoke into the sunlight that filtered through the window.

It must've been something in my voice that made her stop dead and turn around. She stared hard at me. 'Sibisi is coming,' she said. 'We'll celebrate and the old liquor will taste like new liquor, don't you worry.' She walked out of the lounge.

And in walked Makaps — with a white woman in tow, a frizzy-haired Afrikaner with a high-pitched voice and thin legs.

'Hey Scara, my bra,' he said. 'Viva! Viva Sibisi, viva!'

I greeted him softly, searching my brain for an alternative drinking-hole, more deserted than Ma Two-Tone's.

'This is my big bra and colleague,' he told the woman. 'You remember what I told you about the Black Pimpernel?'

'Uhum,' she nodded.

'Well, meet his creator.'

'He's the one!' she said laughing. They were both tipsy.

Makaps took the woman's wrist and raised her hand into the air. He said to her: 'Say "Viva Scara!"'

'Viva Scara!' she said, smiling at me.

He put a hand on my knee and offered his condolences for the death of Gus. 'I saw his picture in the *Black World*,' he said. 'These coloureds are violent. Give me Sofasonke any time. But we'll be voting soon and then we'll move into the suburbs, hey doll?'

'Uhum.'

'Fetch us two glasses, baby.'

While she skipped off to the kitchen, Makaphela turned to me excitedly. 'You want a story, Scara, I got one for you.'

'I don't want no story,' I said.

'Me and Pam, we just got married.'

I stared at him, at the gap in his teeth, his scarred face, his poor clothes. He removed from his pocket his brand-new identity document and flipped to where the marriage certificate had been pasted in — today!

Just then, Pam returned with two glasses and Makaphela helped himself to my brandy, pouring two doubles which could easily have been mistaken for triples.

'To a new country,' she said, 'and a new marriage.'

'Tell him about my mother,' Makaphela said . . . 'no no, first tell him how we met.'

'Even about the . . . stealing?' she asked doubtfully.

'Why not? This man is my brother.'

'He was stealing a car, *my* car, and I caught him red-handed and it was love at first sight . . .'

'Hey, baby!' Makaphela swooned and kissed her.

'Now about my mother,' he said, kissing her again.

'The first time Makaps took me to meet his ma, you know what she called me?'

'Listen to this one, my learned friend,' Makaps said from the edge of his seat, as if he too was hearing the story for the first time.

'Tell us,' I said.

'Miesies Pam.'

Makaps grabbed his Ayers from his head, smashed it into his face and shook with laughter.

'She calls the makoti Miesies Pam?' I said, chuckling despite my mood. It was funny, funny enough to make a pallbearer drop a coffin, and I laughed with them.

'And you know all those apartheid laws, they no more there,' Pam continued. 'But his ma still draws the curtains when we sit close in the lounge so that the police won't see us.'

I drank a toast to their happiness. Then I had to go.

I drove to Zodwa's home. She was playing with friends in the street outside. Engrossed in their game, they at first did not notice the Volksie pull up on the pavement a few metres from their den. I watched their game for a while.

A boy stood in the centre of a circle. Zodwa, barefooted and dusty as always, walked up to him. 'Sawubona, Mr Sibisi,' she said.

'Sawubona, Khensani,' he said. 'What is your order?' My wife's name was now permanent, I realized with a lurch somewhere in my heart.

'Ice-cream,' little Khensani said. 'Two. The milky ones in the cone.'

The boy pulled two imaginary ice-creams out of the air and handed them to her. She took them and licked them both as if they were dripping. The den of kids collapsed with laughter. Then somebody nudged her, and she swung around and saw me. The imaginary ice-creams disappeared and she walked up to the car.

'Have you heard the news?' I asked.

'Yes, Aunty Khensani has got a baby.'

'Have you seen the baby yet?' I asked the question because she did not seem at all excited.

She shook her head.

'Well, would you like to come with me?'

She gazed into my face. Here was a dilemma more monumental than choosing a dress amongst hundreds: the devil was offering her a lift to see her favourite angel. Then she made up her mind and became suddenly excited.

'I must first clean myself,' she said and begged me to wait for her while she ran into the bleakest-looking skull and crossbones on that bleak street.

While I waited for her I continued to watch her friends playing their game. I flipped through an old copy of the *Black World*, pretending no interest at all in their antics. Soon their self-consciousness disappeared and the game carried on. A boy strode up to a group of five or six boys and girls standing expectantly in the den.

'I am Sibisi,' he announced, in a bold, old man's croak, his chest pushed out importantly.

'Viva Sibisi!' his peers chanted.

'What do you want?' he asked them.

'Toast and fried eggs,' said one.

'A police dog,' said another.

'A car and money for movies.'

'Come to my office tomorrow,' Sibisi said gravely.

On the way to the hospital, I warned little Khensani that Khensani might be sad when she saw us.

She just looked out of the window, determined not to talk to me. She wore a clean pink dress and fairly new black shoes. Her hair was combed back and held in place by a blue Alice band.

'How's school?' I asked her.

She did not answer, sticking out her chin the way Khensani used to.

'Why won't you talk to me?' I remembered that my wife would always tell me why she was cross with me; if little Khensani wanted to emulate her, she would have to tell me too. After a while she answered with a question.

'Why did you hurt Aunty Khensani?'

'I did not hurt her!' I said indignantly. 'The comrades . . .' I hesitated, but then decided that she probably knew anyway, '. . . the comrades killed her friend.'

'She says you hurt her very much.'

'I didn't, I was in jail.'

'Even before you went to jail.'

'How?'

'In her heart.' She kept her face turned away from me.

I didn't know what to say.

We drove on in silence until I saw an ice-cream cart on the side of the road. I stopped the car.

'Viva Sibisi, viva!' the vendor said, ringing his bell and strolling over to the car. His cart was plastered with stickers blaring out the slogans of the Movement.

'What's your boss gonna say about all that?' I asked him, pointing at the stickers.

'Hah!' he laughed. 'My boss put them there! Like this we sell a lot of ice-cream. Tomorrow we sell in the suburbs, we take them off.'

'You want ice-cream?' I asked Khensani.

'No,' she said emphatically.

'My boss was wrong,' the vendor laughed, peering curiously at this child who didn't want ice-cream in the middle of summer. He rang his bell to get her attention but she stared stubbornly ahead.

'You know this hospital we're going to,' I said to her, 'it's not Baragwanath, it's a white hospital, very smart. And if you want to go in there you have to have an ice-cream, it's their rules.'

She looked startled, her poise slipping away.

'Ask him,' I pointed to the vendor.
''S true,' he nodded.
We drove off licking our ice-creams.

Khensani was sitting up in bed, holding a baby girl in her arms, a wrinkled little face with damp hair, twitching and frowning as she slept through one of her first dreams. Khensani's hair was also damp and her face looked bruised. When she saw us she looked up with her sad eyes and she cried for a long time, while little Khensani and I held her, weeping too.

When the tears stopped she told me what had happened. Her boyfriend, Themba, had driven her to the hospital this morning to have the baby. As they made their way out of Tembisa, a crowd of youths stopped the car, chanting and dancing and burning tyres in the street, celebrating the return of Sibisi. They demanded to know which political party Themba and Khensani supported. Themba gave the name of the Pan Africanists, Khensani instinctively chose the Charterists, hoping that one of them would be spared. Themba had chosen the wrong one.

'And they put a gun to his head and shot him dead.' Then she cried again. Through her sobs she finished her story. 'More youths came and fought with those who killed Themba. Two of them took Themba's car and drove me to the hospital.'

Later we turned on the television in her room to watch the historic home-coming of Sibisi. Yes, it was the old man I had driven to safety in my car fourteen months ago. Jerry. The name suited him. He sat blinking and smiling behind a bank of microphones, and journalists from all over the world threw questions at him. Scores of cameras clicked and flashed. An image of Gus came into my head.

I heard a voice I recognized and Sipho Ndabeni of the *Daily Star* rose from his seat.

'Mr Sibisi,' he said, clearing his throat. 'The youth in the townships are not so sure about this easily negotiated settlement. They don't believe that you are really Sibisi, the President of the Movement and the man who fought so valiantly in the campaigns of the fifties. That Sibisi was an uncompromising fighter, they say, while you have made deals with the white oppressors . . .'

Sibisi joined in the nervous laughter that crackled through the hall.

'Well, I discarded my passbook a long time ago, so I do not have that crucial document any more to prove who I am. But there is a journalist among you . . .' he craned his neck and looked around the room '. . . he works for the *Black World*. He can attest to my identity. Many months ago, after I had been secretly released by De Vries, he drove me to the border. There have been many rumours about my release but, in answering your question, I can now reveal the truth.'

'Scara,' Khensani said, 'that's you he's talking about.'

'Shh,' I said, turning up the volume of the TV just a little. I wanted to hear what Sibisi had to say.

A hand holding a glass of water appeared on the screen. Sibisi took it and sipped.

'Yes, it was that man De Vries who freed me. But the conservatives in his party were not happy about it and so they kicked him out, claiming that he was a madman. Well, I have had the honour of spending many hours with De Vries, both while I was in prison and during my short exile. We have eaten from the same plate, drunk from the same cup like true African brothers . . .'

Eaten from the same plate, drunk from the same cup, slept in the same bed maybe. Used the same toilet. Where? Some rusty corrugated-iron toilet buzzing with flies, stinking to the high African heavens far away in the bush on the banks of a stagnant green river. Germs, diseases, worms. 'Ordinarily a tapeworm has a double life history.' De Vries's tapeworm lays its eggs in a chunk of pork and dies. Sibisi eats the meat . . .

'Scara,' Khensani was calling to me excitedly. 'Scara, he was talking about you!'

I nodded. I had been dreaming up one of my stories of fantasy and imagination.

'Go,' she said.

I held onto her.

'Scara.' She wanted me to look into her eyes and I did. 'I'll be waiting here for you.'

I smiled and looked out of the window. It was raining outside, even though the sun was shining.

'Khensani,' I said. But Khensani the younger answered, thinking that I had called for her. I decided to ask her a question anyway. I took her over to the window. 'Today is a great day,' I said, 'an important day for all the people in this country. Do you know why?'

'Of course,' she said, 'you and Aunty Khensani have a baby.'

'That's true,' I said, 'but why else is it a great day?'

She thought for a while, scratching her nose. Sibisi was still speaking on the television, the rain came down outside softly wetting the earth.

'Aah, I know,' she said with a sigh of triumph. 'Because the monkeys are getting married.'

'Yes,' Khensani said, 'Umshado weZinkawu.'

A monkeys' wedding. That's what we say when it rains and shines at the same time. It was such a long time since I had heard the saying that I had forgotten all about it.

'I think I'll stay here,' I said, turning to Khensani. 'It's not every day the monkeys get married. Sibisi will just have to wait.'

Glossary

amandla ngawethu (or awethu) — power to the people
Awu — exclamation of surprise
Baba — Father
babalaas — hangover
bakkie — light delivery van
Beloofde Land — Promised Land
boereseun — Afrikaner boy
boerewors — sausage
bra — brother
braaivleis, braai — barbecue
choopa — home-made ice lolly
dhunia — coriander
Dikeledi — Tears
dompas — passbook
donga — dry watercourse
fahfee — Chinese gambling game
gogo — granny
Hawu — exclamation of surprise
hok — cage
indaba — conference
inyanga — medicine man, herbalist
jong — sonny
kwela-kwela — police van
laager — circle of wagons
lightie — young boy
magwinya — deep-fried cake, similar to a doughnut

mahala — free
maheu — drink made from mealie-meal porridge
makoti — daughter-in-law
makulu baas — big master
makwerekwere — (derog.) person from Zimbabwe or Malawi
masala — curry spices
mashonisa — moneylender
Mayibuye iAfrika — Come back Africa
mbaula — brazier
mealie, mealie-meal — maize, maize-meal
mfowethu, mfo — brother
mfundisi — priest
mieliepap — maize-meal porridge
Miesies — Madam
mlungu — white person
Modimo — God
moratiwa — sweetheart
morogo — wild spinach
mossie — sparrow
muti — medicine
naartjies — tangerines
pap — mealie-meal porridge
papgeld — maintenance money (lit. porridge money)
sangoma — medicine woman, diviner
Sê die kaffer moet wegkom van die venster af — Tell the kaffir to
   get away from the window
simanje-manje — a style of dance music
skollie — coloured hoodlum
skyf — cigarette
sputla — cane spirit
stokvel — syndicate or club which raises funds by selling food and
   liquor at parties
Suiwer Wit Party — Pure White Party
Suka! — Go away!
tackies — sneakers
the moer in — furious
tokoloshe — an evil spirit which appears as a short man
toyi-toyi — a dance usually performed during protest marches
tsotsis — thugs
tsotsitaal — black urban argot

Usanana lwam — My little baby
velskoene — rawhide shoes
Vervlaks! — Damn it!
voetsek — fuck off (usually used to chase away a dog)
voorlaaiers — muzzle-loaders
Voortrekker — Boer pioneer
warme klappe — stiff clouts
Wat sê jy daar? — What's that you say?
Watter kak is dit dié op my gesig? — What shit is this on my face?
wena — you
Yebo — Yes
zol — dagga cigarette
zonke — everything